The

ZEN GENE

By

Laurie Valder Mains

ISBN 9780991743902
Canada

The Zen Gene

Prologue

Vector

Victoria BC
July 2020

Tyler knew his plan was good, well except for the part about her dying, that part was not so good.

He studied the data and found that the probability of the formula killing her was low, but low was not zero, and that was the problem. It was her age. The solvents' adverse outcomes data was based on adults not children. The data showed a four percent risk of triggering an atypical immune response which could, in theory, cause anaphylaxis which could be serious if it occurred while she was swimming.

He scanned the roiling water and crowded pool deck and considered the situation frowning when he came to a less than perfect solution. He did not like uncertainties but he realized the chance of her drowning, without being spotted, was low and, assuming the Recreation Centre has an EpiPen, death from anaphylaxis was equally low. He stopped worrying about it, the swimming pool was the right place to do this, and accepting this small risk meant he would finally get started on the program.

There was another issue he needed to deal with, in the last few minutes his body awareness had begun to fade. He'd been lurking in the mostly empty side channel which led to the waterslide and managing sensory issues quite well. At least he was until they announced the opening of the water slide and people began to surge past and some of them brushed against him as they raced to get in line.

He hated being in a public swimming pool but worse than the thought of standing in other people's pee was the slimy feel of their skin; he hugged himself as he leaned back against the edge of the pool trying to avoid contact. The unwanted sensation of feeling skin threatened to send him running from the water.

One reason he hadn't was he could no longer reliably feel his feet touching the bottom. He knew they must be touching because he was standing upright but logic and reasoning were no substitute for actual feedback. He tried wiggling his toes but it was no use, he could not feel them and when he leaned forwards to look and see if they were moving he had the odd feeling he was seeing someone else's toes. He had experienced this kind of disconnection before and he knew if it got worse it would affect his overall awareness and, in this situation, losing track of his hands would be a disaster.

His anxiety which had been steadily building bumped up considerably when he imagined applying the formula to the girl's skin. He shuddered at the imagery and, closing his eyes, tried to calm himself by visualizing the three letter stop condons for his proto RNA. After a few moments of this he managed to shift his focus enough to regain control lessening the storm in his mind.

Being in the pool experiencing unwanted physical contact was distracting but he was determined to proceed, the test needed to be done and it might as well start now. This was the only field trial and he needed the data it would generate. All he had to do, he assured himself, was pour a few drops of the formula on the girl's skin and not get caught. Simple.

The test dose had been ready for more than a month but until an hour ago, when he spotted her heading into the recreation centre, he had no idea how he would administer it. One reason for this was he had never met her, did not know her at all, and had only recognized her from her school photo. He knew nothing about her aside from her name, Katy Peters, her age, twelve years three months, and the fact she was a direct vector to his target.

He scanned the pool again and spotted her and a red haired girl getting out of the hot tub together. Katy was tall and wore a bright green one-piece bathing suit which made her stand out from the throng of kids. When they jumped into the pool and started heading in his direction he decided it was time to get ready. He slipped two fingers into the mesh pocket inside the waistband of his bathing suit and retrieved the vial. He held it out of sight in the palm of his hand and, covering the action, twisted off the white plastic cap.

His fingers were slick and the cap slipped from his grasp and was lost in the water. No turning back now, he thought, placing his thumb over the open end to keep the solvent from evaporating. He watched the green bathing suit coming nearer as Katie and her friend made their way towards the waterslide. The pool was crammed with raucous screaming kids but his attention was only on Katy. As she approached he looked for a suitable place to pour the contents of the vial but quickly realized finding a dry spot on her would be impossible. He barked a nervous laugh struck by the insanity of searching for such a thing on someone swimming.

His plan was feeling less certain by the moment as he scanned her body. He needed to place it where it would not immediately be washed off but as she approached he became keenly aware of the rule that there are places you are not allowed to touch on girls which was an additional complication. He had calculated the solvent needed to be on her skin for a full minute to be effective but achieving that kind of exposure seemed unlikely given that her red-headed friend kept splashing her.

As he watched them approach his pounding heart urged him to sidle closer but, amazingly, Katy came directly towards him walking backwards through the throng of kids. He was confused by this, she almost seemed to be trying to bump into him. He positioned the vial between the fingers of his right hand and watched as she came nearer. He was having trouble feeling his fingers and had to keep looking to see if the vial was still there. Just as they were about to bump he thrust his hand out to fend off the collision. When his palm made contact with her shoulder he tipped the vial and trickled the contents onto her skin. He made sure to avoid the shoulder strap of her bathing suit and managed to pour it all out before she spun around.

"Sorry Tyler," she said.

When she spoke to him years of parental prompting took over and he responded automatically by making himself look at her face. His gaze fell first upon the tip of her nose, then moved to one side of her lower lip where the skin folded, then to the orange freckle on her earlobe, and then to her left cheek which is where he noticed the colour changing. He knew from experience that red meant she was upset and he was in trouble.

He looked away from her but could still feel her gaze upon him. She was looking at him longer and more intensely than most people did and he thought for sure it meant he was busted. He was worried he might have to talk to her and he was greatly relieved when she suddenly spun around and darted back into the crowd. Happy that he had not been caught he watched her moving away while silently counting off the seconds of exposure. He was hoping to reach sixty before she was splashed or dove under the water. As he watched her a thought struck him.

How does she know my name?

He was counting the seconds and wondering about that when the red haired girl came from behind him and banged into his arm sending the empty vial flying from his hand.

"What did you do to Katie you freak?"

Her voice was high pitched and cut sharply through the clamoring din.

"I saw you put something on her. What did you put on her?"

She was loud but he ignored her as he made a reflexive grab for the vial but missed. Over the noise of the pool and the rising pitch of the girl's complaint he clearly heard the "plink" of contact as the vial hit the water. He searched for it but the glass was invisible against the blue bottom. He looked for Katie again, locating her by her bathing suit; she was too far away to see if, during the few seconds he'd been distracted she'd been splashed. He saw her looking back in his direction but not at him she was staring open-mouthed at her red haired friend.

He watched her for a few more seconds before looking down at the water. He was worried a kid might step on the vial and get some of the formula directly into his bloodstream. He continued to ignore the red haired girl as he searched though she was now full-on screaming at him and a lifeguard was approaching.

He stopped looking for the vial when it suddenly dawned on him he'd done it. The trial had begun! Throwing his head back he laughed and slapped the water with his open hands startling the hectoring girl to silence. His barked laugh had a dangerous feral quality to it and his eyes burned with an intensity which caught her by surprise. Instinctively she moved away from him not wanting to turn her back to him until she left the pool.

He was smiling when he noticed the lifeguard pointing and motioning for him to approach her. He began to wade to where she was waiting but before he got there a boy slipped and fell on the wet pool deck and started howling and she left to help him. He turned back in time to see the slender girl in the green bathing suit climb up the steps at the far end of the pool. His eyes followed her slim figure as she climbed the ladder but, unlike other sixteen-year-old boys, Tyler was only thinking about her immune response.

Chapter 1

September 17, 2020

Panjwai district of Kandahar Province Afghanistan

The sergeant dragged a rough sleeve across his mouth leaving a scattering of dark droplets of blood on the material. His lips were dry and painful and his mouth had a nasty burnt taste that, no matter what he tried, he could not get rid of. His mouth was so completely dry when he tried to spit all he managed to produce was sound.

He took another sip from his water bottle, sloshed it around, and spit it out. The night was too dark for him to see it disappear into the parched desert. The water did not help; the taste was still there now with a sharp metallic undertone. As bad as the taste in his mouth was it was the headache that was affecting him the most, the Ibuprofen he swallowed a half hour earlier was not touching it.

He turned his attention to the compound below where the hostiles appeared to be settled in for the night. He checked his watch, twenty-three fifty Kandahar time, moon rise was over an hour ago. It was supposed to be full but with the overcast in this dark corner of the desert it was almost invisible. From where he sat it was a faint blur and did little to lighten the darkness cloaking the desert. He was grateful for that, if he got a shot at the target, the darkness would supply useful cover for them to slip away.

There were three on his team, all of them marksmen placed in strategic positions, ready to provide backup. All he needed was a positive ID and one clear shot and they would break this rebel group's hold in the area. The target was the leader, Ahmed El Ahmed. He was a small man, judging by the photograph passed around at this morning's briefing and, on this occasion, he was being described as a holy man.

This description of Ahmed was a new one but that didn't surprise him. Over the previous three weeks Ahmed had been variously described as, a Turkish mercenary, an Italian missionary, and a UCLA Grad student. All these descriptions supplied by US Military Intelligence. The fact he was given contradictory information prior to this morning's briefing made no difference to him. His job was essentially apolitical; he and his team were the plumbers sent in to unblock the shit pipe of Democracy. He was more than happy to leave the political spin to the spooks.

"The dirty little Turk bastard is trying to make a name for himself in the opium trade," was how Major Wallace from US Military Intelligence described Ahmed on a previous occasion.

He was a career soldier, had seen action in five Middle Eastern and African nations over the last thirteen years. After working alongside his American counterparts for many of those years he'd begun to detect a pattern. USMI officers invariably boiled this type of sanction down to the latest moral outrage politicians were selling the voters stateside. They tried to make killing brown people, like Ahmed, seem like they were saving widows and orphans or furthering Afghan women's rights. Anyone with an IQ over the speed limit knew it was about money, oil, and selling weapons. The unending conflict in the Middle East guaranteed a constant need to replenish expensive weaponry, weaponry that is made in the US.

He wondered what the upside was for Ahmed and his band of rebels. Everyone knows there is no money at this end of the drug trade. Being holed up in a goat barn afraid to stick your head outside to take a piss doesn't seem like much of a life. As he scanned the barnyard scene below his night-vision binoculars turned his bad headache into a brutal headache. He and his team had been in position for over three hours waiting for an opportunity to sanction Ahmed.

The main problem for snipers this late in the Afghan conflict was the spooky and uncooperative nature of the targets. The insurgents learned to be shy about showing themselves out in the open after dark. They knew going outside for a breath of fresh air could be unhealthy; it might easily be their last breath courtesy of some grunt on a hillside a couple kilometers away.

It was an ugly prospect to be sniped. When the 50 caliber slug tumbles into your skull it renders the meat inside into a gray and pink spray and when that hot brain muck splashes your buddy's faces they tend to remember it. Tonight they were close in and, after he puts Ahmed down, he knew the surrounding dunes would explode with pissed-off insurgents; every one of them itching to earn the bragging rights of taking out a sniper detail. When the target hits dirt it's bug-time; running flat out through blackness back to the extraction point and, if they make it, waiting long agonizing minutes for the chopper to swoop in and save their butts.

"Doesn't this guy ever needa take a leak?"

The voice that whispered from the darkness was his wingman Alex Torgesen. Tor was fifteen feet behind him to his left kneeling behind a rock with his night-vision binoculars pinned to his eyes. He was about to respond with something clever when they both noticed a change in light intensity at the rear of the shack. It was a small change but it clearly showed up as a brightening of the greenish fog of the night-vision which meant a door just opened.

They watched in silence as a single ghostly figure with a hood covering its head emerged and walked along the near side of the building. By process of elimination this had to be their guy since all the other men had been out except for Ahmed. No doubt he sent them out to clear the way. He knew Ahmed would eventually need to relieve himself against the same section of wall at the rear of the compound.

He didn't know where the women peed he was just happy it wasn't against that section of wall; it cut his chances of shooting the wrong heat signature in half. The figure walking below believed he was in complete darkness but to the tech-enhanced eyes watching he stood out as if it were daytime. He followed his progress waiting for the Known Combatant Identity Program's clunky algorithm to finish its lethal calculation. It seemed to take a long time but it finally gave a positive ID for Ahmed.
The figure was stopped at the back wall of the compound getting ready to do his business when his ear-bud came to life.

"Ranger one, we got movement southeast your position."
"Copy two, how many, how far?"
He spoke quietly into his helmet mike not certain how close they were.
"Half click, AK and RPG," he said.
"Roger that Slick, we got green for go, eyes on RPG. When you hear my shot light em up," he said.

In the last few minutes, since getting the green light, the headache had intensified and it wasn't from knowing about the rocket propelled grenade lurking nearby, Slick and Kowalski had that covered. There was something about the nature of this pain, he'd never felt anything quite like it, at least not inside his head. It was perplexing; it was physical, sharp, almost like a knee to the groin or a gut punch.

"Roger that," Slick said.

Team Two was situated two klics west of his position with a different view of the compound. They were well placed to cover him and Torgesen plus the far end of the compound that he could not see from his position. It was ideal kill-zone coverage from every direction. He shifted his position and lay prone on the ground behind his weapon. Once in this position he was vulnerable and dependent on Torgesen and the others for protection. From this point on his focus would be on the target alone.

The military issue .50 Caliber Barrett sniper rifle had a hi-tech scope tweaked specifically for conditions of desert warfare. The scope was a technical marvel; so advanced it came with standing orders to destroy it rather than have it fall into enemy hands. It came equipped with an explosive charge set within the instrument's electronics and optics for that purpose. It also had a satellite up-link so the Sergeant in the sky could detonate the charge should the operator become incapacitated. He'd used the weapon many times in practice and in theatre and that explosive charge, a few centimeters from his right eye, was always present in his thoughts when he looked through the hole. If that charge went off, at the very least, it would blind him or, more likely, it would blow his head off. Another perk of being an Army Specialist, he thought. As unpleasant as the idea of it blowing up in his face he would rather die that way than fall into Taliban hands and be tortured to death, or worse, tortured and made to live.

The headache had gained strength and colour in the last few minutes and he was having trouble staying focused on the task. He hoped Tor was keeping an eye out for the RPG because he did not need the additional complication of having the Taliban stumble upon their position. Technically he no longer needed a spotter there wasn't an operational requirement of calling out wind speed or range information. The scope, with its satellite up-link, calculated all of this for him and updated the information in fractions of a second but, with all that, he was glad to have Tor covering his ass, especially tonight.

He tucked the stock tight to his cheek enjoying the familiarity of the act but when he closed his left eye and tried to sight through the scope the vision in his right eye blurred. There was no wind but it felt like a puff of cold air hit his eyeball and made his eye tear up. He felt frustrated waiting precious seconds for his vision to clear. He resisted the urge to rub his eye knowing from experience that could make it worse.

He couldn't wait much longer the target was going to finish and disappear back inside the shack. The sooner he got his shot the sooner he would be back at base where he could grab more pain killers and conk out for a few hours. The intense ache behind his eyes had become more than a distraction; at this point it was becoming an operational concern.

At this range the man was an easy shot for him and when his vision finally cleared the target view was perfect; he could even see the heat signature from his urine stream. His vision was clear but when he tried to focus his mind and concentrate he discovered he had another problem; he could not push past the increasing pain inside his skull. He tried to relax and let muscle memory take over hoping it would carry him to the point where he would regain enough control to pull the trigger. He carefully slipped his index finger onto the trigger; the pull tension was set light and it only took a tiny amount of pressure to fire the weapon. It was ultra-sensitive and he was always careful when he made first contact.

The pain eased a little and things were beginning to come together, he was perfectly sighted on the target with the reticle centered on the back of his hooded head. As he started to put pressure on the trigger he blinked once very slowly and then his eyelid closed and would not open. He was confused and trying to make sense of what was happening to him when a ripping pulse of searing pain gripped him and turned everything inside his head white hot. The pain was staggering. It felt like battery acid had been splashed on the backsides of his eyeballs inside his head; the effect was so real he gagged at the smell of burning bubbling flesh. His face muscles went hard, snapping in to rigid spasm, locking his jaw. He tried to scream but his mouth would not open to allow sound to escape.

"Come on Sarge, make with the noise already I need a take a dump."

Torgesen whispered from the darkness but he could no longer respond, he could not hear him nor could he move any part of his body. The muscles of his torso had contracted and locked together turning him into a hard knotted ball of flesh. What consciousness remained was sealed away locked inside a damaged mind which no longer permitted conscious thought. As his higher functions dimmed there remained only one clear input to his senses and that was the nerve-searing pain alive inside his skull. Within his ebbing awareness he knew he was dying and he welcomed it.

Torgesen realized something was wrong with him and went over and knelt down beside him.
"Ranger two, Sarge has…. a problem. You should do the deed, copy?"

He examined his stricken partner trying to determine what had happened. It looked like he was having a seizure or a stroke and then it occurred to him he might have been bitten by a snake. He briefly turned on his shielded light and rolled him over to check the ground beneath him but there was nothing there. There was no more time to check for bite marks he got his weapon ready and prepared for the shit storm when Slick took down the target.

He readied himself to shoot whoever came their way after the report from Slick's rifle. He selected full auto and clicked off the safety waiting for the shot but it never came. He knew there were at least two unfriendlies nearby but he risked another call. He wanted to know what the fuck was happening.

"Ranger two, this is Tor, the Sarge is T.U. Repeat. Sarge is down," he whispered, "you are 'go' to take out the target. Do you copy?"
He waited but there was only dead air, scary dead air, and then he heard.

"Ah, we got a problem, Tor."

It was Steve Kowalski, Slick's new wingman and he sounded worried.

"WTF Steve?" he hissed.

"I think Slick had a heart attack or something. He's flaked out on the ground kinda curled up," he said.

What the fuck is this Torgesen thought turning back to peer at the dim outline of his Sergeant on the ground. He had no idea what was going on but with Slick and the

Sarge both down that meant he was in command and as far as he was concerned the operation was over.

"Ranger two what's your status?" he whispered.
"Confused, what's yours?" he said.
"Same. Can you see the unfriendlies?"
"Yeah they're closer now at your nine o'clock."
"Ok Steve it's bug-out time. Can you carry Slick back to the E.P.?"
"Yeah, I guess so," he said.
"Okay, go now, don't wait," he whispered.

He was about to put his weapon down and attempt to pick up the sergeant when he heard a voice to his left. Kowalski was right they were close. The shadowy outline of a man with an RPG came into view against the slightly lighter background of the night sky. Torgesen silently cursed the fact he left his night-vision gear on the rock behind him when he came to help the sergeant. The man with the RPG stopped twenty meters away down the slope and Torgesen shifted the selector to single fire and slowly knelt beside his Sergeant. He was concerned that auto fire would draw return fire to his muzzle flash. The bad guy was right there in front of them. This would not be a good time for Sarge to start moaning he thought as he shouldered his weapon and waited.

He saw the outline of the other man walking in their direction but as he watched he stopped moving and Torgesen's blood ran cold as he wondered if they'd been spotted. He waited controlling his breathing; he was counting on them not being able to see any better than he could. The other man was taller and armed with an AK47, and he turned and appeared to be looking directly at him. Torgesen sighted on him and almost shot him but the man jumped when he heard the unmistakable sound of a .50 cal. echoing from the hills west of their position.

That was when another Taliban let out a surprised grunt and gave away his position. It was a third man that Team Two had failed to spot and he was standing less than ten meters away. Torgesen turned in the direction of the sound being careful to move slowly so the insurgent's eyes would not detect his movement.

It took an agonizingly long time for his muzzle to be pointed in the direction of the third man. As he was turning he decided to make a pre-emptive strike and take him out first. He took aim at the centre of the blackness where he thought the voice had come from.
He swiveled his eyes away from the spot and he could almost make out the shape of a man using his slightly more sensitive peripheral vision against the inky blackness of the rocks behind him. He turned his eyes back and placed his finger on the trigger aiming centre mass.

Time slowed as his concentration centered on that chunk of darkness. If the target had not moved away in the last few seconds he would be dead in the next few. Torgesen hoped he would have enough time to turn and kill his comrades. He was about to squeeze the trigger when the night erupted with sounds from the compound below. He could hear yelling and sporadic gun fire from the insurgents and he thought he saw his target move out of position. The man had only gone a few steps when the sergeant moaned.

The insurgent stopped and turned towards them but before Torgesen could pull the trigger and kill him something weird happened. Both his eyes began to flutter wildly and twitch and then shut completely. They would not open. It felt like something heavy was pressing down on his eyes from inside his head. He had an urge to turn his head to see what it was but he was unable to move his neck. He felt something gritty pressing on them squeezing them painfully. He was trying hard to gain control over the situation when his left leg went into a hard spasm. The muscle cramped and locked pitching him forwards. He tripped over his partner and when he tried to recover his balance he overcompensated and stumbled backwards landing on his butt.

He was helpless, he could not open his eyes and he could not move. Like an injured dog struck on a roadway he could not understand what was happening to him, but he was sure it was going to kill him. He couldn't open his eyes and the pain inside his head was shutting out all his other senses. He was balanced on his butt, stunned and swaying, and as consciousness drifted away he thought of his wife Jean answering the phone and hearing his commanders voice. He tipped over and slumped down beside the sergeant no longer aware of his surroundings or the peril they were in; no longer caring.

The Taliban soldier heard him fall and he was pointing his AK at them in the darkness and, though he and the sergeant would never think of it this way, they were extremely lucky that night. Kowalski decided, on his own initiative, to shoot the target before bugging out. As he later told it he nailed the guy as he was opening the door to re-enter the building and shooting him felt so good he decided to shoot the propane tanks next to the goat barn

The explosion distracted the insurgent and the light blew his night vision which kept him from spotting Torgesen and the Sarge lying helpless a few meters away. It was the screams of his burning comrades that made him forget about them sending him running back to the compound below leaving the prone soldiers safe and forgotten.

Kowalski had emptied the fifty shooting the burning insurgents as they ran screaming from the building. He then picked up his partner Slick and carried him fireman-style back to the extraction point. When he got there and realized that the Sarge and Torgesen were in trouble he went back and found them, carrying them out one at a time.

Chapter 2

Our Nations Security

September 20, 2020
Thunderbay Ontario

Lakehead University, Centre for Advanced Genetics

Lee Mann's phone chirped. He grimaced when he saw the screen; he'd been expecting this call and not looking forward to it. His gaze went from the British Columbia area code on his cell to the lab coat hanging by the door. He considered ignoring the call, grabbing his coat, and heading back to the lab but he knew they would keep on calling.

"Dr. Mann?"
"Yes."
"Colonel Western, CFB Esquimalt, your name came up in reference to a problem we're having."

The voice on the phone bore traces of flat prairie in the shape and delivery of the vowels, maybe one generation removed, but still as plain as cow shit on a boot. He spoke softly but the depth and timbre of his voice fairly barked authority. Mann recognized the type; they start out by setting the unspoken but clear expectation of your compliance. Like any seasoned actor or lawyer the practitioner of this technique needs to demonstrate, preferably in the first few moments, that they are superior and you are subordinate. It was clear from Western's first few words, or more precisely the way they were spoken, that he considered him his subordinate.

He cleared his throat, "Colonel, as I told the woman who called yesterday I don't do consultations, I am not a clinician, I am a research scientist and as such I cannot offer you any help."

He hoped his clipped response would help the guy decipher his message, *I will not help you, quit wasting my time.*

"This isn't a therapeutic situation Dr. Mann, at least not directly. We require your help to sort out a problem we are having with one of our members, a problem which appears to have a genetic origin. I am aware that you are not a clinician but we believe this issue may relate to the research you did on aggression."

There it was, confirmed. It was what he suspected all along; his one big mistake as a youthful researcher was to rush to publication and now that mistake was about to raise its ugly head once again. He drew a breath and let it out slowly in an effort to maintain control.

"If you know about my research Colonel you must also be aware that I refused to cooperate with the Canadian military," he said.

He was opposed to Governments co-opting scientific research in an effort to find newer better ways to kill people. He made a decision early in his career not to help them; it was people like Western that caused him to give up on some promising research into the neural-correlates of aggression in great apes. The surprising thing about this call was the military was well aware of his position, he'd made it amply clear to them more than a decade ago.

He was pissed off about this interruption but also somewhat curious to hear what crisis would make them desperate enough to call him. He was not the only geneticist in the country nor was he the most experienced. The only way in which he stood out from the rest of his colleagues was he was the least likely to help them. They probably got turned down by everyone else, he thought, and made a mental note to phone Kerry Laines at UBC and see if they contacted her. He could not imagine what kind of mess they got themselves into but it was troubling to hear it involved genetics.

"Doctor Mann your position is clear but I've been directed to inform you that this is a matter of extreme importance, one which threatens our nation's security," he said.

He laughed. It was rude but he couldn't help it. The guy actually invoked national security. Where do they find these guys, he wondered?

"You need to appreciate our situation and understand that we need your cooperation and we will take whatever steps we deem necessary to obtain it," he said.
"That sounds an awful lot like a threat Colonel."
"Dr. Mann, I hope it will not be necessary to employ the resources available to me to secure your cooperation. There is a military aircraft at TBIA ready to fly you to the west coast as soon as you can arrange to leave," he said.

He was getting a very bad feeling about this.

"I don't need a ride to the coast Colonel I'm not going anywhere," he said then paused and added, "Well actually that's not entirely true. I am going to call my brother in-law and invite him to lunch. You may have heard of him, Robert Doyle, he works for the National Post. Who knows? He might want to write a story about you and your soldier with the genetic disorder," he said.

"There's no need to do that Dr. Mann we're all on the same side and there is something else you need to know. The Minister of Environment, Sid Raines, is at this moment speaking with Lyle Greef," he said.

Mann swore under his breath, he'd just been out name-dropped. Lyle Greef was the Director of the Green Journey Society, a group dedicated to saving the oceans. A multi-billionaire, who made his fortune in container ships, he became a man of vision funding ocean research at major universities all over the world. He was also the principal funder of Mann's current research project; they had recently agreed to a new three-year research grant which started in less than a week.

"I believe they are discussing the possibility of Canada coming on-board to support his Green Seas Environmental Initiative. Mr. Greef has been championing this initiative at the UN for some time and, with Canada's support, he might finally get it passed," Western said.

He felt sick to his stomach. It was Lyle's dream to get this initiative recognized by the United Nations and if what Western was telling him was true there is no way he can hold out against that kind of pressure. The Colonel's underlying message was clear cooperate or lose your funding. He hoped this was a bluff on the Colonel's part but the pit of his stomach did not think it was.

"Nice try but the answer is still no, I will not help you. Goodbye, Colonel," he said.

He ended the call and slumped back in his chair. He was sweating freely and had discovered a rigid knot at the base of his neck which he tried unsuccessfully to dislodge. He found himself once again wishing he'd never written that paper on primate aggression. He was about to get up and go back to the lab when his cell chirped. He looked at it and instantly knew that Western had not been bluffing, the country code was Switzerland, it was Lyle Greef's private number.

Canadian Forces Base Naden, Esquimalt, British Columbia

Colonel John Western put the phone down and looked at Lt. Hunter sitting at the computer console across the room and raised an expectant eyebrow. "Well?"

Patricia Hunter glanced at him and raised her finger to say be patient while the machine did its work. When it was finished she turned to look at him and shook her head.

"We've got anxiety, anger, and stress all within normal limits. Voice analysis indicates 89 percent no deception," she said.

Western's face tightened into a scowl. He did not believe it, not for one second, he was old school and he didn't trust machines and this particular analysis proved he was right not to trust them. Ferreting out lies was a skill he'd spent twenty-five years mastering. It was true he did not get a strong reading from Mann but it was difficult to read someone over the phone, especially someone you've have never met.

You need to see their body language, watch their eyes, and feel their energy to get a good reading. Another reason he did not believe the computer analysis had nothing to do with the technology or what he'd heard on the phone. He did not believe Mann because he did not believe in coincidence and this whole thing was rotten with it.

"What is the latest from Sedulca? Have they come up with anything concrete?" he said.

Hunter reached for a report on the desk and flipped it open and read.

"According to Sedulca they cannot confirm or deny the existence of a paralytic state because they were unable to replicate it in the lab. He believes the problem is they have not been able to create a situation realistic enough to cause the reaction. He is proposing we send the original four soldiers back to Afghanistan on a similar mission and he and his team accompany them to gather data," she said.

Western looked up from the letter he was reading and stared at her.

"Is that supposed to be funny, Lieutenant?"
"That is what he is recommending," she said.
"Freaking psychologist, he's never seen action outside of his lab and he wants to go on a shooting trip to Afghanistan? What does he think they do over there, camp by the river and sing songs?"

Hunter laughed; it did seem an unlikely scenario. A bunch of lab coated medical techs following a sniper detail into Afghanistan. Sedulca clearly had no concept of what a combat soldier's life was like, his knowledge of soldiering probably came from watching movies. She doubted he would last a week in the desert.

Western turned to his calendar and checked his schedule, "Anyway there's no time for field trials. There are lots of people in Ottawa sweating razor blades over this thing and I don't think they fully understand how devastating this thing could turn out to be. The worst part is the uncertainty it raises in the troops. Imagine knowing you might be rendered helpless in the heat of battle, if word gets out we could see mass desertions. Our entire ground force could disappear overnight and I wouldn't blame them. This has the potential to become a huge security problem if we don't figure it out.

I received an update from Kabul last night. Six more have had similar breakdowns since we brought our guys back, which would seem to indicate that this thing, whatever it is, is continuing to emerge. Ottawa has instructed the base commander in Afghanistan to clamp down on rumors in the ranks, place the affected men in isolation, and ship them here as soon as possible. As far as Ottawa is concerned, for the moment, Naden is ground zero and the ball is in our court. I need you to stay close to this Doctor Mann until we can figure out what his role is in this thing."

"You seem confident that Mann will agree to come here," she said.

"He'll be here, I guarantee it." Western grinned at her and added," Did I ever mention to you that I don't believe in coincidence?"

Hunter laughed, "Maybe a couple million times over the last five years but I agree with you this coincidence is unbelievable," she said.

"If everything works out as planned he will arrive tomorrow evening. I want you to pick him up at YVR, feed him a nice meal, and then tuck him in for the night. I've got him booked into the purple room so we can monitor his communications. If he brings a laptop you need to make it go missing long enough for tech services to look at it.

Apply some charm and massage that big PhD ego and let's see what incriminating details fall out of his mouth. After you tuck him in you are leaving for Thunder Bay. I want you to do some digging around. It's going to be a long night you're booked on the red eye out of Vancouver at 1:30 am. I've arranged a jet ranger helo at YVR to fly you to Vancouver to catch your flight to Thunder Bay.

Welcome to Victoria

September 16
8:33 pm PST

The aircraft, a well-worn military version of the Boeing 737 built in the 80s, painted dull grey and lacking in basic amenities, landed hard, military style, on the main runway at Victoria International Airport. It taxied away from the main passenger terminal stopping in front of the Canadian Armed Forces hangar.

When he came down the stairs Mann saw an attractive young woman wearing a uniform holding a sign with his name on it. She was looking directly at him and not smiling. He thought the sign was over-kill considering he was the only non-military passenger on the aircraft.

"Welcome to BC, Dr. Mann," she said.

This was his first visit to Victoria but if he thought he was going to get to a tour of the city he was mistaken. She drove him directly to the Naden Naval Base located in Esquimalt where he was efficiently processed, photographed, and issued a clip-on visitor ID tag with his picture and a bar-code on it. The security officer who processed him was courteous and professional and urged him in the most emphatic terms not to lose it lest he be shot.

She led him to a room with a single bed and all the charm of a prison cell. This was to be his home for the duration of his stay she told him, making it clear he was not expected to leave the base. The single window in the room did not open and it faced away from the ocean overlooking an outdoor storage area.

No ocean view for the lowly conscripted scientist, he thought. She left him in the room to get settled and returned a half hour later and took him to a well appointed dining room where he received a decent meal of fresh poached Pacific salmon. They were in the officer's mess and he noticed other people avoided eye contact with him and no one spoke to him other than the young woman. She told him her name was Patricia.

The dinner conversation she made matched exactly the warmth and charm of the room they assigned him. The truth was he did not mind, looking at Patricia was not painful even if she was grilling him like a mackerel. When he asked her questions about herself or the work she was engaged in the answers she provided were short and designed not to encourage further inquiry. He realized she had been assigned to pump him for information and this set the tone and temperature for their time together.

When the meal was over and the mackerel done, if slightly charred, she glanced meaningfully at her watch and pointed out the time difference between Thunder Bay and the west coast and encouraged him to retire. She marched him back to his room and when the door closed behind him he was sure he heard an extra click. He wondered if she locked him in but he did not check, he was tired and it would not help him sleep knowing he was a prisoner of the Canadian Armed Forces.

Colonel John Western

At eight the next morning a different woman called and told him she would be there in half an hour to escort him to breakfast. She knocked once and unlocked his cell door ten minutes early. She was older than Patricia and did not offer her name or make small talk as he scarfed down his breakfast. When he was finished she led him to an office where a man in uniform sat behind a gunmetal grey steel desk. The demeanor of the man who stood up to shake his hand was not even remotely friendly.

He took note of the fact that Colonel Western held eye contact for a long time, long enough to make him feel uncomfortable and when he looked away he realized that was the point. He introduced himself as Colonel John Western, Canadian Forces Military Intelligence Pacific Fleet. He was medium height, dark haired with grey at the temples, and belligerently unremarkable in appearance. Nondescript did not begin to describe the lack of distinguishing characteristics of the man. His uniform did not have markings to indicate which branch of the Canadian Forces he was affiliated with nor his rank. The only identifying item on his person was a white plastic

name tag with black lettering pinned over his left breast
pocket.

No picture ID for the chief spook, he thought. There was
nothing personal in the office, no pictures, diplomas, golf
trophies, memo board, nothing. He assumed it was a
room used to interview enemy agents or hostile scientists,
which he certainly was. There was no reason to believe
the man sitting behind the desk was named Western other
than that was how he introduced himself and his plastic
name tag corroborated.

"Please have a seat," he said.

He sat in the chair placed before the desk, it was small
and metal and apparently designed to be uncomfortable.

"There is a soldier we would like you to…examine,"

Western began and waited letting his opening statement
age for a moment.

Mann did not say anything in response he simply
continued to look out the single window at the harbour.
He saw two parked warships and a BC ferry in dry dock.
It was a nicer view than the one they gave him and this
room was used to interrogate prisoners. He wondered
what they were trying to tell him. I should ask for a room
upgrade, maybe cash in some Air Miles, he thought
smiling.

He decided, while gazing at the lovely Patricia over
dinner last night, that he had no choice but to grin and
bear it. Lyle Greef made it clear, though he never said it
directly, that if he wanted to keep his research grant he
needed to cooperate with Western. He may as well enjoy
his time in Victoria. The nonsense they told him about
helping them with a genetics problem could not last much

longer. He knew they would eventually get around to the real reason they wanted him there.

"We need to understand what has happened to him," the Colonel paused again and waited for a response but he remained silent.

"The soldier in question was hand-picked for an assignment overseas," he continued as he put on his glasses to refer to a document on the desk, no longer waiting for him to respond. "Pre-mission training took place on this base and he was in good mental and physical health. He was in top shape when he shipped out on an overseas mission. He is thirty-seven years old, married, a graduate of UBC. He has one child, a daughter who is thirteen, and a dog. He lives with his family in a good suburb of Victoria.

He is a career soldier, in for more than fifteen years, and he has seen active duty in several hot zones and performed well. He has not suffered an injury, beyond the usual bumps and bruises, and he has never suffered head trauma. He does not have any psychiatric disorders, does not use drugs, is not secretly gay, and he doesn't have any aberrant sexual behaviours or desires, or money problems," he said.

He sat silently impassively listening as the Colonel described to him, in some detail, an ordinary man.

"While on his last assignment we discovered he has developed a serious problem, one which he did not have on previous assignments. To put it in blunt terms Dr. Mann this highly skilled and experienced combat soldier has lost the ability to carry out the duties for which he was trained. That is to say, he tells us he was willing to carry out the assignment, but when he tried to do so he became physically incapacitated. This occurred while he was on a mission where he was expected to use deadly force," he said.

He found the Colonel's hushed and reverent tone comical and he laughed. The Colonel's lowered voice and whispered words seemed as though he were hesitantly outing a comrade, telling his worst secret, much worse and more shameful than impotence or homosexuality.

"Do you find this situation funny Dr. Mann?" he said.

He looked at the Colonel and could see by the splotchy colour on his face he found nothing humorous about it.

"So find the guy a desk job," he said, exasperated.

"I don't think you understand the importance of what I'm telling you, Doctor. This is a highly trained elite soldier who can no longer perform his duties," he said.

He scratched his head confused.

"Colonel, let me see if I understand the situation correctly. Twenty years ago I did some very preliminary research into aggression in great apes and because of this you believe I can tell you why your soldier can't kill people. Have I got that right?"

"Yes, essentially," Western said.

Western's answer was unbelievable and he shook his head looking at him. What is wrong with this guy, he thought? None of this makes sense there has to be more to it. He decided to force the issue.

"Well, Colonel, it turns out you picked the right guy for the job because I'm a quick study. I have the answer for you," he said.

Western glared at him but said nothing. It was clear he was not used to such blatant disrespect and there was a shaft of hatred in his steady gaze.

"Here is my diagnosis. Before your warrior left for unknown lands to kill unknown people, he caught his wife heroically doing' the neighbour and this, understandably, dampened his enthusiasm."

He leaned back in the chair and expelled a long breath of frustration. What a waste of time, he thought.

"His wife has not cheated on him Doctor," he said. Western spoke with such absolute certainty he suspected he'd checked personally.

"Colonel you are missing my point. It does not matter if his wife has or has not cheated on him. That's not what I am trying to tell you. The point, Colonel Western, is that the human mind is not a perfect sphere of understanding there are dark recesses and sub-basements and all manner of experiential unknowns. My guess, and that is all it will ever be, is that your soldier has a debilitating case of Post-Traumatic Stress Disorder. The point I am trying to make clear is that I understand this soldier is important to your 'mission' but, in this case, it is simply 'too bad you lost one.'

With counseling and proper care people with PTSD can and do recover. I sincerely hope this man recovers but I find it hard to believe that one individual soldier is so important he can't be replaced. I'm sorry I couldn't help you. Please arrange my transportation back to Thunder Bay."

He stood up and looked down at the man seated before him and watched his face as it lost a bit more colour.

Whatever is going on here, he thought, they are taking it very seriously. The Colonel looked like he was making a decision and he hoped he was deciding to either tell him what was really going on here or let him get on a plane and go home.

"Doctor Mann, if Sergeant Peters was the problem we could certainly replace him, but Peters is not the problem."

He waited.

"Our problem is the sixteen other soldiers with the same issue," he said, "sixteen that we know of."

Chapter 3

High Lights

September 20 2020

Tyler rode into the backyard and dropped his bike on the grass the rear wheel still spinning as he ran into the house. The slamming door echoed behind him as he passed through the kitchen and into the living room where he shrugged his book-laden backpack onto the couch. Homework could wait. This was the second week of school and he was already sick of it.

The house was a small post-war bungalow with two bedrooms on the main level and a full basement. It was the style of home contractors were encouraged to build by the thousands for soldiers returning from World War Two. Andrea chose it because the rent was reasonable and she liked the isolated rural location. It looked out upon farm fields from two sides and was at the end of the road so there was little traffic.

His bedroom was in the basement and the first thing he did was check his email. He unlocked his bedroom door and flipped on the light switch which turned on a low wattage lamp and started the boot sequence for his computer. When it booted he typed in his password and checked his email, he was hoping for a reply from Tomo Labs in Seoul. He was sure that Han, the head of research, believed his story that he was a gene researcher at UBC looking for an industry partner for product development. It helped that he had a UBC email address;

he got it by hacking the account of an elderly English Professor.

When he checked his mail he was disappointed there was nothing from Han but then he remembered it was the middle of the night in Korea. Checking the time he estimated he had two hours before Andrea came back from her job. That was good because he needed to turn on the agitators and check temperatures. He wanted to be back before she got home, and two hours should be enough time to do what was needed. It made him anxious if he ran late because he would then have to think up reasons why he was not home when she got back. She would ask him where he was, even if he was only gone for a few minutes, and she no longer believed him if he told her he was next door.

If she did not like his answer she would drive him nuts asking questions. It made his life simpler to just be there when she arrived rather than endure endless grilling about his activities. It would be easier if he could work at home but that was impossible. What he was working on was potentially lethal and he could not take the chance that Andrea might, on the pretense of cleaning his room, break in and become exposed. She'd done it before.

He shut down the computer and relocked the door; on his way out he grabbed a handful of brown cookies and refilled his water bottle. He ate the cookies as he sped down the dirt lane behind the house that led towards town. He finished the last cookie and was sweating in the warm September sun by the time he reached the corner at Munn Road and Steady Drive but instead of turning left towards the city he turned onto Munn and headed towards the industrial section. He rode for another five minutes then slowed his bike as he approached the high wooden fence that ran the length of Layton's Auto and Truck Wrecking yard. He stopped and wiped sweat from his forehead with his shirt sleeve then grabbed the water bottle from its holder and took a long cool pull.

He turned his head and looked over his shoulder to see the position of the sun in the sky. It hung five inches above the aspen trees on the crest of Wilson Hill it was the ideal position. With only two hours he did not have time to waste but the conditions were perfect for a run and he could feel the need draw him. It would not take long to make one pass though there was always the possibility he could get stuck and that would be bad.

He leaned forward with his chest on the handlebar and looked at the shadow cast by his wheel spokes on the gray packed-earth trail. The line between shadow and light was crisp; indicating the high quality of this early autumn sunlight. The familiar pulse of excitement began to tick within him and he shivered with anticipation. The day had been hot and the air was still warm but the prospect of a run in perfect light sent an icy chill of need cascading through him. Before he became completely drawn in by his need he remembered to repeat the safety words Zen gave him.

"Once," he spoke the word solemnly then gazed along the length of the fence trembling with anticipation.
"Only once," he repeated.

When he spoke the words he mimicked the extra emphasis Zen put on them and this gave the words more power, even as his excitement built he could feel his control strengthening. *Only once Tyler. That's the deal, only once. Okay?*
He could hear her voice in his head and he repeated the phrase again.

"Only once."

He spoke the words softly one more time and he was ready. He turned the handlebar to the left, lifted the bike by the seat, and kicked the pedal to spin the rear wheel and shift down to first gear. He dropped the bike and the spinning rear wheel kicked up a rooster tail of dust as he hopped on and began to pedal. He followed the slope which led to the footpath that ran along the fence behind Layton's.

It was a path that generations of kids had used as a shortcut; the soil had been pounded into fine grey dust from shoes and wheels traveling along the gently undulating rise and fall of the land. He checked ahead to be sure there was no one on the path, he almost run into a group of school kids last time. He leaned forward as he peddled putting his face down as near to the handlebar as he could without bumping his chin as he picked up speed.

Ahead he saw the weathered yellow top of the wrecked school bus in the junkyard and he tilted his head up slightly. Turning his face towards the fence he swiveled his eyes upwards and the fence pickets became a blur in the periphery of his vision.

Two more rotations of the pedals and individual fence boards came back clear and sharp in his vision. One more turn and they became distorted like vibrating guitar strings. He was getting close now. He tightened his muscles picking up speed; readying himself he set his jaw; the muscles in his chest, shoulders, and arms ached with tension. Only his legs continued to move freely as he braced himself for the section of fence where it would happen. He held his breath as he entered the long shadow of the school bus. When he emerged at the other end it struck him. Sunlight.

The bike wobbled and he maintained his balance though he was no longer fully in control. The energy of the light flooding his open optic nerve produced voltage sufficient to uncouple much of his conscious awareness from his surroundings. His lower brain functioned as it should and it, along with his forward momentum, kept the bike upright.

The strobe effect of the sunlight coming through the pickets induced v spikes directly to his cerebral cortex which produced the seizure which lifted him from the confines of his body, leaving land and flesh behind and below as he entered a state of flow. The unmediated light shook him violently as the electro-chemical effect infused his mind with raw sensation. His eyes were prisms which turned light into infinite seductive sensations.

The peak came and lifted him away; soaring, vibrating, beyond, to that sweet inner elation. Sky, ground, fence, everything was gone, driven away as he surfed waves of unimaginable sensation. Too soon, far below him, he sensed the path coming to an end, he did not want the sensation to end but he knew it must and he searched his mind for the words Zen made him promise to say to resist the urge to go again.

Only once Tyler, that's the deal, only once, okay?

It was hard to let go but he set his will and forced himself to keep pedaling past the end of the fence, past the gas station on Water Road, past the Hydro maintenance yard, peddling until the tears in his eyes had dried and the sensation ebbed; he wanted more but refused to give in to the need. He was three blocks away when he felt the need let go of his mind and the hollow ache inside him lessen its grip.

Zen taught him to replace the emptiness which followed with pride and focus on the knowledge that he was strong enough to resist it and that too felt good. The further he got from the junkyard the better he felt and the stronger he became. The sweet memory of the sensation sustained him until he was far enough away the danger of getting stuck was gone.

Three years ago Andrea had been frantic and asked Zen to help look for him when he did not come home after school. She found him on the ground next to his bike trembling and insensible. That was the day he discovered the weird light effect and got stuck making too many passes and only stopped when the sun moved out of position.

He had nearly blinded himself and needed to wear dark glasses for months to combat the headaches. Zen was smart about things like that, she told him that she did not understand why he did it but she wouldn't tell Andrea about it because she would freak. They told her he fell off his bike which was mostly true. After his headaches stopped and he could ride again Zen spotted him heading in the direction of the junkyard and followed him. She watched him do it and realized it was probably not harmful if he only did it once.

When he turned his bike around and tried to go again she forced him off the path. She was bigger than him then and easily knocked him off his bike. She sat on top of him pinning him down mercilessly tickling him until he gave up. She called him 'the nerve junkie' for a long time after that.

He did not like being touched but, if he did not exactly like it, he could at least tolerate some touching when she did it. Over the summer she caught him a few more times and came to understand this was something he was drawn to. He could not understand why she wanted him to stop the fence thing; he did not believe it would hurt him. It was only when she threatened to tell Andrea he agreed to a compromise. He could do it once a day. She made him promise he would stick to their deal.

Only once Tyler, that's the deal. Promise me.

He turned onto Enterprise Crescent and made his way past blocks of empty and shuttered industrial buildings then turned left onto Dunstan Road for another block and a half to the factory. He jumped off his bike and pushed it through the hole in the security fence stashing it in the weeds behind the long dead power transformer. His bike would not attract any attention; there was no need to lock it because it blended in with the rest of the junk strewn around the lot.

The transformer had once supplied electricity to the factory, an Agro-Pharm Corporation, which had been a large player on the local industrial scene back in the eighties. Now it was another abandoned piece of twentieth century technology standing sentinel to the massive structure decaying behind it. The pharmaceutical complex was two city blocks long and at least half a block wide with a dedicated spur line for rail cars. Three shifts of workers pumped out billions of doses of hormones for the dairy and meat industry during the late twentieth century.

Until the unfortunate connection between artificial hormones and Alzheimer's disease was discovered hundreds of employees efficiently turned out products which produced generations of out-sized livestock to feed over-sized humans. The physical plant was shut down in 2013, and as far as he could tell, no one had been inside the building since it had been boarded up and abandoned. He discovered it six years ago when he was ten and it had become his private playground.

Cars seldom drove past and there was rarely people around and, as a solitary child, this situation suited him perfectly. He ran his fingers through the waist-high weeds growing along the rail spur which led to the factory's concrete loading dock. He walked down the pathway he'd worn through the Scots broom. Somehow the first year he begun hanging around the factory Andrea found out and forbade him to play there. She made up stories about how they did experiments on children inside the factory but even as a ten-year-old he was bright enough to realize she was making up stories to scare him, and if anything, her efforts made him more interested in the place. It wasn't far from their house and he came most days after school while she was at her job.

Sections of the metal security fence around the property had collapsed and it was easy to get onto the property and once inside there was lots of interesting stuff for a kid to play with. One day while he was looking for materials to build a fort he looked under the long concrete loading dock and noticed a wire grill covering an air vent. He thought the grill would make a good window for his fort and it was easy to get it off using the pry bar he found on one of his earlier adventures. It was not until the grill was off that he realized the vent provided an entryway into the building. Going inside the first time had been terrifying and had almost killed him.

He walked to the loading dock and squatted down amongst the tall weeds and waited a few moments watching the road and the surrounding buildings. He wanted to make sure there was no one hanging around. Satisfied, he crawled underneath and duck walked over to the vent. He removed the metal grate covering the air duct leading to the building's basement. He knew it was unlikely anyone was watching him but he was being more careful after the incident in lab four. The meatpacking plant across the road was shut down and boarded up long ago like most of the industrial buildings in this part of the city but he was careful about not being observed.

The vent, eighteen feet long, led to a basement utility room. His first time going in he discovered the vent had a deceptively gentle downwards slope which turns vertical at the twelve foot mark. He'd crawled into the vent in complete darkness and was surprised by the sudden drop off. He fell down the vent and came to a painful stop when his head slammed into the solid steel grating that covered a huge fan at the bottom.

Plummeting face first down eight feet of ventilator shaft into complete blackness had almost killed him. His out-stretched arms slammed through the gaps in the fan cage and dangled in the blade space below and his face and head bashed into the steel cover. If the fan had been turning his arms would have been sliced off like two sticks of salami at the deli. His head hit hard enough that he lost consciousness for a while. When he woke he was dazed and in pain and nearly passed out again but he forgot about the pain when he realized he was trapped upside down inside the vent. He came close to having an all-out fit of hysteria but managed to regain control of himself.

He struggled and pushed until his body moved back and little by little he worked his right arm free of the grate. He rested for a while because he was having trouble catching his breath in the tight dusty confines. He was wondering what to do and thinking about the fact no one knew where he was.

In desperation, though he was stuck head down inside the shaft and it was hard to move at all, he managed to free his other arm from the grate. He began to search along the sides of the vent as far as he could reach with his fingers until he came across something that felt like a crack.

He realized it was the folded seam in the galvanized sheet metal of the vent. He tried to judge where the crack was relative to his foot and began to kick furiously with the heel of his sneaker. The noise was deafening and the dust he loosened made breathing difficult. He had to stop frequently to catch his breath but fear soon had him back at it. It took long agonizing and painful minutes until he felt the metal seam begin to part and spread open. It took more long choking minutes to widen it enough to work it back and forth with his hand.

When the whole section of vent gave way and split open he kicked like a madman until he was able to squirm and wriggle his body backwards and out through the opening. Half in and half out of the vent he twisted around so he could sit upright in the open hole and this allowed the blood to drain from his head and let him catch his breath. He was relieved until he realized he had another problem. When he stuck his leg out of the vent, no matter how hard he stretched it, he could not feel the floor below. He did not know how far down it was or what piece of machinery was waiting to impale him. He sat for a long time trying to decide what to do.

It was not a decision between two courses of action because when he tried to climb back up the vent he discovered he could not. There was nothing to grab onto, the vent had smooth metal sides. Being the only logical choice open to him, he got ready and held his breath and jumped into complete darkness. He remembered wondering how he would explain his injuries to Andrea. He got lucky, the floor was only a few feet below him and mercifully clear of debris but that was still not the end of his problem. It took him a scary half hour of feeling around in the dark to find his way up to the main floor of the factory, and though he knew they were not true, during that half hour of blindness the stories Andrea told him about them experimenting on children came back to haunt him.

That first time inside the building he had been badly spooked and when he found the stairs leading to the main level he ran around inside the factory like a caged rat until he found an emergency exit with a push bar that would open. He was glad to see the blue sky and his trusty bike that day but like most kids he was more curious than cautious and that first time going inside did not deter him from going back.

He climbed the concrete stairs from the basement and stepped through the door stopping to marvel at the amazing light show of streaming sunlight angling down from the ruined roof onto the floor of the factory. For two city blocks random columns of brilliant golden sunlight poked through holes in the roof creating a fantasy realm of dust-speckled beams.

It reminded him of St. Mark's Cathedral downtown. Andrea took him there a few times and told him he was baptized there but he could not remember that. To him it was a building with pictures on the windows and a lot of soggy old people that tried to touch him. They stopped going and Andrea admitted that she only took him there to "keep up appearances," whatever that meant. She did lots of stuff like that, he could not understand why she did those things but he found it easier to go along with her rather than have her repeatedly try to explain it to him and getting upset when he still did not understand.

He walked into the section of the building that housed the rows of chemistry and biology labs. The lab he used was closest to the basement stairs. He picked it because of that and because it contained the best stainless steel work counters. The room was fifteen by twenty with one boarded up window. When he began the project he cleared and then maintained the pathway on the concrete floor from the basement stairs to the door of his lab. He wet mopped it with bleach and water every few days.

He was careful not to track contaminates into the lab because you never knew what spores might be in the dust and thus traveling in the folds of your clothes. It would be ironic if, after having searched everywhere for the Hantavirus it showed up accidentally in his lab media and made him sick. There were plenty of rodent droppings in the building but as far as he could determine not the virus. In every direction the factory floor was mounded with loose and drifting piles of debris that came from the ruined roof and deteriorating walls. No matter how hard he tried to avoid it each time he walked in the building he would raise dust storms in his wake.

There had been several laboratories to choose from and he picked Bio Lab Eight because of its counters and proximity to the basement door. He spent weeks cleaning the lab and scrubbing the stainless steel counter tops with bleach.

He decided to paint the floor with white garage-floor enamel because he could not get the old concrete clean enough for his purposes. The lab once had lots of equipment but it had all been removed when they closed down operations; he saw the outlines of equipment that once sat on the floor and counter tops.

When the lab was clean and ready for use he began to search the other rooms in the building for useful equipment. There were pieces here and there and though he didn't always know what they were used for he dragged them to his lab.

A month after he began his project he came across a locked storeroom with a jackpot of instrumentation. It took him a noisy exhausting hour of bashing the lock on the door to get in but once inside he found all kinds of cool stuff. He dragged the bigger pieces using an improvised dolly made from his old skate board.

As he learned more about genetics on-line he tried different experiments and steadily found or improvised the equipment he needed to do them and soon he had a well equipped biology lab. It was well equipped except for a few key items which he could not find. He could not obtain an optical microscope or a computer that wasn't ancient but while he was searching he found something amazing in the basement beneath lab three.

It was only accessible by a locked stairway inside the lab and when he first saw it he did not understand what it was until months later when he saw a photo of the same machine on-line and discovered that it was a scanning electron microscope.

It was after midnight on a school night when he found the photo but he could not wait until school ended the next day to go back and see it and he snuck out. The first thing he did was search the device for a manufacturers tag, it was an Electroscan, scanning electron microscope, the date of manufacture read Mar 1997, but any hopes he had of using it were dashed when he read the power requirements. A large diesel generator could not supply enough power to operate it.

He retrieved the key to his lab from its hiding place behind an old polished brass fire extinguisher which hung on the wall next to the door. He unlocked the door but before he opened it he plugged in the ends of an extension cord poking out from under the door and waited until he heard the fan inside. It was a household fan he found on Recycle Sunday. It was missing one side of its safety grill but it worked.

It was big and efficient and strong enough to supply two psi of positive air flow inside the lab without drawing much current. The positive air pressure helped to discourage dust infiltration when he opened the door. The factory behind him was a million cubic feet of disintegrating building and there was dust and debris constantly circulating in the air.

While he was putting the lab together he also searched for a live wall receptacle to run equipment. In five years he never found a single hot receptacle, though he actively searched whenever he went exploring in the building. Like everything else, when they decommissioned the building they shut down the power supply. The only place he found live power was in the security shack at the front gate of the factory and it was a long way from lab eight. He bought five one-hundred-foot extension cords from Canadian Tire and laid them on the ground from the guard shack to the lab. It cost seventy-five dollars to buy them.

He had the money but he forgot there was sales tax on top of that and he had to think up a good reason to ask Andrea for five dollars. There were times he almost gave up on the whole idea because things like floor paint and extension cords were costing a lot of money. When he laid the cords on the ground he worried the bright orange colour would attract attention and he painstakingly covered every inch of cord with dirt or other junk to obscure it.

He replaced the key behind the fire extinguisher; it was a bit of luck when the last workers left the factory they inserted the keys into the lab door locks. The individual laboratories were all built as standalone sealed structures within the factory and time and exposure to the elements had not wrecked their roofs like it had the main factory roof.

He slipped a pair of elastic shoe covers over his sneakers before he entered. He stole a few pair from the swimming pool change room last July. They were for use at the pool to keep people from tracking dirt onto the pool deck with street shoes, they also worked well at stopping him from tracking dirt into the lab.

He opened the door and was pleased when he felt the gentle puff of positive air flow. Walking into the dark room he went to the main work bench and clicked the switch on the power bar. Three low volt LED lights came on and pulled the lab and equipment out of the murk into sharp focus. He waited a few moments for the computer monitor to flicker to life before he booted the computer. He found lots of monitors on sight but they were all ancient CRT types and they sucked power like crazy.

The one he picked was the newest of the bunch but even so the resolution was fuzzy and indistinct no matter the refresh rate. On his travels through the ruins of the factory he never found a usable computer so he built his own based on an old IBM desktop.

He used the IBM to control and monitor the electrical power distribution and processes in the grow room. He built it with bits and pieces of hardware people threw away and the only part he could not find was a decent motherboard. The motherboards and chip sets he found in the factory storage room were of no use because of their age. He solved the problem by removing the board from his home computer and convincing Andrea it was blown and needed to be replaced. It took a while to get her to spend two hundred dollars for a new one but he used his best motivator. He needed it to do homework.

That ploy worked almost every time but he was careful not to over use it because it could lead to a discussion about his grades. He smiled as he recalled the day they went to Cyclops Computers at Hillside Mall and she put the new motherboard on her credit card. The guy who sold it to them winked at him and grinned when Andrea wasn't looking and Tyler thought about trying for a new more efficient power supply but he did not like the colour her face turned when she saw the bill for the motherboard.

The monitor woke giving off that weird smell of old electronics and when the IBM booted it grudgingly displayed a colour bar graph showing temperature and humidity readouts over time in lab seven, the grow room next door. The readouts were for the three dishes of agar growing version x. He could see the last dish in the row was showing a temperature decrease of .07 degrees. He read back through the trace and it showed a sine wave of variation over time which he knew matched the refrigerant compressor cycling on and off in the bar fridge.

It looked like every time the fridge cycled the last dish would lose a percentage of heat and the losses were adding up. This was unfortunate because he did not want to lose any of the variations of this generation. He checked to make sure the fridge was not cycling at the moment then turned the switch to start the agitators in the solution tanks.

He thought about writing a subroutine to automatically shut the fridge down during agitation but he was afraid it would have little effect and would require him to leave the computer running, which would use up any electrical savings. He could not hear the agitators vibrate but he saw the voltage drop by the usual amount. He counted to fifty while they vibrated and as he watched the last dish lost another full degree.

Hazen Michaels

Zen sat with her legs up and ankles crossed on the kitchen table eating an apple trying to force herself to concentrate on reading the first section of her homework assignment. She was bored senseless, her mom was away working, and there was no one around to talk to. She called her friend Becka earlier but they could not talk because her mom answered and said she was expecting a call.

She could not understand why Becka did not have her own cell phone like everyone else on the planet. She stared drearily out the kitchen window and sighed. She remembered she was supposed to rake the leaves before her mom got back and she craned her neck to see if the maple was finished dropping them. She knew from experience there was no point in starting until they had all fallen.

The kitchen window looked over Tyler's house next door and she wondered if he was at home. She could go and hang out with him for a while but he was not much of a talker unless you wanted to talk about science or television shows and she was not sure she was that desperate. They'd grown up next door to each other and their moms were good friends and like a lot of single parents they helped each other out with childcare. Her mom was a long distance trucker and until she was old enough to stay on her own when her mom was working she basically lived with Tyler and Andi.

When she turned thirteen, her mom decided she was old enough to babysit Tyler while Andi was at work during the summer holidays. For two summers they spent almost everyday together and during that time it had never occurred to her to question why Tyler would need babysitting at eleven. It didn't matter why because she was earning money and happy to goof off with him. She got up and stretched her arms to take the kink out of her back from sitting and she noticed she was almost tall enough to touch the ceiling lamp if she stood on her tiptoes.

She was sick of trying to make sense of the French Revolution and she flipped the textbook onto the large pile of textbooks she needed to read in grade twelve. What was the point of learning French history when even the French couldn't make sense of it, she thought. She was desperately in need of amusement; she'd already flipped through all the television channels at least five times finally turned it off in disgust when she could not find anything to watch.

She'd spent an hour painting her toenails and listening to music and was considering taking a bath and washing her hair when she saw Tyler fly out the back door and grab his bike. As usual he was in a big hurry. She had not spent much time with him lately mostly because she was seeing Lonnie Davis, at least she had been up until a few days ago. On the first day of school he sent her an IM and broke up with her so he could go out with Linda McFadden. Guys could be such jerks, she thought. She watched Tyler riding away and on a whim decided to follow him and see how he was doing with his fence thing. She was not exactly sure what the fence thing was about but after finding him twitching and semi-conscious on the ground she was pretty sure it was not good for him.

She'd asked Mr. Phillips in her *Introduction to Psychology* class about the incident without saying who she was talking about, like he couldn't guess, and he gamely played along and asked her if her friend was disabled because what she was describing sounded like self-stimulating behaviour. He told her he learned about self-stim when he worked part time in a group home for mentally challenged adults while he was going to university.

Self-stim, he explained, is a repetitive action some people with developmental disabilities engage in. It can occasionally help them to organize their thinking by limiting sensory overload but it can also be a destructive counter-productive behaviour depending on what type of stim it is and how often they do it.

The end of period buzzer came before she could ask him anything about developmental disabilities and the school year ended before she could talk with him again. It didn't matter anyway, she knew there was nothing wrong with Tyler. He was a bit weird in some ways and sometimes he was hard to understand, but he was definitely not mentally disabled. In some ways he was the smartest person she knew.

He had a tough time at school but in some subjects, like science, he was a wiz. She had been struggling to understand the genetics module in grade ten science class and he helped her pass the course and get an A. He knew the answer to every single practice exam question in the text book and he showed her how to think about genetics in a way that made sense to her.

She went into her room and dug through her jewelry box on top of her dresser and found a hair band. She tried to brush through her hair but gave up and slipped the band around it turning it into a frizzy Rasta-style ponytail. It was a tangled mess but it would make riding her bike a lot easier. Her hair was greasy and she didn't want it in her face while she rode it was too disgusting. She needed to wash it but, like the French Revolution, it could wait.

There was no need to hurry to catch up with Tyler she knew where he was going. She got her bike and arrived at Layton's fence just as he finished his run and was moving past the far end. She hung back out of sight wondering if he would go again or if he was keeping to the deal they made. She waited and when he kept going she was pleased with herself for the progress he'd made.
At first she was pleased but when he kept going she began to wonder, as he sped away, where he was going. When they hung out together they usually headed to Black Bear Park or the Seven Eleven or the Recreation Centre. She watched him turn in a direction no one ever went and she suspected he'd spotted her and was trying to ditch her so he could do his fence thing again.
She was not sure why the idea bugged her so much but it did and she decided to follow him to see what the little freak was up to. She turned the corner onto Dunstan Road which led into the industrial park in time to see him go through a hole in a fence.

She watched him stash his bike behind an abandoned building and she ducked down when he turned and looked back in her direction. She watched from the weeds as he walked to the side of the building and, after looking around once more, dropped down into the tall grass alongside a loading dock. At first she thought he was having a pee until she reminded herself boys do not squat to pee, and giggled at her mistake. Maybe he was doing number two, she thought, yuck! She waited a long time but when he did not stand up again she went to investigate. When she arrived at the place she saw him crouch down he was gone. She looked around mystified.

The area around the factory was huge and mostly covered with weeds and Scots broom but she could see no obvious place he might have gone. She checked but his bike was where he'd left it. When she squatted down in the exact spot he had she noticed the area in deep shadow under the loading dock between the building and the train tracks.

From her vantage point she could just make out the bottom edge of an opening in the wall, and she walked over to the loading dock and bent over to take a look. There was something under there and she crab walked under the dock to where she found an air vent cut into the buildings concrete foundation covered by a metal screen. The screen was part of the ventilation system which presumably led into the building. Her legs began to cramp from crouching and she got on her knees to examine the screen.

It looked secure enough until she put her fingers through the holes and gave it a little tug and it came off in her hands. Her eyes had adjusted to the shadows under the loading dock and she could see faint scuff marks and loose dirt on the bottom of the vent. The trail of dirt inside the vent led away into darkness and she figured he must have gone into the building through the vent.

What the heck is he doing in there? she wondered.
She was not sure what to do next; she listened but could not hear any sounds coming from inside the building. She decided to crawl in a little way and see if she could find out what he was up to. She did it partly from curiosity and partly because, now that she knew he was inside, she felt responsible for him.

He was a pathetic nerve junky and she did not want him to get hurt or get in trouble. As a thirteen year-old she had felt responsible for him and the reason was his mother Andi. It used to drive her crazy the way Andi would talk to her mom about Tyler. She talked as though there was something wrong with him and to her thirteen year-old mind it meant she did not love her own kid because he was a little bit different.

Simply thinking about it now made her angry even though she realized that she was wrong about Andi, she does love him. She knew that what she was feeling was responsibility; once you feel responsible for someone the feeling doesn't go away just because they get older. She leaned the screen up against the side of the building and stuck her head in and looked down the vent. She listened hard but could not hear him or anything else inside the building.

It took a few minutes to screw up her courage and crawl further into the open vent. It was large enough for her not to feel claustrophobic but it took a few tries to figure out how to get her body into the right position to do it. She did not see how he'd done it and naturally crawled in head first.

It felt like it was getting tighter as she crawled forwards on her forearms and knees and the further she went the darker it got. She'd gone about ten feet and had not noticed the vent was beginning to angle downwards. She kept moving slowly forwards and just before she reached the drop off she noticed her weight was now mostly on her forearms. When her arms hit empty space the angle combined with her momentum continued to move her forwards until she slid then fell into terrifying blackness. She barely had time to scream before it was cut off in a spasm of pain as she slammed into the bottom.

She was stunned, when she hit the bottom it knocked the wind out of her and she panicked desperately trying to draw air into her lungs. She was not badly injured in the fall; Tyler had stuffed the bottom of the shaft with packing material to break his own fall when he entered but he knew the trick and entered feet first. She was stuck upside down in the vent and did not have enough upper body strength in her arms and chest to push herself back up the shaft even with all the adrenaline wildly coursing through her system. Upside down and in complete darkness panic seized her and when she regained her breath she screamed. She gulped air and bellowed fully locked in the grip of fear that she would never get out.

She was dizzy and feeling sick from being upside down and screaming when a terrifying thought entered her mind. What if Tyler did not come in here? What if he has already left and no one finds her and she dies in here alone?

At the exact moment she realized she was going to die alone something brushed the bare skin of her ankle. She shrieked as madness took hold and she thrashed, kicked, and screamed and lost what little control she had as she imagined a rat crawling up her leg.

"Zen what are you doing in there?"

She sobbed with relief when she heard Tyler's voice.

"Help me Tyler. Please!" she shrieked. "I can't get out." Her trembling voice echoed pitifully inside the vent and her upside down face streamed hot tears and her inverted nose leaked snot. He reached inside the opening and felt around trying to figure out how she got herself so jammed up and how to get her out.

"I need to push you back up," he said.
"Please hurry," she wailed.

On tip toes he reached his right arm and shoulder into the opening. Although he had powerful arm, chest, and back muscles, when he tried to lift her up the shaft he could not lift her high enough to free her arms. He changed his position so both arms could reach inside and he awkwardly angled his shoulders into the irregular opening.

He grabbed her where he could and again began to lift her. She was calmer and had stopped sobbing now that she knew she was not going to die and there was no rat. After a few minutes of him grabbing and tugging at her.

"I am going to kill you if you keep doing that."
"What?" he grunted.
"Grabbing me there," she said.

He finally managed to lift her high enough to release her locked arms from beneath her. Once her arms were free and he got her legs started out the opening she was able to scramble out on her own. It was only after the ordeal was over and she was standing beside him in the inky darkness that she began to shake uncontrollably. She was standing close enough for him to feel her trembling.

"What's wrong?" he said.

She was badly frightened by the experience and the hit of adrenaline from the shock and fear continued to jangle her nerves.

"Nothing," she said.

She sobbed her response and bumped against him in the darkness and then stayed pressed up against his side. She could sense him bristle at the close contact, she knew that he did not like to be touched, but noticed he fought the urge and did not move away as he normally would. Amazingly he seemed to understand that she was upset and needed to be near him and for this she was thankful.

"Why were you in there, Zen?" he said.

"When I saw you heading for Layton's I followed you. What are you doing in here anyway?" she said wanting to shift the focus to give her time to regain her composure. "Promise you won't tell?" he said.

His face was near hers in the dark but she could not see him. It reminded her of when they were kids and used to talk in the dark at bedtime and promise not to tell. In his case this meant not telling Andi.

"Okay?" she said.

She was not sure if it was the shock of nearly dying or the complete darkness but she was suddenly aware of the closeness of his face to hers.

"You promise you won't tell anyone about this place," he said.

He said the words softly and his mouth brushed her cheek as he spoke. The intimacy of the situation along with the darkness helped to calm her and lessen the grip of fear. Being together this close in the dark and silence heightened all her senses.

"Yah okay," she said, whispering her response though she had no clue what it was she was agreeing to. She was experiencing confusion and, more surprisingly, strange new feelings for him; she found herself wishing he would put his arms around her and hold her. She was shocked by this errant desire, wanting to be held by him arose from out of nowhere and she put it down to the after-effects of almost dying. She attempted to put this weird desire out of her thoughts.

He did not hold her but he did find her hand and held it to lead her carefully through the basement to a staircase which lead to the building's main level. She felt oddly safe when he took her hand in his, it was true she had a bad fright when she was stuck in the vent but what she was feeling now was not fear or gratitude. It was something else. As they walked she thought about what that 'something' might be she also thought about the intimacy of his touch when she was stuck in the vent and was unprepared for what she saw when they stepped through the doorway.

She almost swooned at the dazzling scene of hundreds of golden shafts of brilliant sunlight streaking down through holes in the roof.

"Holy shit Ty it's beautiful," she said and there were tears in her eyes.
"Holy shit," he agreed.

She was transfixed by the scale and eerie majesty of the sight. It was purely breathtaking. The interior of the ruined building, far from creating a vision of dystopia, displayed a vision of magical fantasy.
From the outside the building had looked like the holographs she'd seen of decaying industrial cities in the northeast United States but inside it was transformed into an enchanted castle of golden light. She stood gazing in wonder until she noticed that Tyler was still holding her hand.

It spurred her to act and she stepped in front of him and pulled him forward into a rich mote-speckled beam of light and the sensation was wonderful.
The sun bathed their upturned faces as she drew him closer and with arms wrapped around his waist she held him tight as they shared this sweet intimacy, swathed as they were in the warm embrace of angled sunlight. It did not last long as he began to squirm but that was okay she was happy he tolerated her touch for as long as he had. She could feel his discomfort build until it became too

much for him and his eyes lost their dreamy glaze and took on the 'trapped animal' look he got when he was agitated.

He stepped away from her and said, "You promised. Don't tell Andrea or mom, okay?"

She laughed when he said that; it was odd how after all these years he still called her mom "mom." He never called Andi "mom" and it was not until she was older that her own mom explained to her how much this hurt Andi. She knew instinctively he never did it to hurt Andi it was just the way he learned things. He thought that her mom's name was "mom" because that is what she called her.

"Okay, I promise. What's the big secret anyway? Have you got a grow-op or something?" she said.

She was kidding but she looked at his eyes wondering what the big deal was and why he was adamant about her not telling. She could easily understand him not wanting her to tell Andi but he must be extremely worried if he did not want her to tell her mom.

"What's a grow-op?" he said.

The blank look on his face told her he was not kidding, he did not know what a grow-op was and it reminded her that, for a sixteen year-old boy, he was pretty clueless.

"Never mind it doesn't matter," she said.
"Come with me and don't make dust," he said.

After he had released himself from her embrace he surprised her by taking her hand again to lead her along a cleared pathway through the factory to a door marked Lab Eight.

He told her he was getting ready to leave for home when he heard her screaming. She watched him retrieve the key from where he stashed it and then plug in a cord lying on the floor. She laughed when he insisted she put shoe covers over her sneakers before he opened the door.

"Don't touch stuff, okay?" he said.

She nodded her assent and felt a puff of air touch her face as he opened the door to his big secret.

"Holy shit! Tyler, what the heck are you up to?" she said.

Chapter 4

Jonas

Sept 22, 11:15 AM
Naden Naval Base
Esquimalt, British Columbia

Mann stared out the window for a full minute before speaking, "Colonel I agree you have a serious problem on your hands but why pick me? I am a researcher I don't do field work and, more to the point, I have not worked on any aspect of aggression for years. There must be a hundred different avenues of investigation you could try before looking for a genetic factor. Do you have a specific reason to suspect there is a genetic factor?"

He was feeling guilty about the way he acted earlier, it must be a scary prospect having your soldiers infected by an unknown and possibly weaponized virus.

"Yes, but don't ask me to explain it to you," Western said.
"Is there someone working on this I can speak with? Maybe that will speed things along?"
"Yes, there is and he is an old friend of yours, Jonas McLean."

He spun around and looked at Western's face for the first time since losing the staring contest. He had managed to avoid a rematch up to this point but now he had no choice but to look because, if he heard him correctly, things had taken a decidedly weird turn.

"Colonel the Jonas McLean I knew is dead, he died five years ago. He suffered from schizophrenia and my understanding is he killed himself. I read his obituary in the Toronto Star," he said.

He watched the man's face trying to determine if this was some elaborate distasteful joke but Western gave nothing away. His mouth showed a trace of a smirk which held a hint of disgust; he could not tell if it was for the suicide or Jonas.

"Mr. McLean is not as dead as the papers reported. He is here working for us on classified human factors research. He knew it would blow his cover but when this problem came up he suggested we contact you."
"You're telling me Jonas McLean is alive?"
"That's correct."

He considered this for a moment and found himself shaking his head in confusion. Nothing Western said so far made any sense so why should the news of a fake suicide be any different?

"Okay Colonel, I never saw his body, if you say he's alive I can't argue the point and I don't need to know or particularly care what the false suicide report was about but none of this alters the fact that Jonas McLean, my one-time graduate student, suffers from severe paranoid schizophrenia and I can assure you he was not faking that."

"We came to realize early on that there would be challenges working with him but in his own unique way he is quite brilliant. And in this particular situation he was our only option because we knew you would not freely cooperate with us, given your history. We were aware that he worked closely with you on aggression mapping; he recalled a fair bit of the detail but...," he said.

"But he never understood the data in depth and that is why I'm here," Mann finished for him.
"Yes, that is correct," he said.

He looked at Western and laughed, it was a belly laugh with tears and all and it took him some moments to recover himself.

"Colonel," he said, "you have absolutely nothing to worry about. You have assembled an elite team of scientists consisting of the mentally unstable and the pathologically unwilling. I wish you good luck you are going to need it."

He laughed even harder when he saw the sour look on Western's face.

Western cleared his throat and tried a new tack. "We have the affected soldiers in isolation and we are keeping them away from each other," he said.

"Are you afraid of infection or conspiracy?" he asked and this time it was the Colonel's turn to smile.

"It crossed our minds there might be some kind of conspiracy but we scratched that idea. These men are full-time career military personnel and they are as mystified as anyone by what has happened. We've determined that whatever the agent is causing this problem it is almost certainly spread through human contact."

"Colonel, virology and epidemiology are not my field of expertise but as far as I know there are no known viral or bacterial agents, man-made or otherwise, that can cause the effects you've described. My advice to you is to look for another factor. Have they been exposed to radiation? Maybe it's a thyroid issue. Was this a deep-sea diving mission? Maybe they were not adequately decompressed," he suggested.

He was thinking out loud and tossing out random ideas and possibilities until he looked over and saw a thin smile on Western's face and realized how deftly he'd been hooked.

As a research scientist asking questions and suggesting possible solutions to problems was his natural state of being. Western had expertly laid the trail of crumbs that led him into this trap. He was a little embarrassed at how easily he'd been worked but, he had to admit, he was intrigued by the problem. If a man-made agent, such as a weaponized virus, has interfered with these soldiers on a genetic level and he could discover what it was this could certainly be important for the safety of soldiers. If it was not man-made but a naturally occurring phenomenon it could turn out to be a unique scientific discovery. Either way it was a fascinating problem.

He looked at the parked warships and came to a decision then laughed mirthlessly at the power of his ego to let him to be dragged into something which had the equal potential to be career ending or Nobel producing.
"What tests have been done on them?"
"I can't tell you."

For his part Western was maintaining a magnificent poker face and as infuriating as the man was he had to admire his nerve.

"How am I supposed to do anything useful for you if you won't tell me what's been done so far?" he said.
There was that smile again.
"Are you agreeing to help us Doctor Mann?"
He looked at Western and frowned, confused.

"You have it set up that I have to help you if I want to keep my grant money. What else do you want?" he said. He was irritated by the man's smug game-playing face. "I need you to sign these documents here, here, and here," Western said pushing a sheaf of papers in front of him and indicating several places where he wanted him to sign.

"What is this?"
"A confidentiality and non-disclosure agreement and part 4 of the official secrets act of 1971," he said.
"I suppose I must sign this if I want to get back to my life." He picked up the pen and made a few chicken scratches where indicated.
Western picked it up and examined the scrawl. "Dr. D.F. Duck." He laughed mirthlessly and jammed the papers into his briefcase.

"It doesn't matter what name you sign Doctor Mann if you fuck with us we will bury you so deep even God will need a flashlight to find you."

"I am a scientist Colonel and I can assure you there is no God and people like you are good and sufficient proof of that."

***

Jonas McLean was younger than Mann by five years but when he walked into Bio Containment Lab 1, in a building safely sequestered out of harm's way at the extreme south end of the massive Naden Naval Reserve, his first thought was he looked ten years older.

He had never been large but now, bent and stoop shouldered, he seemed almost tiny. He looked life-beaten with a grim and deeply weathered face the product of living rough for years. His voice matched his face, it sounded as weathered as he looked.

"It's been a long time, Lee," McLean said and held out his hand. He was surprised by the strength in his grip, "You look good for a dead guy, Jonas," he said and laughed at his joke. Jonas did not smile.
"I was in a mental hospital for a few years and then I lived on the street," he said. "My father was ashamed of me when I got sick. After I was released I left Ontario living rough on the coast; it was not until years later that I learned that he'd placed the obituary."

The blue of McLean's eyes deepened when he said this and he felt bad about his joke until he realized this was exactly what McLean had intended.

"Where did you learn to work that emotional capital Jonas in the nut house or bullshitting the dumpster cops?" he said.

Jonas shrugged and smiled winningly and said "It worked well on the young nurses, at least for a while, the street cops not so much."
"Are you medication compliant?" he said.

He asked the question not unkindly he simply needed to know who he was talking to. He had some practical experience with the illness. His uncle Dave on his dad's side was schizophrenic and even as a little kid he knew when Uncle Dave was off his meds the difference in his personality was night and day. The medication helped to smooth him out but he was never free of the illness until one cold day in January when his uncle rose early, ate a hearty breakfast with his mom, then went down to the basement and put his father's shotgun in his mouth.

"I wouldn't be here if I wasn't," Jonas said.

He saw McLean glance at Western when he spoke and he realized their working relationship was probably an uneasy one. Western did not strike him as being tolerant of difference. The Colonel went to the door and opened it.

"I'll leave you to get reacquainted. There will be a team meeting after lunch in my office I'll see you there Dr. Mann. Jonas, I want you to come to my office for a few minutes before you leave for the day," he said.

After Western was gone he said, "What kind of bullshit did you feed them to get them to drag me out here?"

"I had nothing to do with it. They informed me you were coming. Believe me I had nothing to do with it. I suppose they think you've cracked the aggression placement problem. I told them they were out to lunch and you would sooner set yourself on fire than work for them but no one listens to me," McLean said.

"Are all military types' like Western or is he an outlier? This is an interesting problem but he seems way more freaked out than I would expect." Mann said.

"Yes military types are an intense bunch but I suspect he is a little more desperate than most," said McLean as he strolled over to the lab window and gazed out at the same dry docked ships but from a different direction. "Not that I blame him, it must be a daunting prospect to have an army unable to fight, anyway I'm happy to see you again Lee I never had a chance to thank you for having me committed. You saved my life. I know I was out of my mind at U of T and you helped me more than my own family. I would not be alive today if it weren't for you. Thank you."

He joined him at the window and gazed at the navy ships and remembered the good times they had in the lab together before Jonas became ill. He could not imagine what horrible demeaning things he must have endured since he last saw him. It would be devastating to go from bright young graduate student with a promising career ahead of him to living on the street as an untreated schizophrenic and the occasional unwilling guest of the judicial/mental health system.

When they worked together at U of T he never thought of McLean as being particularly unstable until one morning when he came to work and he found him wandering the corridors confused, half dressed, and mostly insensible. At first he thought he was on an epic drunk but he soon figured out he was in a dissociative state. He managed to get him into the university van and drive him to the Emergency room at Toronto General Hospital. When he spoke with McLean's admitting Doctor in the Emergency room the Doctor said he thought it was probably schizophrenia which, he told him, often strikes people in their early twenties.

He recalled that McLean was particularly good at statistics and everyone knew proficiency in statistics was a precursor to schizophrenia.
"You would have helped me Jonas, if it were me in trouble. In fact you helped me a lot and for that and more I believe we are even," he said.

Jonas had been solid for him when his girlfriend dumped him for someone else and his world tumbled out of control. He had been planning to ask her to marry him but one day, without warning, she broke up with him and left town. It hit him hard and Jonas was a rock the whole time. He wanted to steer the conversation away from those uncomfortable and hurtful memories and he changed the subject and got down to business.

"Tell me what happens to these soldiers when they try to… perform their work?" he said.

He tried not to think about the fact that killing people was their occupation. McLean rolled another chair up to a computer station and motioned for him to sit.

"What we know is mostly self-reported. The affected soldiers, with minor variations, describe the problem as beginning with a nasty headache. It is unclear if it would be considered a migraine because none of them suffered migraines prior to this event. They reported that the headache intensifies as they prepare to do whatever Government sanctioned act of violence they are about to undertake, presumably kill someone. The pain increases as preparations progress until it tips them over and they reach a point where they mentally and physically shut down.

The effect was discovered at an inopportune time during a sniper mission. Of the four soldiers involved three of them suffered debilitating reactions to identical situations. The scenario I was given was they were deployed in an unnamed foreign country preparing to assassinate someone in order to maintain our freedom and democracy when this group incapacitation occurred.
The leader of the mission is Master Sergeant Mike Peters and he described the pain he experienced in his head as bad then worse, quickly becoming unrecoverable. When it struck him he thought the self-destruct charge in his rifle scope had detonated," he said.

"Rifle scopes have self-destruct charges?" he said, astonished.

"We are living in the technological age Lee," McLean said and continued, "Obviously he later determined this was not what happened. There was no detonation and he could offer no other explanation for this reaction and neither could the others. The other effect they all reported was odd and we are having trouble sorting out its significance. Along with a debilitating headache, the soldiers experienced an inability to open their eyes."

"Was that a reaction to the pain?" he asked.

"We are not certain yet but my guess is no. This eyelid effect can last for some considerable time after the head pain subsides. One of the soldiers was unable to completely open or control his eyelids for more than two days. Imagine a soldier in combat who, when he attempts to fire his weapon, is struck blind for a few hours to several days. Now you can you see why Western was concerned enough to kidnap you.

Our medical team ran exhaustive tests, including f MRI, known pathogens, viral, psychological, everything they could think of with no conclusive results. One finding that is interesting but probably meaningless is the unexpected concurrence of higher than normal poliomyelitis antigens in all the soldiers including the unaffected fourth soldier.

None of them were given booster shots for polio for this mission, it is believed they must have encountered a hot carrier either enroute or in country and this exposure activated their immune systems. The good news is their immune response was normal and none of them contracted polio. That was the only anomalous physical finding."

He thought about what Jonas was telling him but he was confused. Something about this did not track. Why would three out of four soldiers have the problem and not all of them?

"Was the unaffected soldier able to act normally? That is, aggressively?" he said, the concept of normal behaviour clearly did not apply to this group.

"Yes. As a matter of fact he saved the other three. He basically wiped out a group of heavily armed insurgents and then carried his buddies out one at a time to safety," he said.

"You mean he traveled back and forth physically carrying these guys?" he said.

"Yes. It was close to three kilometers each trip," he said.

That is an incredible feat of endurance, he thought, "Can we ascertain if they were all exposed at the same time to the polio virus? Four people simultaneously becoming positive for the polio antigen doesn't jibe with my understanding of how the virus usually works. It sounds more like a deliberate infection," he said. "Were you able to determine if they were in physical contact with someone who was infected on the ground in Afghanistan like a cook or a physician?" he asked.

McLean laughed and then winked at him.

"Who said anything about Afghanistan? And no there was no contact we could determine," he said. They were both getting into the hunt and it was a bit like old times. "Were the relative levels of antigen the same in all the subjects?" he said.

"I don't know but I'll find out," Jonas said.

"So after reviewing their data this is all you've found?"

"I've looked through the entire series of medical test results with Lieutenant Sedulca, the lead investigator, at least a dozen times, and after many hours of pouring over the results I found nothing that caught my eye or interest with the possible exception of Lieutenant Sedulca," he said grinning.

"Well that's a good thing as far as I'm concerned because if the problem was easy I would be pissed off. What is she like?" he said.

"Short and sweet like me," he said.

While they were talking Jonas reached into his pocket and took out a crumpled piece of note paper. On it he scrawled, 'Be careful what you say they are listening'. He put the paper back in his pocket and motioned to the computer screen in front of them. It was one of half a dozen computer screens in the room which all showed the same scene. He pressed a key and the video showed an adult male lying on his left side curled into a tight fetal ball on a standard hospital bed.

His eyes and mouth were clamped shut and he could see the soldier's straining bulging jaw muscles. It looked like every muscle in his body was clenched. His whole body was in spasm as he writhed in pain. It was video footage from the oldest of the stricken soldiers taken while he was still in Afghanistan.

"I suppose by now you've realized the military types think this has something to do with our work at U of T," McLean said.

"No shit, Sherlock," he said.

McLean laughed.

"Okay, Lee. I will leave you to it. I'm going to see what the big cheese wants and then I'm off to another meeting. You can stay here the whole day if you want. Everything we've done is on the computer. See you later," he said.

McLean headed to Western's office, knocked on the door and let himself in. Western was sitting at his desk and had a scowl on his face when Jonas sat down.

"Let me tell you what I know about Lee Mann. I understand you were hoping he would be some kind of criminal mastermind and the creator of this thing but I'm afraid you're gonna be disappointed," Jonas said.

Western turned away and stared at his computer screen he did not like McLean; as far as he was concerned the guy was a freak and nothing more. He tolerated him because he was ordered to bring him on-board. Someone in Ottawa insisted McLean be part of the investigation ostensibly because of his research background but

Western suspected McLean was connected to someone high up at National Defense HQ in Ottawa. If he could figure out McLean's Ottawa connection he might find a way to get rid of him, but without knowing who it was, it could be a bad move to dump him. Anyway he might need him if things go wrong with the kid. He let him prattle on about Mann not listening waiting for him to finish.

"Okay Jonas thanks for the update. Have you arranged things regarding the kid? If we need to grab him you and Sedulca have to move fast."

"We'll get him and stash him just like we discussed but I'm hoping it does not come to that," Jonas said.

"Me too."

Western had found a way to compromise both of them so they would not pose any threat to his plan. He let them believe they would be in for a cut of the proceeds when he sells the kid's formula. Using their greed to draw them in and control their actions was expedient for now. He would deal with him and his friend Sedulca later after the deal was done but for now he would let them assume all the risk.

If things don't go as planned and they run out of time they will need to grab the kid and stash him away until he can arrange a sale. It was a smart move to get them to do the dirty work, if they are caught and charged with kidnapping, nothing will lead the authorities back to him. If they get caught it will all be on them, a plot hatched by the bent psychologist and the schizophrenic biologist. No one will doubt it, especially after he releases the video tape of their pillow talk: lying in bed conspiring to kidnap a sixteen-year-old kid.

It amazed him how lax people were about their home security. They had no idea they were under surveillance, they simply assumed because they were 'in on it' they were safe. He let McLean babble on for a few more minutes then sent him away. What he needed was for him and Sedulca to isolate whatever it was the kid created. If he could get his hands on the formula he would not need them and there would be no reason to grab the kid.
It made him sick to be in the same room with McLean. When the time came he would enjoy putting his knee on McLean's neck and ridding the world of one more disgusting degenerate.

Western found himself grinding his teeth and slamming desk drawers searching for cigarettes until he realized what he was doing. He could not understand the craziness that swept over him. He was in a rage, ready to throttle McLean for no reason and the weird part was he had not smoked for twenty years. He was becoming alarmed by these weird uncontrollable thoughts and impulses.

Yesterday he almost destroyed the dashboard of his car smashing it with his fist when a car cut him off in rush hour traffic. When he caught up to the car at the next traffic light he realized he had pulled his service weapon out of its holster. He did not know what he might have done if it had not turned out to be an elderly woman driving. He put the incident down to stress from this kid thing, there was an awful lot riding on it, possibly everything.

***

Frank Sedulca held the door open for Jonas as they walked out of the lab building. They did not try to maintain the pretense they were just friends. Officially the Canadian Military no longer cared about sexual orientation as long as it did not interfere with their work.

"What did you think of Lee Mann?" McLean asked as they got in Sedulca's car.
"I only caught a glimpse of him but he doesn't do anything for me. He did not strike me in any way whatsoever," he said, "so he was your big crush back at U of T eh?"

McLean shrugged, Lee never suspected it but it was true he'd been attracted to him all those years ago.

"Well you know the thing about straight guys; they don't all suck," McLean said.

They laughed at the joke though they'd both experienced the pain of rejection after falling hard for a guy who either did not get it or was repulsed.

"So what is going on, why is Colonel Klink so hot for us to grab the kid?" Sedulca said.

"Things are developing fast. If it goes off the rails he thinks grabbing the kid is the best way to control the formula. We haven't been able to figure it out and we're running out of time. If the circle of people who know about this gets any wider we could be shut out of the money.

I have no problem with grabbing the kid, this virus or whatever it is, will be worth millions maybe billions to the right people. Western's Pentagon buddy thinks he can make a deal with an American defense contractor that he knows so, for now, we play it cool and do what Western wants," McLean said, "if the Americans won't pay the Chinese or Russians will and if we control the kid we won't need Western to make the deal. We will simply hand him over and believe me, those countries won't have any problem getting the formula out of him."

Chapter 5

Porno?

"Let me see if I've got this right," Zen said. She had a grin on her face and was watching him from the corner of her eye as she removed the elastic band from her ponytail. She shook loose the long strands then bent from the hips as she tossed her hair forward. It was long and thick but because she was tall it did not touch Tyler's spotless floor. While her head was down she attempted, unsuccessfully, to comb the large knots out with her splayed fingers.

Her face was hidden from view by the mass of curly brown tangles but the rest of her was visible and he found his eyes drawn to this interesting shape. She caught him checking her out and that made her smile. After falling down the ventilation shaft she knew there would be no putting it off she had to wash her hair when she got home. There was a bumpy line of yellow and purple bruises forming on both her forearms which she had not yet noticed.

"You found this stinky old laboratory and decided to become a mad scientist?" she said. "Is that about right?"

Straightening up she faced him and used a single raised eyebrow to emphasize her doubts regarding his sanity.

"Tyler, you helped me with my genetics paper but you totally flunked grade seven science. What makes you think you can do real science? Don't ya have to be like a scientist or something?" she said making quotation marks in the air.

She continued to tease him as she gathered her thick tresses and re-applied the elastic band creating a messy ponytail.

"I got a C," he said.

He was not defensive about many things but Andrea gave him a hard time about his marks and behaviour at school and he was sensitive about it. Zen knew that raising the subject of school was almost the only way to get any reaction from him. Like an older sibling, she knew exactly how to push his buttons, and she used his problems at school to get him worked up and talking.

"It was a C minus and you totally flunked," she said, walking as she talked, moving freely around the lab looking at stuff and occasionally wrinkling her nose. "It certainly is clean in here, not like your funky bedroom," she said.

He shrugged, "It needs to be clean," he said.

She continued to wander around the room examining everything but so far keeping her promise not to touch anything. She was amazed by the elaborate secret world he created for himself. It reminded her of how little time she spent with him in the last few years. She knew he was into science, he has science stuff all over his bedroom, but she had no idea he was into it this much.

This looked like a real laboratory. Aside from the times he helped her with her genetics assignments he never talked about science with her but then he never talked about much of anything. She knew it was not fair and she should not tease him about his school work because he was trying hard to get it right.

She suspected it was not the work he had trouble with but the teachers. They did not understand him and they split into two groups; those who thought he was doing it on purpose to piss them off and those who considered him learning disabled. She spun around and looked at him and was pretty sure he was checking her out again.

"Please tell zee members of zee jury vut monster you are cre-a-ting here Herr Doktor Tylershtein?" she said.

Pointing her index finger at him like a lawyer in a bad daytime drama then grandly gesturing around the room to the various pieces of scientific equipment with her other hand.

"Unt vere did you get all ziss fanshy shmanshy schience shtuff anyvay?" she said.

He laughed at her crazy accent but continued to watch her nervously as she roamed about the lab. He was enjoying her performance but he was worried she might touch something or open something. He never thought about anyone coming into the lab and if he had it certainly would not be Zen, she was too unpredictable.

At any moment she might do something completely crazy. There were dangerous things in the lab and exposure to some of them could make her sick. The problem of how to explain what he was doing, and why he was doing it, was occupying him, he realized, now she'd seen his lab, she would not be put off.

He was hesitant to say anything at all in case she told mom because for sure mom would tell Andrea. He was aware, from his past attempts, that he had zero talent for deception and less than zero if it was Zen he was trying to deceive. She always seemed to catch him whenever he lied so he decided to tell her the truth.

It was the best solution; he would not have to make anything up, and she would not understand the science anyway. The events leading up to his decision to build the lab were continuous and linear in his mind. He had trouble judging where to jump into the explanation so he began at the beginning.

"Remember that time Andrea went to Edmonton and I stayed with you and mom?" he said.
"Yeah, I remember, that was a long time ago," she said.

She was curious how anything that happened five years ago could possibly relate to what he was doing in this place.

"You told me your father was killed in a war." he said.
Zen's face reddened and she stopped flitting about the room alert to what he was saying. She'd forgotten she told him that and watched his face for a sign of what she thought was probably coming. She remembered the exchange clearly. When she was thirteen and he was eleven they were reading comics on her bed and out of the blue he asked about her father.

She lied and told him the first thing that came into her head. He caught her off guard with the question and she was flustered and made up a story about him dying in a war. She did it because she did not want to tell him what actually happened to her loser father. She hoped he'd forgotten about it but now it looked as if he was going to call her on it. Why else would he bring it up?

"When you told me what happened to him I didn't know what it meant so I looked up war online. I found out a lot of stuff about it but I could not find the reason it happens. The thing I kept seeing was people all seem to agree it is a bad thing but it keeps happening all the time. I found data online about violence that said it is a product of biology. When I read that I came up with a plan of how to stop it," he said.

"Stop what?" she said.

She was listening carefully to him because she thought he was talking about her father but she had obviously lost the thread of the conversation.

"Stop war," he said.

"What are you talking about Ty? No one can stop war. It's been going on for like a billion years." She looked at his eyes to see if he was talking about war or something else. "You know," she continued, "like World War One and Two and all the other littler wars. Geez Ty don't you know anything? It's impossible to stop people from doing something they really like to do," she said. She was relieved that, for the moment at least, he did not seem to be talking about her father.

"I did it," he said.

"Did what?" she said thinking he was onto yet another topic then she saw him make a gesture, pointing to the battered bar fridge with fake wood siding on the door. It was sitting all alone high up on a pile of bricks at the far end of the main workbench.

It was emblazoned with yellow caution tape from the dollar store and secured by a school combination lock and a two yard long piece of heavy chain he found outside the factory.

"I stopped it," he said.

She looked to where he was pointing and laughed playing along with his joke. She went up on her tip toes and performed a gangly long-limbed pirouette and then glided, not ungracefully, across the room to stand before the bar fridge. She examined it for a moment then, leaning over, delicately placed one hand on top and used the other to dig a knuckle into her cheek in an attempt to look coy.
Dramatically sweeping her out-stretched hand across the front of the fridge she seamlessly morphed into Debbie Darling the beautiful game show demonstrator. She favoured the audience with her most dazzling television smile.

"Here we have it ladies and gentlemen. Take a look at what the delectable Debbie Darling has displayed for us in our grand prize showcase number one. That's right folks you heard it here first. Our very own Doctor Fryin' Pan, the world's weirdest mad scientist, has invented…" she paused for dramatic effect, "THE END OF WAR!"

He laughed at her performance. He loved it when she did one of her over-the-top television personas, Debbie Darling being the best. He clapped his hands with polite but appreciative applause when she took a bow.

"Zo mein Herr Doktor Hamburger unt Fries, how does ziss magical potion of yours verk?" she said. She was having great fun teasing him but she could see he was enjoying it too so that made it okay. He was laughing at her outrageous German accent.

"How it verks?" he said.

"Yes Mr. flunked grade seven science the world wants to know," she said. She pretended to hold out a microphone for him to speak into but he did not get the microphone reference so she crossed her arms and challenged him with a raised eyebrow instead.
"Well?" she said.

He looked at her and tried to determine what he should tell her but then decided it didn't matter what he said she wouldn't believe him anyway.

"It's complex," he said.

"Try me," she said evenly.

He looked at her but avoided her eyes as he began to explain.

"I re-purposed a common virus as a vector for 9800 base pairs of reptilian DNA which codes for mRNA when activated and instructs neuronal growth in the basil ganglia," he said.

She listened and her mouth fell open. It took her a moment to recover and, in an effort to hide the fact she did not understand anything he said, she responded by saying, "You are a totally weird science junky Ty." She laughed and before he could react she skipped over to him and put him in a headlock which she could do because she was taller than him. She tried to give him an Indian hair burn but he shrugged her off and sidestepped away patting down his hair.

"Anyway you shouldn't be messing with viruses. They are bad for people and some can even kill ya," she said, "or worse," she added darkly.

She had resumed her natural place of dominance as the older and wiser of the two.

"What are you really making here?" She said this because, after thinking about it, she concluded he was trying to put her off with his crazy answer to confuse her.

He was engaged in wondering what was worse than dying and he regarded her warily as he leaned against the far edge of the countertop ready to move away if she tried anything else. He was attempting to think up another way to explain it to her but he couldn't come up with anything so he began to imitate Mr. Davies the science teacher. He pretended to adjust his glasses and checked to see if his fly was open multiple times and she recognized him right away and laughed. Mr. Davies' self-conscious mannerisms were famous at school.

"Nnnnot all vvvviruses kkkill," he said, clearing his throat like Mr. Davies did. "Ahhh ddddidn't you ahhh bbbbarf vomit your guts out for a wwweek few days last NNNNovember winter? Well, Ms. ZZZZZen, that was a vvvvirus, a bug if you will, and you ahhh ddddidn't even dddddie. TTTThere you hhhave it." He took a deep bow and made a big show of checking his fly one last time. "No, I didn't die, but believe me, for a while there I wanted to. And stop with the Mr. Davies stutter already. He can't hhhhelp it yyyyya know," she said.

They both laughed.

"It's okay. The virus I used was modified by someone and it was never a killer; I only use it as a kind of mailman," he said.

"A mailman, what kind of dopey virus is that? Does it only strike at Christmas time?" she said and laughed at her joke which he didn't get. "So what do you call this mailman you invented?" she said.

"Poliomyelitis-Okinawa ribonucleic acid, I call it POrna for short," he said.

She looked at him to see if he was kidding and when she saw he was serious she guffawed. She laughed until tears streamed from her eyes and she could hardly catch her breath. When she did, she said "Porno, you called your invention Porno?" She hooted again and bent over holding her stomach because she was laughing so hard it was starting to hurt.

"What's so funny?" he asked.

She had laughed so hard she needed to pee. In between hoots she asked him where the washroom was. He was torn because he did not want her wandering around inside the factory alone but he wanted to check temperatures again before Andrea got home. He only had about ten minutes before he would need to leave. He did not have time to show her where the washroom was so he told her to grab a flashlight.

"It's dark inside," he said
She made a face when he said that. She did not like the sound of it but she badly needed to pee and she grabbed one of the flashlights piled on the counter top and turned to go.

"Try it," he said.

She tried it and the battery was dead and she tried another and another until she found one that worked. By this time she needed to find the washroom in a big hurry but before he would tell her where it was he made her promise not to raise a lot of dust. He also handed her a small electric lamp to take with her to test any outlets she found in the washroom.

Though he had been working and playing inside the building for years he never once ventured into the women's washroom. It was one of Andrea's rules she taught him when he was a kid, and though he was desperate for an electrical source, he would not break the rule. Before she left he warned her not to go near lab four with the duct tape on the door. He made her promise.

When she returned from the washroom he noticed she cleaned the tear smudges from her cheeks. When he asked about power in the women's washroom he was not surprised when she shook her head. "And there's no water either," she said a little peeved that he failed to mention this important detail.

"Thanks for trying. I have to go now Andrea will be back soon."

As they were leaving she said, "How do you know it works?"

"What?"

"So this Porno of yours, how do you know it works?" she said.

"It's POrna and I tried it."

"You tried it?" she said.

"Yes."

"You tried it on yourself and because you haven't started a war you think it works?" she said wondering how anyone could be that dense.

"Not on me."

"So who did you try it on?" she said.

"Katie Peters."

She looked at his face to see if he was joking.

"Tyler what are you talking about?" her voice was hushed with concern. "Did you do something to Katie?"

"I put POrna on her," he said thinking she would find it funny because she laughed before.

"Tyler, listen to me. Did you do something to that girl?" she said. Her voice was serious and she was not smiling anymore.

"Yes. I saw her going to the pool and I put POrna on her shoulder when she bumped into me."

"Oh my God," she said backing away from him. "That's why you were asking me all those questions about her."

"Yes."
What on earth did he do to Katie? An alarming realization dawned on her. Mike Peters will kill him if he did something to her.

"Oh my God."

Chapter 6

Andi

September 23
CFB Naden
9:00 am

It was the morning of his second day in British Columbia and he was already sick of military food. He was picking at his breakfast in the Officer's Mess when a different woman came to get him. This one was wearing a name tag that read "Jones" on her uniform blouse and she came to tell him Colonel Western had called an emergency meeting.

When he arrived at the meeting there were two other people in the room along with Western. He'd seen the other men before but had not been introduced to them and he noticed he was not being introduced this time. The conference room in was in the sub-basement of a concrete building designated C Con. The room was windowless and it had a creepy confined feeling._

"We've discovered an outside connection," Western said jumping right in. "Last July there was an incident involving Sergeant Peters' daughter. She came down with a high fever after swimming at a public pool." Western was looking at him as he spoke.

"They took her to Royal Jubilee Emergency where she was hospitalized for three days. They treated her for high fever and delirium associated with exposure to the polio virus."

He noticed that Western was still staring at him and seemed to be waiting for a response so he complied and gave him a *'so what'* shrug.

"She was swimming," he continued," with a friend and the friend reported she witnessed an older boy putting something on the Peters' girl in the pool. Sergeant Peters dismissed it at the time because his daughter considered this friend and her story to be unreliable. Our people interviewed the daughter and the other girl; the girlfriend clearly recalled the incident though Ms. Peters remained doubtful about the whole thing. The boy was identified as a sixteen-year-old Tyler Worthy. He lives with his mother in a rented house in the West Shore area of Victoria."

Western stopped talking and he looked up and noticed he was staring at him again. The pause and staring continued for some time and he was becoming uncomfortable.

"Colonel, I'm sorry but I'm not following this. What has this to do with your soldier problem? Maybe this boy did something to the girl, but so what? I admit the polio connection is interesting but polio cannot create this problem we are seeing in your men. None of this tracks. I think you are making an error pursuing this line of investigation."

Western regarded him with an unreadable blank stare and as he watched his face it looked like the Colonel was trying to come to a decision about something.

"Dr. Mann, there is another reason we wanted your help with this problem. It turns out you are acquainted with this boy's mother."

Western was watching his face waiting to gauge his reaction to this news. The others in the room were also watching him.

"Acquainted? What does that mean? Is she a colleague or something?" he asked. He did not like the way this thing was going, it was obvious he was set up but he still did not know why.

"Andrea Gayle Worthington." Western said the name watching his reaction.

"Andi?"

His eyes bore the unmistakable inward look of someone recalling a memory from a long time ago and that, unfortunately, was not the reaction Western was hoping to see. He was looking for signs of guilt not the innocent surprise he saw now. The doctor did not attempt to deny knowing the woman which was, as far as he was concerned, almost certain proof he was not in on it. He was no actor and this was no act. Clearly Dr. Mann was not involved and his reaction proved it.

"She changed her surname to Worthy after she left a marriage that turned bad. Her ex-husband was a drug addict and according to Ministry documents tried to kill her while on a drug rampage. She suffered injuries from the assault and the ex is now in prison. It appears she was not willing to take a chance that he would find her when he got out so she and the kid took off.
This happened in Montreal fourteen years ago and she has been keeping a low profile in Victoria ever since. She works as a cashier in a local grocery store and neither she nor her son has any presence in police, family services, or court records. Murphy," he nodded at the taller of the two men in the room, "followed a hunch to see if she changed her name. That was how we connected her to you by

tracing back through her name change to her marriage and then U of T. and that is where your name popped up," he said.

Mann glared at Western, "You've known about this connection all along and that's the real reason you brought me out here." He shook his head in disgust at this pointless subterfuge. "I have not seen Andi Worthington for years. It's true we dated for a while but we split up many years ago. That was great detective work Colonel you definitely nailed my ass on this one."

Western's face darkened.

"Doctor Mann, you must admit it is a strange coincidence, you being the aggression guy and your girlfriend's son being the delivery boy, wouldn't you agree?"

"First of all Colonel, I am not the 'aggression guy' as you like to call it. I stopped that research long ago mainly because of people like you. Yes, it is a coincidence that I know the boy's mother but I have never met him and wouldn't know him if I saw him. Please listen carefully to what I am saying Colonel Western, I did not create a virus that suppresses aggression but if I could create such a thing I definitely would. The reason I have not created it is the same reason no one else has, it is simply not possible."

He watched as Western stood up and walked around the table to where he was sitting and for a brief instant he thought the man was going to strike him. He definitely looked like he was ready to hit someone.

"I don't think you understand the situation here Doctor Mann. You are not getting the big picture. The fact that you know this woman is enough for most reasonable people to assume you had something to do with this." He considered Western's words and their implications for a moment and then gave him a sympathetic smile.

"I can see your problem Colonel you need to blame someone. I would consider it a singular honour to accept responsibility for putting an end to aggression. That is not such a bad way to be remembered." He laughed at the look of discomfort on the Colonel's face. "The only reason I don't walk out of here right now is I'm interested, as a scientist, in discovering what has caused this problem. Who knows? Maybe the world is about to become a less violent place. No more armies, war, or murder. Wouldn't that be a refreshing change for humanity?"

Western stood up and walked over to the door and put his hand on the knob. "How would you feel about making contact with the boy's mother?" he said.

He had to hand it to the guy he never gives up. The idea of seeing Andi again after all these years made him uneasy. There was no scientific basis for wasting any time on this kid thing. It was a complete wrong turn and he wondered why Western was suggesting this reunion with her. He had an uneasy feeling the Colonel was once again holding something back.

"I'm sorry Colonel but I'm not interested. You are wasting your time with this polio thing."

"There is something else you don't know Doctor Mann. The boy's father is Julian Froste," he said.

He was getting out of his chair but stopped when he heard the name. When he and Andi were both attending the University of Toronto Froste was a twenty-three-year-old

French national living in Canada attending U of T on an international scholarship. He was famous on campus as a math genius of the first order.

"So Froste is this boy's father and he is now in prison?"

"No. The boy's stepfather is in prison. No one knows where Froste is he never returned to France he simply dropped off the grid. We think he might be using the boy but for what purpose we don't know. Look at your friend Jonas sometimes people with big brains do poorly in the real world. If Froste is involved in this you have to agree that it is much more likely a mind like his could come up with an anti-aggression virus," Western said.

"Froste was brilliant and yes if anyone could it would be someone like him. But he was a mathematician not a biologist and I still don't believe what you are suggesting is even possible. There are too many variables to deal with when considering the biology of aggression," he said.

"Will you go and talk to the mom?" Western was pushing hard to close the deal and he wondered why. He thought it over while Western and the others watched and waited for him to make a decision. He was curious about the real reason he wanted him to see Andi. The idea that her son was somehow involved in all this was nonsense and a complete waste of time but it was the thought of seeing Andi again that was working away on his resolve. She was the woman who broke his heart and he was not sure if he could stand the pain of seeing her again or if he could trust himself to be an adult about it when or if he discovered the reason she dumped him all those years ago. He was surprised how much it still hurt to think about her.

He did not believe Western about any of this because, so far, nothing he told him was true. He made up his mind to do it because he once had strong feelings for Andi and Western was after her son. He was not sure if what he was feeling was love or hate but deep down he knew he needed to find out why she left him.

"I will see her if for no other reason than to eliminate her kid from your shit list."

"Don't give me that Doc. You wouldn't miss this for the world. You are in this until the bitter end because now you have to know if it is true or not. Admit it," he said.

He looked away from him and grunted his agreement. It was true enough he was hooked on the problem but he was not happy about having it continually pointed out to him. He wanted to know what was going on and if Andi was his connection to continue working on the problem, so be it. He was not happy about working for Western but for now he would go along with the program.

Chapter 7

Old Wounds

Andi had always been tall and slender with bright elegant eyes. She was still slim but she moved with a life worn heaviness and her beautiful eyes seemed flat and lifeless. He suspected it was the result of her life choices. It can't be easy being a single parent these days, he thought.

He watched her from the corner of his eye as he loitered in the frozen food section glancing over his shoulder as he pretended to shop for frozen lamb pieces. She looked wonderful to his eyes and he feared he had not aged quite as well as he was screwing up the courage to approach her. The mere sight of her made his palms sweat. She did not notice him, she didn't seem to notice anyone; she was mechanical and absent in her actions as she performed her tasks.

Her hair was short and darker than he remembered, he saw what appeared to be part of a tattoo on her neck above the tan collar of her Ralph's Food Market smock. That's new, he thought, but corrected himself, for all he knew the tattoo could be many years old. He watched her give another lifeless smile to a customer. He wondered what kind of hell she'd been through in the years since they were together.

How did Andi, who used to be so full of life and eager for knowledge, end up this way? When they hung out together at university and then later, when they saw each other more seriously, she had been a free-spirited girl with a sharp mind and wicked sense of humour. Their time together was mostly wonderful but he remembered how occasionally a shadow would overtake her for a day or two. When he asked her about it she alluded to, but never explained, some difficult family situation. It was obvious that, whatever it was, it affected her deeply but he, being young and self-absorbed, was incapable of meaningfully probing this area of her life.

His palms had turned cold and clammy standing by the cooler watching her. A sure sign, he thought, that this was going to end badly. On his way to see her, after picking up a rental car and receiving instructions on how to find the store, he tried to convince himself that he was doing this for Andi and her son. He knew that wasn't true. This was for his benefit alone plain and simple. After all these years he still wanted to know why she rejected him.

Andi's House

Five hours after his less than convincing acting debut at Ralph's where he'd pretended to run into her by chance while in Victoria for a science conference, he was standing beside Andi in her kitchen. She was surprised to see him at the store and distant at first but she took her lunch break early and they talked for thirty minutes in the coffee shop next door. Getting up to return to work she said goodbye but stopped and looking back at him smiled rather sadly and invited him to dinner and meet her son Tyler.

The house at the end of Taylor Road was small, peaceful, and homey looking with vines growing over the front stoop and a frayed rope swing under an ancient maple tree in the side yard. There were only two other houses on the quiet semi-rural street and he could imagine her son playing ball hockey on the empty road. It looked like the kind of place a kid could grow up and have a happy secure childhood. As he approached the front door he wondered if Tyler was that happy kid or the unknowing dupe of a sick and angry father.

"I'm glad you stopped to say hi Lee. It's been a long time," she said.

Andi's voice was as warm and intimate as he remembered and she looked the same as when they were together and in some ways better. She wore the same French perfume, light and flowery, and when he closed his eyes he was transported back in time. Dinner was over and they were standing in her kitchen shoulder to shoulder cleaning the dishes like they did in his apartment so many years ago.

"I am too," he said but he could not bring himself to look at her, he felt guilty about deceiving her. He realized this was likely to end badly but, for the moment at least, he was enjoying their time together.

They talked non-stop through dinner catching up on each other's lives and now there was a lull in the conversation. The silence made him aware of the growing ache he felt. He needed to say something to take his mind away from the memory-pain of losing her and he spoke without thinking it through in a halting emotional voice, "I felt bad that we never-", he shuddered to a dismal stop as he let the unformed thought fade and die. He was embarrassed when he realized too late that she would likely interpret what he said not as sentimentality but as a pathetic needy plea. If nothing else the words served to lessen the emotional pressure building inside him.

"I know what you mean, it feels the same for me, funny how life goes, eh?"

She spoke in a dreamy distracted way and he was uncertain what she meant. She seemed to be agreeing with him but he had the feeling she was thinking and talking about something completely different. The hopeful surge of emotion he felt met the crevice of despair when he took it to mean she did not feel the same way about him. He saw her looking at him and when the corners of her mouth came up in a wan smile it buoyed his spirit. Her beautiful soulful eyes filled him with fresh imaginings and reset the faltering tempo of his vacant heart. Her smile had the power to make him believe, however fleetingly, in the possibility of once again finding love and happiness. He was surprised when he realized just how much he still desired her. She had once completed his life; filled it in a manner he never truly understood until she was gone.

Silent, standing beside her, he could feel the warmth radiating between them, thick with memories of past intimacy. The love he felt for her was the sweetest he'd ever known, it was a bond he had never experienced again; though he looked for it in others it was lost to him. The silence grew between them and felt like they both had more to say but could not bring the words. Andi stepped away to look through a drawer and the moment was gone, the air changed.

"What do you think of Tyler?" she said.

"He is a nice kid. He doesn't talk much does he?"

"He's always been quiet. Boys are less verbal than girls. I seem to recall you telling me that once," she said smiling as she turned away.

The memory of that conversation rushed back to him like it had been standing in the wings waiting to come on stage and remind him of their intimate past.

It had been a snow day in the city. Toronto was buried and classes were canceled. They spent the day lying around his apartment reading, eating, and making love. It was near midnight when she asked if he was mad at her about something.

"No. Why do you ask?" he had said.
"Well you haven't said anything for over an hour. I thought you were mad at me for something."
He remembered closing his book, rolling over and tickling her.
"Boys don't need to talk as much as girls" he'd told her.

He found himself blushing at the memory of what they did after the tickling and he wondered, somewhat hopefully, if she had reminded him of that particular night on purpose. She was watching his face and when it turned red she laughed. Hanging the tea towel on the stove door handle she asked if he wanted a beer. They sat comfortably together as two old friends on the couch in the living room gazing at the fields across the road, listening to jazz on Seattle's KPLU, and talking about yesterdays.

It was nice recounting histories to each other after all these years though they steered clear of the topic of her breaking up with him. She seemed to know a lot of his history but he knew next to nothing about hers except that which Western told him and he wondered now how much of that he could believe. He guessed she had followed his career online, which was not difficult to do in the age of Google. He noticed that what she volunteered of her own history was heavily edited. Nowhere in her narrative did a violent ex-husband make an appearance but he was not surprised by this omission, why would anyone bring up someone like that. She mostly talked about Tyler and the troubles he was having at school and how he was socially awkward and preferred not to be around people.

"The only real friend he has is Zen the girl who lives next door. She used to babysit him for me," she said.

The way she said it made him think she was not completely sure what to think of their friendship.

"Is she a lot older than him?" he asked.
"Two years," she said.
"Are they dating or anything?" he asked.
"Wow. Where have you been, Lee? Kids don't date anymore they hang out in big groups and take turns randomly hooking up with each other."

She smiled when she said it but then her face changed again and she looked thoughtful.

"Anyway, it's not like that. They're friends anyway I think she is dating someone. It's only that Ty is kind of ….vulnerable," she said.

"To the wiles of an older woman?" he said.

"I guess I'm being a mom," she said.

He was fairly certain that he was not getting her underlying message, there was something in her voice that made him ask.

"What is it?"
"I was thinking about something. Do you remember telling me about your cousin Ryan?"
"Robin," he corrected.

"You told me about the weird thing he used to do. How he would go to the park and lie on the ground and watch the swings and the merry-go-round for hours at a time," she said.
"Yeah it was a big deal for him when he was seven or eight, he eventually grew out of it. Now I believe he's into helicopters and trains. He lives in a group home in Hamilton and the last I heard he was doing well. Why were you thinking of Robin?" he asked.

■■■

Andi turned her face away from him and looked out the window. The sun was setting over the hay fields across the road and she gazed upon the changing coral hue without seeing it. She was not sure what she was trying to ask him. Lee had always been a perceptive guy and maybe he would be honest with her if she just came out and asked him. The problem was she was afraid, the questions she needed to ask him felt life-altering. Her fear of what his answers might be disturbed her deeply. The truth was she wasn't sure she wanted to know the answer.

"Do you think there is anything- wrong with Tyler?" she said. She did not look at him when she spoke and her voice was soft and filled with emotion.

"Do you mean Robin kind of wrong?" he asked.

She nodded, she couldn't find the courage to say it out loud in case she started crying.

He was quiet for a moment aware of her anxiety and conscious of her fragile emotional state. He cared about her and wanted to consider his answer carefully before responding. Tyler seemed a typical enough teen but from what she told him it sounded like his teachers were concerned he might be learning disabled. He knew enough about school culture to understand that teachers often speak in coded deniable language when discussing the problems of a student with his parents. He did it himself with some of his college student's parents.

"Do you think there is something?" he said.

He was probing for her understanding of the situation because it could save him from sticking his foot in it.

"I know there is something different about Ty, but I don't know what it all means," she said
"He seems normal to me but I'm no expert. Why don't you have him assessed by a psychologist? If he has some kind of learning issue it is much better to find out what it is and get to work on it and if he doesn't you can stop worrying about it," he said.

They sat in silence for a few minutes.
"That makes a lot of sense. I suppose I've been afraid to find out."

She looked sad and upset and without thinking about what he was doing he put his arm around her shoulder. It was a natural gesture of comfort and she seemed to welcome it as she relaxed into his embrace. It was nice to feel how well they still fit together. It was a familiar feeling and a welcome one. It had been some time since either of them had shared any kind of closeness. After a while she put her arms around his waist and her head on his chest and they held each other comfortably until Tyler came into the room and turned on the television.

He observed that the boy did not seem to notice he was holding his mother. At first he put it down to a teenage boy trying to be cool but after a while he began to feel uncomfortable with him sitting on the couch acting like they did not exist. The science show he was watching drowned out the jazz music they were listening to and he slowly broke their embrace. Andi seemed to emerge from somewhere far away, she had not noticed Tyler come into the room. When she realized he was there she leaned over and ran her hand through his hair. Although it was cut short he quickly moved to smooth it down. It was the kind of thing any mom would do partly out of affection and partly to get a response.

"Tyler did you know that Lee is a scientist?" she said.
"Yes," he said.

His answer was a surprise to her and not what she had expected. She had tried to engage Tyler in conversation while they ate dinner but he did not say much at all. She was sure they had not mentioned it to him.

"How do you know?" she asked
"He had a paper in the August 2014 edition of Gene Science Review."
Andi looked surprised then looked at Lee who nodded.

"What did you think of my article?" he asked.
"You were wrong about the gram negative staining but sort of right about the amino acids."

He looked at Andi and smiled when she made a face and shrugged her shoulders.

"What makes you think I was sort of right about the amino acids?"

Tyler didn't take his eyes off the television or hesitate when he said "I mean you were right at the time but the formulation data has changed, and now you are wrong," he said.

He smiled at Andi and winked and said, "Tyler do they teach advanced genetics in grade ten science class?"

"I don't know."
"Ty spends a lot of time on the computer. He likes to read about science. Don't ya, Ty?"

He never responded to her because he was busy channel surfing while a commercial was on. The kid seemed to be watching three different shows at the same time. He was intrigued by the way Tyler answered his questions without any hesitation. At the very least it seemed to indicate some basic knowledge of genetics. He decided to ask a few specific questions that no high school science class would teach.

"Tyler can you tell me what the LAMC gene does?" he said. Again without any hesitation the boy answered.

"It codes for brain convolutions in some mammals."
"What is PCR?" he said.
"Polymerase chain reaction."
"What does it do?" he said.
"It reproduces segments of DNA."
"Have you done PCR?" he said.
"Yes but only for single strand mRNA."

He was watching television and not paying Mann any attention beyond what minimal politeness required. "Tyler is there a genetic basis for aggression in mammals?" he said.

"Obviously."
"Is it possible to alter aggression using discreet gene manipulation?" he said.
"Obviously."

He stopped asking Tyler questions when he noticed the look of alarm on Andi's face. Andi grabbed his hand and drew him up off the couch and into the kitchen.

"What was all that?" she said.

She looked concerned, confused, and a little pissed off. He thought about how to answer her question then grinned and said "I think I can safely say that Tyler is not like Robin."

"Are you saying his answers made sense?" she said.

"Obviously," he said, mimicking Tyler's deadpan delivery and smiling. "That's one smart kid at least where genetics are concerned."

"Well if he's so damn smart why is he flunking all his classes?" she said whispering thinking Tyler was in the house but he'd left at almost the same moment they had. He considered her question, he could hear the frustration in her voice.

"Has he had an IQ test? It is possible that regular school is meaningless to him. He might only be attending school because it is required," he said.

Andi did not look at all happy when he said that. "I suppose I should be thankful he is not intellectually challenged," she said.

He noticed that, at the moment, she did not look or sound thankful at all.

"Sometimes bright people have difficulty fitting into the typical world. Ordinary people often don't make sense to someone who is intellectually gifted. I don't know exactly how intelligent Ty is but he definitely knows something about genetics. It is difficult to gauge how deep his knowledge runs and it is often the case that clever people can acquire enough jargon and basic information to fake their way through a casual conversation on a complex subject without having any real depth of understanding. Exactly how much a boy like Tyler can teach himself by surfing the internet is unknown but, with the wide range of open lectures from major universities and the right kind of mind, the potential could be unlimited," he said.

"Do you think his knowledge is shallow?" she said.

"I don't know," he said.

"What does your gut tell you?" she pressed.

She was asking him for his assessment of Tyler and he felt like he was entering dangerous territory.
"We didn't talk long enough for me to accurately judge the depth of his knowledge, but based on how quickly he responded to my questions, he does appear to have a good grasp of the concepts. His lack of hesitation when answering questions is what makes me think that," he said.

"I don't know whether I should feel relieved or not. You don't make being gifted or intelligent sound very attractive," she said.

He looked into her eyes and said, "I don't know whether you want me to tell you what else I noticed but there is more."
"Tell me what? " she said.
"I noticed that Tyler does not express emotion. For one thing he calls you Andrea and not mom and when he answered my questions about my article he did not try to spare my feelings or soften it when he told me I was

wrong. It was simply a fact like the atomic weight of plutonium," he said.

He paused to gauge how well Andi was taking this information. Her eyes were bright with understanding and emotion but thankfully not tears or anger. He saw the inward-looking cast of her eyes and knew she was thinking about Tyler.

She had always wondered why he never called her mom. She told herself the reason was to punish her for her mistakes. She tried unsuccessfully to clear the emotion from her voice.

"It bothered me that he never called me mom but I got over it. And I know what you mean about the emotion thing. A doctor called it 'low affect' but I knew it was more than that. There was something that happened that worried me. When Tyler turned fourteen he asked me to buy him a pet iguana for his birthday. He never showed any interest in pets or his birthday for that matter so I bought it for him.

I know this sounds weird but the next day, while I was at work, I think he killed it. I never saw it again and he refused to talk to me about it. It scared me that he could be that cold. I did some reading about child development and one book said a lack of emotion combined with the killing of family pets is a precursor to other behaviours. Worse behaviours," she said.

Chapter 8

Babysitting

September 20
10:10 am

Sergeant Daniel Nichol was dripping with sweat from the heat rising off the tarmac at Victoria International Airport. He was waiting for the grey military issue 737-100 to come to a stop. The petroleum smell of jet fuel was overwhelming and with not a hope of a breeze he would soon be soaking wet in his winter-weight tunic. He wondered if he would make it through the day without a change of clothes. He watched the ground crew push the stairway up to the aircraft and the passengers begin to dis-embarked.

Lieutenant Patricia Hunter was the last one off the aircraft. She was arriving on a direct flight from Thunder Bay and because he did not recognize her from Naden he assumed that was where she was stationed.
She has a good name for a spook he thought when he saw her spot the cardboard sign he was holding with her name on it. He checked her out as she walked towards him and decided if she didn't turn out to be a muddy-stick this could be a decent assignment.

"Sergeant Nichol?" she said.

She needed to shout over the sound of a nearby aircraft. He nodded and they shook hands. He almost saluted but she was in civvies and he was not sure what the protocol was for lady Intelligence Officers like maybe it would blow her cover or something. Luckily she stuck her hand out before he needed to make the decision. Her only luggage was a military issue backpack that a crewman handed to him. Nichol shouldered the bag and lead the way to the parking area.

"Tell me Sergeant, how did you get stuck with this babysitting job?" she asked.

They were in the line-up of cars to exit the airbase. She was a smallish woman, maybe 5'4", and she wore tight jeans and an Expo's baseball jersey. She was maybe twenty-five, wore her hair short and efficient, and seemed to be friendly enough. She out ranked him which called for some caution on his part. He knew nothing about the assignment other than he was to pick up a Lieutenant named Hunter at the airport and assist as required.

When she said babysitting his first thought was she was referring to herself, as in maybe she was an army brat with a pretend rank, but that seemed unlikely. She was younger than him but not by much and she could have easily earned her rank. He was chewing on an answer when she said

"You don't know what our assignment is, do you?"

"No, Ma'am. My orders were to pick up an officer named Hunter and cater to her every whim. I was told it was strictly on a 'need to know' basis," he said smiling.

She turned her head away from him and smiled. The Sergeant was kind of cute for a grunt.

"People call me Trish," she said.

This was the way superior officers set the protocols for their interactions for the duration of the assignment.

"I'm Dan," he said.

"Well Dan let me fill you in. Do you have any experience in covert operations?" she said.

"No. I was Military Police for five years with a few courses on anti-terrorism tactics but nothing undercover," he said.

Good, she thought. His answer was honest and not the balls swinging GI Joe crap she usually got from career soldiers. It looked like Western had picked a good man for the job.

"We've been assigned to do surveillance on a sixteen-year-old underachiever named Tyler Worthy. How does that sound?" she said.

He glanced at her to see if she was serious.

"Working for the Canadian Armed Forces I accept there is no assignment too menial or operational directive too insane for the elite higher-ups, in their finite wisdom, to request of the junior ranks," he said. He was treading dangerously close to the acceptable limit of disrespect but when she laughed he knew she worked her way up through the ranks and earned her commission. He relaxed now that he knew they shared common ground. It was obvious she retained the innate distrust the lower ranks held for command.

"The boy is intellectually challenged which is pc for retarded these days. My boss believes he may be in cahoots with his father a French national named Julian Froste. Froste is an immediate apprehend for visa violations," she said.
She held up a photo for him to look at and Nichol glanced at it.

"He looks too young to be the father of a sixteen-year-old," he said.

"It's an old photo. He is thirty-eight and heavily involved in bio-terrorism. He went underground and no one has laid eyes on him since the late nineties. Basically our job is to sit on this kid for a week or longer to see if Froste turns up. The kid's photo is from school and is believed to be accurate," she said and held up Tyler's grade five class photo.

"Handsome kid, he doesn't look retarded," he said as they drove towards the city, "where do you want to start?"

"We will find our baby but first I need some coffee," she said.

Nichol signaled a left and turned onto Weston Avenue and drove up to Tim Horton's and got in line at the drive-thru.

"Dan I thought we were going to get along," she said.

"What? You don't like Timmy's," he said genuinely surprised.

"I said I need coffee Sergeant. I know you can do better and don't try to foist Starbucks on me either it could result in a reduction in rank," she said.

A woman who knows what she likes, he thought, this might be fun after all.

The Factory

All the seams around the door into laboratory four were sealed with shiny grey duct tape. Sergeant Nichol aimed his flashlight playing the light along the seam whistling softly.

"They must have used a whole roll. They obviously don't want anyone to get inside," he said.

Hunter was standing behind him when he reached out to try the door handle.
"Wait Sergeant," she said. "There might be another reason it's sealed like that, maybe they don't want something to get out?"
Nichol reflexively yanked his hand away from the door handle.
She held her light up to the frosted door glass but could see nothing within the lab.

"Let's keep looking," she said, "it's obviously not in daily use so we can come back to it later if we need to."

He was happy to keep moving. He was not particularly freaked out by germs but he knew nothing about biological weapons except for what he saw in combat training films from the Vietnam era. One memorable scene showed a naked Vietnamese girl writhing in the dirt with her skin bubbling and boiling off her face and body. There was no sound track to that part of the film but you did not need sound to hear her screams. Horrific sights like that early in his military career made a lasting impression. He dedicated his time in the military to avoiding unnecessary risks especially when it involved things he knew nothing about. Chemical and biological warfare were two of those things and so far that policy had worked well.

He was happy to follow Hunter's lead as they continued to explore the ruined factory. they followed a rough pathway through the debris past a row of labs. None of the lab doors were locked and when they looked inside all they saw were dusty empty rooms until they came to number eight. The first thing he noticed was the floor in front of the door to lab eight was clean down to the bare concrete and a pathway had been cleared to a doorway marked basement.

She nodded and he reached out and gingerly tried the door knob and was relieved to find it locked. He ran the beam of his light all along the seam of the door but there was no duct tape. He noticed the male and female ends of an electrical cord jutting out from under the door. They looked newer than anything else they saw inside the factory.

"I'll bet this is where they… do... whatever it is…they do," he finished lamely.

She gave him a look and almost rolled her eyes but smiled instead and gently nudged him out of the way. She was trying to kick the eye-rolling habit it was fine at thirteen but did not play well as an adult.

He watched her kneel down before the door handle. It took her less than a minute to efficiently pick the lock. Her 'cred' rose considerably in his mind along with the unhappy realization she was way out of his league. When he heard the lock release he moved forward to open the door.

She held up a hand to stop him as she removed a P232 Sig Sauer pistol from a waist holster and chambered a round. He watched her walking ahead of him for the last half hour and did not realize she had a weapon stowed on board. She clicked the safety off and looked at him and nodded for him to open the door. He held his breath reached out and pushed it open. There was a bit of resistance from the snug rubber seals around the door. There was no one in the room and he resumed breathing when he realized the door was not booby trapped.

They entered and he held the light for her as she checked out the lab. He was not in a hurry to discover any deadly bugs and he was happy to let her do the exploring. She was leaning over and looking through a stack of boxes with her mini flashlight in her mouth when he remembered the plug that was sticking out from under the door. She did not need his light for the moment and he stepped back outside the lab to examine it. Someone had neatly cut the seal away from the doorway just enough to let the cord ends through. Without thinking he plugged the two ends together. They both jumped when the large fan in the corner of the lab roared to life.

"That's interesting, a positive airflow set up," she said giving him a long look to see if he had done it on purpose. "Please don't touch anything else Sergeant Nichol," she said. The tone of her voice and the use of his last name made it abundantly clear it was not simply a request.

She wasn't a scientist but she was thinking a lab this complex could not be set up by a mentally challenged sixteen-year-old. Someone, presumably the kid's father, had the knowledge necessary to build a biology laboratory. Neither she nor Nichol had much beyond basic high school science but they agreed this looked like an active working lab.

That knowledge did not make her feel any better about what they might find in the lab with the duct-taped door. She took a small camera from her jacket pocket and shot photos of everything while touching nothing. She glanced at her watch and decided they'd been there long enough. She did not want the boy or his father to catch them inside the building. They were about to leave and relock the door when she spotted a video cable plugged into the computer and wondered where the camera was located. She found a power bar under the countertop and clicked it on.

Some dim low voltage lighting came on immediately and the monitor began to flicker. She had not planned to boot the computer in case it was checked to see when it was last used but this was too tempting. She hit the power button on the old IBM desktop computer and waited while it booted. It took a long time but it came to life and requested a password. She took the key-shaped thumb drive from her pocket and inserted it into a USB port. The computer rebooted but this time without a password request. She found the icon for the video camera and clicked it. When the video feed came online they both stared at the mostly dark screen trying to figure out what they were looking at. Then she got an idea. She told Nichol to go back to lab four and shine his flashlight at the frosted window on the door. When he did she saw flashes of light on the screen.

"Stop moving," she yelled to him through the open door. "Okay now move slowly to your right."

He complied.

"Now down a little," she said.

He complied and the dim image on the screen brightened and inky shapes became clearer and she watched as something on the lab floor congealed into a meaningful shape.

"Oh oh what's this," she said.

Chapter 9

The Truth Hurts

6:30 pm

They were in the kitchen when he decided it was time to come clean and tell her why he was there. It was a confession he was not looking forward to making but he knew it would only be worse if he let the deception continue.

"There is something I need to tell you. It's about today. I didn't run into you by accident," he said.

She was already upset and she physically recoiled when he said this backing away from him with a look of shock on her face.

"I'm here because Tyler is in trouble," he said.

"What the hell are you talking about?" she said.
The look of shock on her face turned to fear.

"I was contacted by the Canadian Forces Military Intelligence unit in Esquimalt. They are convinced Ty is involved in some kind of terrorist activity," he said.

She stopped with her arms folded across her chest facing him from across the room.

"Is that supposed to be funny? I think you better leave," she said.

"Andi, this isn't a joke. It's serious. I'm here to help Ty," he said.

"Help Tyler?" she said angrily. "You told me you didn't know I had a son.

Those were your exact words and now you tell me you're here to help him?"

"You don't understand," he said.

"You lied to me today and now you're telling me you work for Military Intelligence and Tyler's in trouble. You call that helping?" she yelled.

"No, Andi you don't understand. I don't work for them. I'm an instructor at Lakehead College. They came and got me. My name came up in relation to you because we knew each other in Toronto. I agreed to come here to convince them that Ty had nothing to do with it. There is no other reason. When they told me it was you I knew I needed to help you. Colonel Western told me Ty is involved in some kind of bio-terror attack on his troops," he said.

"What are you talking about? What does Tyler have to do with bio-anything?" she said. She was angry but at least she was listening.

"They think he is somehow involved in terrorism," he said lamely.

"Terrorism, what kind of idiot would think that? He's sixteen years old and failing grade ten. What kind of terrorist does that make him? Does this have anything to do with him being on the computer all the time? Has he talked to someone online? Is that it?" she said.

"No. This is more serious than that," he said.

"Why are you doing this? What's in it for you?"

The hurt sound of accusation in her voice cut him deeply. "Nothing, there is nothing in it for me. What should I have done? Walk away? Ignore the whole thing? I know what these guys are like, they believe Tyler is involved in this and they won't let it go."

"I would have told you!" she said.

"What was I supposed to tell you? That the Canadian Government thinks your son is a bio-terrorist? I was just going to forget the whole thing and tell Western to piss off but after I talked with Ty I realized that he knows something about genetics and knowing that Julian Froste is his father….well I wasn't sure what to think. Maybe Ty is being used by him or… I just didn't know what to think about any of this," he said.

Andi looked at him with unshed tears in her eyes.

"His father?" she said wiping uncried hurt from her eyes, "You are his father."

The impact of this revelation staggered him and he stumbled backwards as though struck physically as she turned away from him. Running to her bedroom she slammed the door behind her. Stunned to silence he leaned against the counter for support as emotion welled within him. His mind reeling he went from disbelief, to the mere possibility, then acceptance as the truth crystallized within his heart. There was something familiar about Tyler, he'd felt it the moment he saw the boy, and now he knew what it was. A moment ago he understood his life completely, he knew the safe boundaries of the loops and pathways on which he traversed his world. It took only four words to shatter this illusion and slam him headlong into reality. He felt as though, up to this point, he'd been living in slow motion but now, jolted awake, he was emerging from the long stupor of his former life. He drifted through the house and stopped pale and shaken before her bedroom door. His logical mind still sought to explain it away, this can't be right it makes no sense.

If I am his father why didn't she tell me?

Before he'd completed the question within his mind his heart revealed the answer.

She never loved me.

He whispered to her closed door still reflexively holding onto the last shred of his former life.

"They told me his father was Julian Froste."

His voice trailed off. The words he spoke served only to repeat what he now realized was a cruel lie. He could not have named the exact emotion he was experiencing at that moment, but thinking about it afterwards he realized it was all of them.

He opened the door.

Chapter 10

The White Van

7:30 pm

Zen stormed around inside her bedroom picking things up and throwing them down again. She was searching for the blue and white top that she knew was somewhere amid the tangle of clothes on the floor. She was frustrated from looking for it and in a full-on rage throwing anything she could put her hand to. When she threw the iPod her grandpa gave her on the floor she stopped and flung herself onto the bed and screamed into her pillow.

When she was done she was surprised to discover how much better she felt. She knew it was pure drama queen stuff but it worked to calm her and now that her thinking was clearer she realized the anger she felt was not over the missing top, it was Tyler. She'd been frantic worrying about Katie all the way home until she remembered seeing her at the mall with her mom just a few days ago. She was no longer concerned about her being sick but it bothered her that Tyler would even do that to her. She was not exactly sure what he'd done but she knew it was probably dangerous and definitely illegal to infect innocent people with his stupid virus.

She knew it would drive her crazy if she did not do something. She could not tell Andi about it because she would go nuts on him and he would never trust her again for ratting on him. It was frustrating trying to have a normal conversation with him but she knew she had to do something. She had to talk him out of doing his weird experiments before he made someone really sick or got into serious trouble. She was so angry it made her cry to even think about him; she was angry and worried that something bad would happen to him.

This couldn't wait. She pulled on her blue hoodie and stormed out the back door. There were no lights on in his room in the basement and she didn't bother to check upstairs. The lights upstairs were off and she figured Andi stayed late to work overtime and that was why he was able to go out in the first place.

She leaned over the fence and scanned the backyard and did not see his bike anywhere. Grabbing her bike off the back porch she rode towards the old factory figuring he might be there playing with his germs. She rode fast spurred on by equal parts anger and worry. She rode past the fence behind Layton's Junkyard and shook her head at her silly mistake, it was dark he wouldn't be there.

She set off for the old factory dreading the idea of entering it through the vent. She decided she would pound on the door until he opened it but when she crossed the train tracks across from the factory she stopped in her tracks. There was a van parked outside the building and two people wearing green coveralls and clear plastic facemasks were taking Tyler's stuff out of the building. She dropped to the ground with her bike squatting in the weeds and watched as they removed the contents of his lab.

"Holy fuck!"

She assumed they were police though she could not see any markings on the van. She waited for the moment when they were both inside the building and crept forward to look for his bike where he usually stashed it. She was relieved to see it was not there but she was too afraid to crawl closer to look inside the van and see if they had him locked inside. She crept back to her bike and dragged it along the ground until she was around the corner of the adjacent building. She rode back to his house praying he had returned.

She was upset about seeing the police and wondered what kind of trouble he was in. Seeing those people dressed in coveralls and facemasks had scared her and she was in a panic wondering where he was. She could not stop herself from imagining him locked up in the white van and she was sobbing by the time she rolled through the front gate into Andi's yard.

Bad Choices

Andi's bedroom was unlit, she was sitting on the edge of her bed with a wad of tissue in her hands, her nose red and eyes puffy.

"I wanted to tell you," she said her voice soft; calm now her anger replaced by sadness, "it was all wrong, the wrong time… for everything," she sobbed into the clump of tissues.

"What was more important than telling me about our son?" he said.

His voice was low; the words he spoke held no judgment in them. There was no anger or accusation in the question he simply wanted to know what it was about him that made her reject him as a father to Tyler.

She shrugged her shoulders, defeated. She felt stupid and worthless in his eyes. Looking back now it was easy to see that she made bad choices and reacted stupidly to everything. She was twenty-one when she got pregnant and she believed that having a baby would destroy their lives. If she had the baby, and they stayed together because of it, she knew they would end up hating each other just like her parents. She did not want that for herself or for Lee and she decided on her own to have an abortion. She did not tell him about the pregnancy because she did not want him to be involved in the decision. It was hers alone.

She had convinced herself she was doing the right thing for both of them. She would take care of the problem and things would go back to the way they were but it did not work out that way. When the time came to have the abortion she could not go through with it, she ran from the clinic in tears. It was the loneliest time of her life. She felt like she was stuck, she could not go back to Lee and she could not go through with the abortion so she did the only thing she could think of, she ran away. She traveled to Montreal to have the baby and after he was born she held onto the fantasy that Lee would come and find her and they would make a life together. It was a silly childish fantasy, he had no idea where she was or even why she left him. After a while the fantasy faded when she realized it would never happen. She became reckless and dispirited drinking too much and bedding anyone who came along in an attempt to ease her pain and fill the emptiness she felt.

She bounced from one toxic relationship to another until the day she woke up in the ICU at Montreal General Hospital with a concussion. When she regained consciousness she did not know where she was or what happened. She could not see, her eyes would not focus, and that experience frightened her, but much worse than that, when her vision cleared, there was a hard-eyed social worker from the Ministry of Child Protection waiting to talk to her. The teenage babysitter she left Tyler with for a few hours had called the Ministry when she had not returned after three days.

The social worker took him into custody and he was living in a foster home. He was not yet two years old and the Ministry woman was threatening to make application to the court to take him away from her permanently. There were papers laid out on the table ready for her to sign to give him up. She screamed at the woman and pushed the papers violently away. She lied and told the doctor that she was assaulted which she probably was though she had no memory of it. After telling the lie she told the social worker she was calling her lawyer and threatened to go to the media with her story if the ministry did not back off. Three days later the same woman returned Tyler to her with a stern warning that she would be watching the situation. As soon as she could arrange it she and Tyler got on a bus and left Montreal for good. That had been a turning point in her life.

The possibility of losing Tyler scared her and she worked hard to clean herself up and get her life back on track. She landed in Winnipeg for a week staying with her aunt and while she was there she decided to move to British Columbia. They traveled west in an old campervan and toured around the provinces looking for a home but it was not until they took the ferry to Vancouver Island that she truly felt safe. Vancouver Island was as far away from her troubles as she could be and still live in Canada. The Island was a place where no one knew her and she was unlikely to ever run into anyone from her past.

Fatherhood

He was still standing at the threshold of her bedroom looking in when she began to speak. He had not seen her room before but he would have recognized it, she had a way of turning a room into an extension of herself. He saw the bits and pieces of history strewn about, the landmarks of a life constantly lived and oft renewed. His eyes came to rest upon a photograph in a silver frame on her dresser and he recognized it immediately.

He felt the air in his lungs thicken and his eyes sting as he was flooded with memories. It was a photo of them at Niagara Falls and from across the room he could see the loving smiles on their faces. He recalled how Andi had asked a teenage girl to take their picture while they kissed. They kissed dramatically and passionately and the girl was so enthralled she forgot to take the picture. They were deeply in love and laughed and posed for her again this time smiling and holding hands. They laughed when the girl's mother dragged her away giving them a nervous look and a wide berth for the rest of the weekend. It was a wonderful memory rich with tender feelings. Looking at the photo sent him back to a time when he could experience real joy and had the expectation of a happy life. It made him sad to consider how little happiness he'd experienced in the years since that photo. Andi watched him through her tears as he gazed at the picture. She kept it all these years and sometimes felt foolish, ashamed, and angry for being such a sentimental fool. Five years ago in a fit of anger she threw it into the garbage but fished it out again when she was overcome with emptiness and grief. She looked at his sad down-turned face and saw tears in his eyes and it surprised her. She had convinced herself long ago that he did not feel anything for her because he never tried to find her.

"I'm sorry," he said.

He sat on the bed beside her as sadness welled up within him for all that had gone. Regret remained his most faithful servant attending to his pain and loss, sidestepping any possibility for relief or for happiness. No wound or scar or deep regret came to his heart as painfully as the love he'd known and lost for this woman. Losing her is what he regretted most and his arms ached to hold her and undo this hurt. He wondered again why she rejected him as father to their child and this time when the word "father" appeared in his mind he broke down and wept covering his face with his hands.

She watched his shoulders slump and felt his sorrow. She pulled his hands away from his face to look into his eyes and only then did she realize what she'd done to him, to both of them.

"I am so sorry Lee, I didn't know," she said.

They sat side by side grieving for the lives they could have had but for fear and pride.

"I thought you met someone," he said.

She shook her head sadly and her eyes bore the look of someone gazing inward. She had tried to give him that impression at the time but now she could not remember why. It was more of her dismal thinking she realized. When she found out she was pregnant it affected her mind in odd ways, the worst was her unreliable judgment and a tendency to make disastrous snap decisions.

"I missed you for so many years after," he said. "I was in love with you."

She heard the emotion in his voice and knew the words he spoke were true and this knowledge broke her. Her shoulders trembled as she sobbed and he put his arm around her and held her with great tenderness. In her youth, though she knew by most standards she was attractive, she had a hard time believing anyone could love the person she was inside. This belief grew in her mind until she assumed anyone who said they loved her was suspect in motive or simply blind to her true ugliness.

She created an impenetrable loop of self-defeating logic which kept her from being hurt but also kept her from accepting love. It worked well until she met Lee and it only took a month for her to fall deeply in love with him. The depth of her love for him scared her but she hid her insecurities from him and risked it all on his heart.

***

7:50 PM

The house was dark when Zen knocked on the front door and she was startled when a man opened it. She had never seen him before and fear made her back away. She thought he was connected with the police and the white van. She took another step backwards and was about to turn and run when she saw Andi. It was a relief to see her until she realized Andi had been crying and this scared her even more because Andi never cried.

What's wrong, Zen?" Andi said.
She was alarmed by the appearance of the girl. She could see she had been crying. Her eyes and face were red and puffy and there were wet smudges on her cheeks. She was balanced on one foot on the bottom step of the porch ready to bolt.

"Where's Tyler?" Zen blurted.

"I don't know, down in his room. Why? Is there something wrong, Zen?" she said.

The pitch of Andi's voice climbed higher with concern matching the girl's.

"I need to talk to him," she said.

"What's wrong? Why do you need to talk to him?" she said.

"Nothing," she said and she turned to leave. "It's nothing."

"Zen, wait," she said.

She ran out into the yard and grabbed the girl by the arm.

"Do you know something? Has something happened? You have to tell me!" she yelled.

He watched the exchange between them. At first the girl cowered under Andi's verbal assault but then she stiffened and it looked to him like she might deck Andi if she did not let go of her arm.

"It's nothing," she said. "I need to see him that's all," Zen said.

He could see the girl was barely holding it together and she would not look at either of them.

"Zen, please come inside," Andi said.

Though she let go of the girl's arm it was clear from her voice she would not take no for an answer. Zen thought about it for a full minute and then reluctantly laid her bike back down on the lawn and followed them into the house. She was young enough to still feel the need to defer to the authority of an adult. He got the impression the girl did not like Andi and it was something that existed long before this situation.

"Zen, this is Dr. Mann," Andi said.

The girl did not lift her eyes from the floor to look at him; she mumbled something he took to be a greeting.

"Dr. Mann is here to help me and Tyler, especially Tyler," she said.

They waited for the girl to respond but she remained silent hovering close to the safety of the front door. It was obvious she did not know who to trust and he decided he better say something to break the ice.

"I know what Tyler has been doing Zen and you aren't ratting him out by talking to us. He might be in serious trouble," he said.

He let that sink in and the girl shifted her position uncomfortably but said nothing.

"Tyler is in trouble," Andi said, "and the only way we can help him is if we all tell what we know. Okay?"

"I promised. I gave him my word," Zen said.
Her voice was tiny and uncertain her resolve wavering under their gaze.
"Before I go downstairs and get him please tell me why you are upset and looking for him," she said.

"There were police at his lab and they were taking his stuff," she said

"What lab?" they said in unison.

Chapter 11

You Should Run Now

6:21 PM

Hunter placed the call to Western and he answered on the second ring. She did not sugarcoat it.

"We followed the kid to an abandoned factory and found a body inside," she said.

"Whose?" he said.

"I don't know but it looks like it's been there a while," she said.

"Did you check for ID?" he said.

"We did not touch it, I saw it on closed circuit video. It's in a room and the door has been sealed with duct tape," she said.
She outlined what she discovered and waited patiently while Western thought this news over.

"Where is the kid now?"

"He left with his girlfriend an hour ago," she said.

"Girlfriend, Jesus how many people are in on this thing?" he said.

"I don't know. The kid and the girl were the only ones we saw," she said.
The line went quiet for a few moments while he thought that over.

"OK here is what I want you to do. You and your partner… what's his name?" he said.

"Nichol," she said.

"Okay, I want you and Nichol to go back in and remove the corpse and anything else that might implicate the kid. Clean his traces in and out of the building whatever and where ever and make sure you get all his lab equipment out. I will arrange for a secure space in Building Six at Nadon, Nichol will know where that is. Don't bring the dead guy wait until dark and dump him in the woods somewhere. Head towards Sooke there are lots of quiet places out there. When you're done send Nichol back here with the lab stuff and you stay on top of the kid. You get all that?" he said.

"I don't have biological warfare training and neither does Nichol. The lab with the corpse is sealed for a reason. We will need some kind of biohazard technician for this job," she said.

"No, this needs to stay in house. I'll arrange some protective gear for working with hazardous materials for you and Nichol. You're a smart girl. You'll figure it out," he said.

"Okay. Got it," she said.

She was not sure she did get it. There was obviously something big going on here and the self-preservation voice inside her head was saying "Whoa! Wait a minute!"

"One more thing," he said. "Can Nichol keep his yap shut? Is he solid?"

"He's your guy Colonel. I only met him a few hours ago but I guess he's okay. I'll talk to him," she said.

"Good. I don't know him. He was a name on a list. You can hint at some stripes if you need to. Call me as soon as it's done and remember to leave the kid alone and do not let him catch you in his lab. I'm hoping he will show up, find his stuff gone, and behave himself until we can figure out what his role is in this.
My guy is plugging all the kid's details into the system; give me the street address of this lab and we can monitor police communications and give you a heads up if we get a hit. In the meantime, if you get any indication the police are looking for him, I want you to grab him and get him out of town. This kid is potentially very important. How big is he? Can you handle him?" he asked.

"He is solidly built but Nichol is huge, it shouldn't be a problem," she said.

"Make sure he doesn't hurt the kid. The lab stuff and the body are important but the kid is the priority. Does he have a computer?" he said.

"Yes," she said.

"Make sure you grab it and bring it directly to me. The kid and computer are top priority," he said.

"Got it," she said.

She waited for Western to hang up before turning off the digital recorder she had plugged into her cell phone. She stuffed the phone and the recorder into her pocket and went back to the car. She worked for Western and liked him well enough but something about this was way out of whack. Kidnapping an underage civilian was not only beyond his authority it could earn them all ten years in prison. She would definitely enjoy this assignment now that there was a potential for action but she was not stupid. She recorded their conversation because it was clear she and Nichol would need extra insurance if the shit hit. She was grinning broadly when she got back in the car.

"New orders Dan boy," she said. "It looks like this babysitting gig might turn out to be interesting after all. Got any germ phobias I should know about?" She laughed at the look on his face and added "Relax, this is going to be fun. We're going to need a van and some other stuff."

Nichol started up the car and drove them to the motor pool at Naden where he parked his car as she signed out a white unmarked panel van. She did not know how long they would need it so she had him top up both the propane and gasoline tanks to be safe while she went to pick up two biohazard suits with masks and re-breathers. She tried a few on deciding on a small for her and simply asked for the largest one for Nichol.

Their next stop was the Canadian Tire store in View Royal where she paid cash to buy gloves, three boxes of extreme duty garbage bags, two heavy-duty flashlights, a bunch of packs of pre-dampened disinfectant wipes, a dozen rolls of paper towels, three one gallon jugs of bleach, two gallons of household grade ammonia, and a small roll of heavy gauge clear construction plastic and tape to wrap the corpse for transport. She sent Nichol to the garden centre for industrial wand sprayers, the type used to apply pesticides.

7:50 PM

Sergeant Nichol backed out through the fire door with Tyler's old style IBM desktop computer in his arms. The air had cooled after the sun went down but it was a sauna inside his bio-suit. The plastic visor of the mask fogged every time he came outside and he needed to continually remove it to clear the condensation. By the time he turned the corner heading for the van the visor had fogged again. He did not stop to clear it this time and was almost at the van before he noticed there was someone standing behind it.

He knew Hunter was inside the building so he stopped and pulled the mask down to see who it was. The kid they were following was standing behind the van watching him. He appeared to be waiting to speak to him because he was looking at him and pointing his finger at the rear of the van.

When he came closer the boy said "How long has the fridge been unplugged?"

Nichol moved cautiously, putting the computer down in the weeds at his feet then smiling slowly approached the kid ready to give chase. As he walked towards him he was thinking it was unusual that the kid did not seem nervous. He did not back up or run which is what he was expecting and he did not seem the least bit afraid of him. By any standard he was a big man and he knew most kids would have bolted at his approach. The fact that he didn't made him pause and wonder if he was armed. He was wearing a T-shirt and jeans but it's not difficult to conceal a small knife.

"What's your name, son?" he said.

Tyler did not answer. He remained quiet standing at ease looking towards the back of the van. He slowly shifted his gaze back and forth between the van and Nichol. His police training took over and he was thinking about the possibility of incriminating testimony.

"Is it your refrigerator?" he said.

The boy ignored the question.

"How long has the fridge been unplugged?" Tyler said.

The kid's voice was oddly inflected and too calm, almost indifferent. He found his behaviour unnerving and he wondered if the kid was high on something and that was why he was unafraid. He was trying to sort this out, he did not want to do the wrong thing and screw up this assignment not that he had any inkling of what was going on here or why they were following a kid. He glanced at his wristwatch.

"I brought the fridge out about ten minutes ago. Why do you want to know?" he said.

As he talked he edged a bit closer to him and was now standing between him and the back of the van. He was standing close enough that Tyler had to crane his neck to see past him.

"You need to remove it from your truck," he said. Tyler pointed his finger at the van.

"What?" Nichol said. He was confused by the kid's warning and the deadpan lack of emotion he showed when he gave it. If he was trying to suggest the van would be damaged by a bar fridge he would have to put a little more anxiety in his voice because he wasn't buying it.

He saw Hunter emerge from the building with a cardboard box in her arms and she spotted him talking to the kid. She put down the box she was carrying, pulled down her mask, and moved to flank Tyler so she could tackle him if he tried to run. Nichol noticed the kid did not turn his head when she came out and he knew he must have heard her. His lack of normal reaction was spooky and he stopped advancing, he was thinking maybe he did not want to take on this weird unpredictable kid. He was beginning to wonder if the kid knew something he and Hunter did not. That thought did not raise his confidence level.

"Where is the fuel tank?" Tyler said.

"Why are you asking? What has that got to do with anything?" he said.

Nichol was nervous and becoming angry he did not get the point of the game this kid was playing and it was pissing him off. The kid was making him look like a fool in front of Hunter and he did not know what to do about it.
He had to hand it to the little fucker, if he wasn't packing a weapon he definitely had a gnarly set. He saw the kid tense up and take a quick step backwards looking at the closed rear door of the van. He turned to face Nichol and spoke in the same flat unemotional voice.

"You should run now."

With that the boy spun around and darted away from him and the van. Sergeant Nichol's long experience and instincts as a Military Policeman took over and he chased after Tyler instead of looking at the van. That decision saved his life.

Hunter noticed the teen was not surprised to see that she had crept up behind him. He never slowed or changed direction as he charged head down full tilt straight at her. He was bigger and heavier than her and looked solid. She tensed her muscles calling on her combat training as she prepared to tackle him low and take out his legs.

He was moving fast and anticipated her move, like a mind reader he waited for her to leap and when she was airborne he abruptly changed direction sidestepping her. After neatly deking her out he kept moving without breaking stride and quickly left them both behind.

Hunter was expecting to hit a running kid but found clear air instead and landed hard on the packed dirt of the boulevard. Her head and face were down and her body flat on the ground when time on the fail-safe device ran out. It was that bit of luck that saved her life.

The mechanism inside the fridge ignited releasing the chunk of magnesium which burned through the plastic dish of virus. It continued to burn hot, melting the bottom of the fridge. Inside Tyler's lab the bar fridge had been carefully positioned on top of five layers of fire brick to dissipate the heat after sterilizing whatever was inside but inside the van there was nothing to stop it.

The magnesium burned through the sheet metal floor beneath the fridge turning it to flaming molten steel which dripped onto the top of the full propane fuel tank suspended beneath the vehicle. The explosion that followed was powerful.

Aided by gasoline from the other tank and the jugs of bleach and ammonia the detonation blew the van apart and leveled the fence and guard shack. The shockwave continued to expand and intensify as it broke windows in buildings for blocks in every direction.

Sergeant Nichol was ten meters from the epicenter, his broad back exposed to the full impact of the blast. He was upright when it blew and the shockwave picked him up and shot him through the air. He did not know he was flying because the initial impact rendered him unconscious. He was limp; a two hundred and thirty pound projectile of traumatized flesh held together by his bio-suit. When he came down his head contacted the blunt edge of a concrete curb. He would have died instantly if he had not given chase and moved that much farther away from the van, but as it was he was gravely injured.

Tyler felt the hard kick and intense heat of the blast on his back as he ran. He'd run far enough from the van to significantly lessen the impact of the explosion. He was thrown down hard to the ground and rolled a considerable distance but he survived. Aside from road rash he was not injured and he sprang up and ran to his bike and pedaled for home. He did not look back to see the devastation. He knew the magnesium inside the bar fridge had burned through the floor of the van into the fuel tank.

He designed the fail-safe device to burn extra hot to destroy the virus stored inside the bar fridge if the power went off. It worked perfectly except he had not foreseen anyone moving the fridge. He could smell the residue of unburned gasoline in the wind howling past him as he drove his bike forward.

Hunter was pounded hard by the blast but remained conscious. She was lucky that most of the force flew over her while she lay face down on the ground. She was badly shaken but managed to regain her feet to survey the damage and assess the situation. The van was in two sections.

The lower half with wheels was ablaze and the other section which included the roof and sides was upside down twenty five feet from where the van had been parked. She located Nichol amidst the burning debris at the side of the road. She patted out the fire burning his hair and checked for vital signs. When she determined he was alive she grabbed his collar with both hands and dragged him away from the smoldering wreckage.

She pulled him non-stop for half a block then turned down a narrow lane dragging him into the rear parking lot of an abandoned machinery factory. Thank God it's dark, she thought. When she stopped she slumped to the ground exhausted. Adrenaline had driven her forward and now that they had cover she collapsed beside him. Her hearing was affected and she was in pain and stunned from the effects of the blast. She controlled her breathing and concentrated hard listening for the sound of approaching sirens. She knew the next few minutes would be critical to resolving their situation and she needed to work out a survival plan.

She heard sirens but could not estimate how far away they were or from which direction. Her hearing had been damaged by the compression of the air during the blast. Partly because there was no real alternative she decided it was best to hunker down and wait it out. She was rapidly recovering from the worst effects of the explosion but she had to consider the fact that her judgment might be impaired. Her concern now was how long she could wait before seeking medical attention for Nichol.

She could see him writhing as he began to come round. His lips were moving like he was trying to say something but she could not hear him. She needed to start planning a way to get them out of the area. She would explain the van by reporting it stolen but she could not allow the local authorities to find her and Nichol, injured and wearing Government-issued biohazard suits outside a building where a body would eventually be discovered. That damning combination of facts would be tough to explain to the local police.

She tried to remember if she closed the fire door at the factory before the blast. If she did not maybe the explosion slammed it shut. She checked Nichol over for damage and through the shredded biohazard suit she saw lots of small cuts and pieces of debris embedded in the skin of his back but no big bleeders. He appeared to be relatively okay though groggy and disoriented and likely concussed.

She was fairly certain the materials in the cardboard box she was carrying from the lab would not mean much to the police and it was likely blown all over the place. She had no doubt at all the contents of the van were destroyed in the blast but she worried the kid's computer hard drive might have survived.
The spot where it sat on the ground was way too hot for her to try to retrieve it. It was not much of a decision to leave it and run.
She thought about having dragged Nichol away from the scene and was amazed by what the human body can do when adrenaline kicks in but now she was in a lot of pain as a result.

They were safe enough for the moment behind a small building that once was a supply shed of some kind. There were more sounds coming from the vicinity of where the van blew up. Either her hearing was clearer or there were a lot of Emergency vehicles arriving she could not tell which. She was beginning to relax a little when she heard the sound of a car engine approaching the shed where they were hiding.

Chapter 12

Not That Kind of Doctor

8:10 PM

Tyler came in through the back door and when it slammed they all jumped. Andi ran to him, "Where were you? I thought you were in your room." she said. She looked him over and saw his torn clothes and the road rash on his arms and hands. He smelled of smoke and gasoline and she noticed his hair was singed at the back. "What happened to you?" she said.
He ignored her questions as he looked at each of them in turn with his gaze stopping at Mann.

"Someone is hurt," he said.

"Who's hurt?" Andi said. "Was it the explosion we heard?"

"Someone is hurt," he said to Mann, "bad."

"I'll call an ambulance," Andi said.

Her voice rose in pitch and took on an edge of panic as she spoke. She was increasingly alarmed by what was happening but when she stepped to the phone Tyler grabbed it first and stopped her.

"No. Dr. Mann will help," he said.

"What do you mean, no?" she said. "You said someone is hurt. Lee is not that kind of Doctor."

"Dr. Mann will help," he said turning away from her heading back to the door.

She ran over to him and grabbed his arm and turned him to face her. They were about the same height but he was wider and heavier.

"You aren't going anywhere until you tell me what is going on," she said.

He ignored her protests and gently peeled her hand from his arm. He turned and faced her looking directly into her eyes and kept them locked on hers, something he rarely did and the directness of his gaze caught her off guard.

"Andrea will sit down."

Tyler pointed to the chair where she usually sat and she reacted like he'd slapped her face. He never spoke to her this way and she was shocked and a bit afraid of him. It took her some moments to recover and then she tried to reason with him but he simply stared at her and pointed his finger at the chair. His meaning clear, sit down.

"I think I should go and see what this is about," Mann said getting up and putting on his coat. "I won't let anything happen to him. You and Zen wait here and don't worry. We'll be right back," he said.

Before Andi had a chance to recover from the shock they were out the door and sitting in his rental car.

"Where to?" he said.

Tyler said nothing, he pointed in the direction he wanted him to drive, and then he turned his attention to the car radio. He scanned up and down the frequencies and settled on a station that was playing a type of music he could not readily identify. With pointed directions and a few grunts Tyler led them to an industrial area of the city. He motioned for him to slow down and then he pointed to a narrow lane and directed him to drive around to the back of the building. It was a short concrete lane with grass growing up through the slab joints which led to an employee parking lot at the rear of a large factory that was no longer in business.

The rear parking lot appeared empty but he told him to stop the car and turn off the motor. They were beside a weathered wooden storage shed up against the railway tracks at the back of the lot. Tyler jumped out before the car stopped and he watched the boy run across a single set of railway tracks to the rear of an adjacent building which faced onto a different street. It took Tyler less than a minute to locate them. He knew they could not get far. He found them lying low amongst the broom growing behind a low concrete wall.

Hurt and Hiding

8:20 PM

Hunter was holding her breath partly from the pain but mostly to hear what was happening around them. She hoped Nichol would not pick this moment to start moaning. She did not want to clamp her hand over his mouth but she would if necessary. They did not have great cover but she could not move him again. There was no way she could drag Nichol another centimeters. Listening hard she tried to figure out which direction the vehicle was coming from. She knew it was nearby but that was all. Her heart rate spiked when she heard the engine shut off and a door slam.

She was already in damage-control mode trying to anticipate what would happen next and she was about to toss her unregistered and illegal weapon into the weeds. She was reaching to unclip her gun when the kid stuck his head over the top of the wall and scared the shit out of her. When she saw him she reflexively jerked backwards and the sudden movement sent a searing jolt of pain through her rib cage and her vision grew ugly black spots and she came close to passing out.

When her vision cleared and the pain subsided she looked up and he was standing there looking down at her. He wore an expression on his face which was impossible to read. She did not know what to make of this weird kid showing up again. She didn't know if he now had a weapon and came back to seek revenge for taking down his lab or if he was going to help them. Whatever else he was the kid was definitely way out there.

She didn't take out her weapon because, in spite of everything that happened, it did not feel like he posed a threat. She could see by his face he was thinking about something and then he thrust his open hand towards her.

"Come wiss me if you vant to live."

She could not stop herself from laughing and it hurt like hell. Her eyes did not leave his face and she noticed that when he said the line from Terminator he never cracked a smile. It was like he believed the words he said. The pain, the situation, and the weird kid combined to make her feel disconnected from reality and slightly giddy.

She could smell the creosote from the railway ties and the acrid smell of urine on Nichol's clothing and the colours around her seemed to intensify as the unreality of the day kept unfolding. It was like being in a weird non-plot surrealist movie. Her head was pounding from the blast pressure and she briefly wondered if she sustained a head injury and was imagining this whole thing.

She figured she had a broken rib from the fall and judging by the pain there could be more damage. Pain, she realized, was a handy way to gauge the truth or substance of reality. She was trying to think of something to say to the kid when Dr. Mann stuck his head over the top of the wall.

"Patricia, what a nice surprise."

When he examined Nichol and he did not like what he saw. Tyler was right he was badly hurt and fading in and out of consciousness. It took a lot of effort but he and Tyler managed to drag Nichol over the tracks to the car and lift him onto the back seat. He could not imagine how Hunter dragged a man this size as far as she did. When they tucked Nichol's legs in and let go of his torso the orientation of his head shifted and his eyes popped open and swiveled around alarmingly just before vomiting all over the rear seat of the car. Tyler thought it was funny and laughed and he shushed him to be quiet.

The area was overrun with police and fire fighters and he did not want to attract attention. He went back over the wall and gently helped Hunter to her feet. He let her stand unaided and watched her for a moment but she looked like she was going to pass out. He supported her as they walked to the car.

"I'm okay," she said.

Her words were grunted through clenched teeth which adequately portrayed to him the amount of pain she was experiencing and the fact she was definitely not okay. There was no room in the back and he asked Tyler to get into the car first so he could put Hunter on his lap but he flatly refused to do it. He had to let go of her to adjust the car seat back as far as it would go. While he tried to talk Tyler into holding her she fainted and Tyler instinctively grabbed her before she fell.

From there it was easier to convince him that, since he was already holding her, he should drag her in on top of him. He helped him pull her dead weight onto his lap. He could see that having her on top of him made him uncomfortable. While they were driving Hunter regained consciousness and began to move around and Tyler squirmed beneath her trying to limit contact.
For a moment he worried the boy would open the car door and toss her out. When she regained full consciousness she sat still hugging her chest trying to minimize the movement from the bumpy road they were traveling.

"Your friend needs medical attention and so do you," he said, "how do you want to play this?"

"We can't go back to the base because of the van and we can't show up at Emergency in bio-gear," she said. Her words were puffed from her mouth through a tight jaw in short sharp breaths.

"I have a change of clothes at the motel. They should fit him." he said gesturing over his shoulder at Nichol out cold on the back seat. "What are you wearing underneath?" he asked.

"Underwear," she said.

He drove them out of the area being careful to avoid the street with the burned out van. There were firefighters working at putting out the grass fires from the explosion. He took out his cellphone and called Andi. He assured her over and over again they were both fine and when she slowed down on the questions he asked her to bring a pair of jeans and a top to his motel room and a first aid kit.

His request prompted more questions but he lied and told her there was a police car up ahead and he needed to hang up. His room at the Thunder Bird Inn was at the back of the motel well away from the road. He was glad they had some cover from prying eyes as he and Tyler awkwardly carried and dragged Nichol out of the car and into his motel room. He was surprised when Tyler went back out to the car and picked up Hunter and carried her in.

The motel room was adequate for one person but it felt small with four people. Tyler helped Hunter to sit on a chair at the table and held her shoulders until he was sure she was stable and not going to fall over. Then he grabbed the remote control and lay down on the bed beside Nichol and began to channel surf.

Mann pulled the privacy curtains closed and sat down in the chair across from Hunter. He saw her swaying as she sat trying to maintain her balance as she faded in and out. They did not talk much. Andi and Zen showed up ten minutes later and they were shocked by what they saw when they entered the room. He expected a few tense moments when Andi arrived, worried she would react badly knowing these were the people threatening her son. It was obvious they were no longer a threat to anyone and he was relieved when he saw her smile at Hunter, because that meant she'd decided to help them. Andi helped him walk Hunter into the small bathroom and sit her on the toilet. When they were all crowded into the bathroom Andi said, "I'm Tyler's mom Andrea."
It seemed oddly formal given she was undressing her at the time.

"Patricia Hunter," she said.

She shook Andi's hand and winced painfully from the effort. He helped Andi gently peel the bio-gear off her and then left the tiny bathroom while Andi taped her ribs.

He started working on Nichol, first removing the mask and breathing gear that hung around his neck. By the time Hunter walked out of the bathroom unassisted he'd helped Nichol to sit upright on the edge of the bed. He steadied him as the injured man slowly gathered his wits.

Andi came out and began to carefully peel off his bio-suit as Nichol more or less regained consciousness. He was able to help them by following simple instructions like lifting his arms. Andi needed to cut some of the suit away to get it off and when she examined his wounds she decided there would be better light in the bathroom with which to dig out the pieces of shrapnel and debris from his back. He helped her get Nichol to stand and they guided him unsteadily into the bathroom.
They got him seated on the toilet leaning forward with his arms on the tank and one shoulder against the wall for support. Andi opened her first aid kit and took out bandage scissors and efficiently cut off the remains of his T-shirt which had been shredded by the blast. When he saw that Andi had things under control and no longer needed his help he went out to help Hunter get dressed. He opened the paper bag of clothing Andi brought for her to wear.

She could not freely move her arms because of the pain in her rib cage. She was shivering in her underwear sitting on a chair with her chest half wrapped with a tensor bandage. He took the clothes out and helped her to slip into the jeans and T-shirt Andi provided for her. The clothing was too big for her but that was good because tight clothes would have been painful to put on. When he was finished dressing her he helped her sit down again in the chair.

Zen was lying on the bed beside Tyler and they were watching television. He noted that Tyler did not look at Hunter when she was in her underwear; she is an attractive young woman and he could not believe a teenage boy would miss that opportunity. He noticed that Zen took a look but not Tyler.

"Tyler, could you turn to a news channel for a minute," Hunter said. Her whispered words were panted in short sharp breaths.

"I want to see what they are saying about the explosion."

He did not acknowledge her request but he did grab the remote and flip channels until he found a local news channel. They were not talking about the van explosion; he waited only thirty seconds before he turned back to the show he and Zen were watching.

She was about to make the request again when Andi came out of the washroom and Zen moved her legs so she could sit on the side of the bed. She was facing Mann and Hunter and spoke in a low voice.

"He's changing," she said by way of explanation. "He's in bad shape. I don't know why he's able to talk let alone move around." She continued to speak low so Nichol would not overhear but she could see Hunter was having trouble hearing her and she spoke up.

"I checked his eyes and I think he has suffered a brain injury, his left pupil is fixed and unresponsive. He needs immediate medical attention," she said looking directly at Hunter, "What do you want to do?"

"I'll think of something to tell them on the way to the Emergency room," Hunter said and started to stand up but Andi stopped her with her hand on her shoulder.

"He is going to be in there a while please tell me what is going on, what do you and your partner have to do with my son? I don't understand any of this." Her voice was soft and she was requesting this basic information like any parent would when their child is involved.

Hunter considered her request for a long moment and then made a decision she hoped she would not come to regret. She decided to tell her some of what she knew, not because she was obligated to her, but because she felt she owed it to Tyler. He did a remarkable and courageous thing; he came back to help them when most people would have left them behind.

"I won't tell you who we work for beyond the fact it is a Government agency. Here is what I know. We were assigned to do surveillance on Tyler Worthy, a sixteen-year-old who may be involved with a terrorist cell. His father is the leader of this cell and he has made some kind of bio-weapon. Nichol and I picked up Tyler's trail at your house this afternoon," she looked at Andi to see how she was taking it," and we followed him and watched him enter an abandoned pharmaceutical factory. He was inside for a few minutes and when his girlfriend showed up," Hunter nodded towards Zen," they were inside for about an hour and then came out and rode away on their bikes. After they left Nichol and I entered the factory to have a looksee. We found a sophisticated lab set up inside which was obviously in regular use. There was a computer, as well as a padlocked bar fridge wrapped in yellow caution tape," she said.

"I got it at the dollar store," Tyler said. He was lying on the bed and he did not look away from the television screen when he spoke. The adults all looked at him surprised that he was monitoring their conversation.

"I reported what we found to my superior and he instructed us to re-enter the factory and take the lab apart and transport the pieces to a bio-safe location. It was while we were disassembling the lab that Tyler came back. He was near the van speaking with my partner when I came out of the building. I heard him tell Nichol to run a moment before the van exploded. I did not know what happened to Tyler. He was gone when I recovered from the blast. I dragged my partner away from the blast site because I did not want to explain to the police what we were doing there. I don't know why the van blew up but I think Tyler does. That is all I can tell you," she said.

Andi's face had turned ashen at the mention of the explosion; they had all heard and felt it at her house. This was not the kind of situation most parents find themselves in and she was searching for a way to understand what was happening. She turned and looked at Tyler; she had not spoken to him since he ordered her to sit down an hour earlier.

"Do you know why the van blew up Ty?" she said.

"Yes," he said.

She waited but he did not expand on his answer.

"Why did the van blow up Tyler?" she said.

"He unplugged the fridge," he said.

"Was there a bomb inside the fridge?" she said.

In her heart she did not want to hear the answer but she had to know if her son was capable of building a bomb.

"No," he said.

"What was in the fridge?" she said.

"Viruses," he said.

"So what made the fridge explode?" she said.

"The fridge did not explode," he said.

He answered like this fact should be obvious to anyone.

"So what made the explosion?" she said.

"Fuel," he said.

Mann could see that Andi was beginning to lose control of her temper and butted in.

"I think I understand what happened. Something in the fridge was supposed to destroy the live virus if the power went off. Is that right, Tyler?"

"Yes," he said.

"It was a fail-safe device. It began a countdown when the fridge was unplugged and unfortunately for your partner, when he put the fridge in the van, he must have placed it directly over the vehicle's fuel tank. When the failsafe device ignited the magnesium, which burns extremely hot, melted the bottom of the fridge and burned through the metal floor of the van and into the fuel tank. Am I right Tyler?"

"Yes," he said.

Andi was shaking her head in shock.
"Where the hell did you learn to do that?" she said.

"YouTube," he said.

There was a pause in the conversation and Mann was not sure if this was the right time to bring up the subject of the Peters girl but he could not imagine a better time because, for once, Tyler was talking.

"Tyler, last July did you put something on a girl at the swimming pool?" he asked.

He noticed Zen dart a worried look at him.

"Yes," he said.

He watched Andi's mouth fall open, the sudden change of direction and the fact Tyler admitted doing it, caught her off guard. Her face contorted with anger and she was about to say something to him but he caught her eye and vigorously shook his head at her to warn her off. He did not want her to sidetrack this discussion.

"What did you put on her Ty?" he said.

"POrna," he said.

"What the hell is that?" Andi yelled angrily as Mann grabbed her hand and squeezed.

"Poliomyelitis-Okinawa Ribonucleic Acid," Tyler said.

He was trying to keep Andi from reacting but when he heard Tyler's answer it was his turn to have his mouth fall open. Western's infected soldiers had elevated antibodies for polio. It took him a few seconds to recover from this stunning revelation. The line of thought he was pursuing was completely derailed by this startling information and he was trying hard to sort out what it meant. He slowed his thinking and smiled. I must not have heard him right, he thought.

"Tyler," he began again carefully choosing his words "are you saying you put polio virus on the girl?"

"No," he said.

"What did you put on her?"

"POrna," he said.

"Is that a virus?" he said.

He was not consciously aware of it but he had been slowly shaking his head from side to side in disbelief at what he was hearing. He found it amazing that a kid could make up a story like this. It was incredibly detailed.

"Dr. Ok created it," Tyler said.

Andi looked at Mann and shrugged her shoulders as if to say, who is that? He was completely baffled by what he was hearing and he was thankful Andi was showing restraint because he knew she was upset and this was a lot to digest.
"Do you mean Dr. Okinawa, the geneticist?" he said.

"Yes," he said.

He looked at Andi and explained.

"Dr. Okinawa was a well- known geneticist in the seventies. He was brilliant and eccentric and some say 'certifiable' but he was also way ahead of his time and nobody disputes the fact he was an amazing theorist. I read some of his early work before he became completely radicalized in his thinking. He was clearly ahead of his time in his approach to genetics. Luckily for humankind his ideas depended upon theoretically possible techniques and tools which hadn't been invented yet," he said.

He turned his attention back to Tyler.

"What happened to the girl you put the virus on?" he said.

"Nothing."

He was wrestling with Zen for the television remote control as they talked. She wanted to switch to the news channel again and he wanted to watch The Simpsons.

"What was supposed to happen to her?" he said.

"Nothing."

"Why did you do it?" he said.

"She is a vector."

"A vector how?" he said.

"Her father is a soldier."

He was feeling increasingly anxious with each new question. Tyler's answers solidified in his mind the belief that what he was hearing was true though all his training and experience told him it was impossible. It felt like he was looking over the edge of the abyss and he was starting to feel very dizzy.

"Was something supposed to happen to her father Ty?" He was working hard to keep his voice steady and his tone even.

"Yes."

He found himself in the weird position of being both impatient and afraid to hear the answers to his questions. He was frustrated by his halting conversational style though he realized the boy was not doing it to piss him off as some teens might, it was simply his extremely frustrating communication style. His tortured communication was likely compounded when, from an early age, the adults in his life gave him grief for it. This was likely the reason he was reticent to speak with adults.

"What was supposed to happen to him Ty?"

Tyler never took his eyes off the screen when he answered.
"Grow receptors in his basal ganglia to receive an endogenous molecule that controls eyelid activation."

He jumped up from his seat and went to the end of the bed and stood in front of him. He wanted to look at face. He was trying to read the boy's expression to grant himself some relief from his growing apprehension. Tyler was not smiling or laughing and there was no "gotcha" grin on his face.

"Tyler, are you telling me you created a molecule which causes people's eyes to close?" he said.

"Soldiers." Tyler was trying to look beyond him because he was blocking his view of the television.

"I don't understand, what is the difference between people and soldiers?" he said.

"Combat soldiers produce +.023% more ATs 51-a in the ventrolateral part of their ventromedial hypothalamus." He clearly thought this would be sufficient to explain everything.

"ATs 51-a sounds like a neuropeptide designation. Is it?" he asked.

"Yes."

He swallowed the square lump of air in his throat as the carnage to his world view continued to happen.

"What does it do?" he said.

"It suppresses an autonomic stress response."

"Does POrna suppress or express this molecule?" he said.

"*ATs 51-a* is an endogenous peptide which when expressed is a reliable precursor to aggression."

"Okay, I think I'm following this, *ATs 51-a* is a biological indicator that the body is preparing for fight or flight, so what does POrna do?" he asked.

"It instructs cellular growth."

"What kind of cell growth?" he said.

"Reptilian glial cells."

He looked at the boy.
"Are you fucking kidding me? Is this a joke, Tyler?" he said.
Tyler shook his head.

"You're telling me you created mRNA which causes cellular growth in reptiles?" he said confused.

"No."

"In humans?"

"Yes."

"You mean it grows brain cells in humans that alters eyelid control?"

"Yes."

"That does not make sense Tyler, humans don't have reptilian glial cells," he said

"Human glial cells do not recognize the mRNA as reptilian."

He went and sat back in his chair and laughed. This is a joke. He is kidding me, he thought. It's all wrong. If this kind of genetic manipulation were possible it would not be a teenage boy in a home made lab doing it. What the heck is going on here?
None of what he was hearing could possibly be true yet how did he know the soldiers were unable to open their eyes and what about the polio antibodies? He wiped sweat from his brow and tried to relax.

"How did you know which genes to manipulate?" he said.

He wanted to tease the details from him and look for the inconsistencies he knew had to be there.

"The iguana sequence was completed in 2008."

"Tyler," he said smiling with relief because this was the inconsistency he was looking for, "Reptilian mRNA will not work with mammalian DNA."

"I modified it."

"Modified it how?" he said.

"Chirality," Tyler began but he did not finish as a crash came from the bathroom and Mann and Andi ran to see what happened.

They found Nichol unconscious on the floor. Talking to Tyler would have to wait they needed to get him to the hospital now. Andi helped to drag the unconscious man out to the car, and after putting down two motel towels to cover the vomit from his last ride, they managed to stuff him in the back seat. Before he left for the hospital Andi drew him aside.

"We need to talk and I have to get these kids home. Come to my place when you're finished at the hospital." She embraced him and they held each other for a moment. "I think you should check out of here and stay with us." She looked into his eyes and he kissed her once then turned around and climbed into the car.
He was tired and driving carefully and thinking about Andi's invitation when Lt. Hunter cleared her throat.

"Dr. Mann, there is something I didn't tell the boy's mother. The reason we were ordered to clear out his lab was we found a corpse. Someone, presumably Tyler or his father, used duct tape to seal the room off with the body inside. We did not try to identify the body but I suppose it could be the boy's father.
Western wanted to be certain the police did not find whatever it was they were cooking in that lab. I didn't want to mention this in front of the boy's mother. She was upset enough without hearing that news but I thought you should know," she said.

"What body? Are you saying Tyler killed someone?"

"I don't know the answer to that question. All I know is we plugged a video feed cable into his computer and it showed a corpse on the floor of lab four and the door was tightly sealed with duct tape. The corpse, from what I could see, had been in there for a long time, it looked quite deformed. When I told Colonel Western about it he ordered us to clear the factory. He wanted to ensure that nothing would lead the police to Tyler if the body was discovered. Until I heard you questioning him a few minutes ago I had no idea why Western would take such a crazy risk. Messing up a civilian crime scene is a serious matter but now I think I understand why he did it. What I do not understand is why Tyler came back for us. He had no reason to help us. We were stealing his stuff. Nothing he did makes any sense to me, what is his deal anyway?" she said.

He thought about that as he turned onto the highway heading south. He was about to say something when they came up beside a police car and they both stiffened. It would not be easy to explain why Nichol was lying unconscious in the backseat. When the black and white turned a corner and sped away they both let out a long breath and relaxed.

"All I can tell you is he came home shortly after we heard the explosion and told us someone was hurt and needed my help, not his mom or Zen, me. It was as if he knew I was connected to you but there is no way he could have known. It is impossible to explain what drives him, you may have noticed he doesn't talk a lot or explain things in detail, so it was odd how insistent he was that I help you."

They drove along in silence for a while.

"He isn't connected with a terrorist cell is he?" she said.

"Clearly not, the bio-genetic thing he's been working on is his idea alone and there is no mysterious terrorist father pulling the strings and using him as a delivery boy. The bullshit story Western told you is the same one he told me. As for the girl she is not involved in any of this she is simply his friend and guardian angel," he said.

By the time they arrived at the Emergency entrance Hunter had her cover story ready. Keep it simple, she thought, Nichol fell off his motorcycle and banged his head. She hoped some sharp nurse would not be suspicious about all the shrapnel holes on his back. She would explain her busted ribs by telling them she was on the back of the bike.

He stopped outside and ran in to get help to move Nichol. He helped Hunter out of the car while two hospital attendants lifted Nichol off the back seat and onto a gurney. He walked her into the waiting area and found her a seat and knelt down in front of her for a moment to make certain she was not going to faint then he wished her good luck and left.

He did not stick around to find out if the medical staff bought her story. He needed to talk check out and get to Andi's house. What Hunter told him had just made Tyler's problems a lot worse. He knew that sooner or later Hunter would call Western and report to him what happened and he needed time to come up with a plan. He was on his way to the motel when Andi called him.

"There is a new problem. On the way home Zen was asking Ty questions about Katie Peters. She asked him if he infected anyone else with POrna and he told her that he had infected her with it last winter," she said.

"Oh no, how did she take the news?" he said.

"Not well, she is hurt and angry. He tried to explain why he did it but it just made things worse," she said, "I'm afraid she might call the police. Thank God her mom is on the road or it would be game over for Tyler."

"Damn," he said.

"I'm on my way over to talk to Zen now to see if I can calm her down. When you get here could you talk to Ty and find out what he did to her and if there is some way to fix it?" she said.

Andi sounded exhausted and overwhelmed.
"I'll talk to him and I'll speak to Zen too and see if I can help her with this," he said.

"Thank you, Lee. I need help with this, I don't understand what he has done or why," she said.

He drove back to his motel to check out before going to Andi's house. A plan was beginning to take shape. He needed to straighten out this mess to keep Tyler out of prison. He felt bad for Zen but at the moment he had no idea how to help her and he could only manage one crisis at a time. He went into the room and packed his suitcase and grabbed the discarded bio-suits and facemasks. He paid and checked out of his room and then returned the car to the rental company and paid the yard kid extra for cleaning out the puke. He told him he could keep the motel towels and laughed when the kid sarcastically said, "Gee, thanks, Mister."

He rented their smallest moving van and threw his suitcase and the bio-suits into the back then headed for Andi's house. He got lost on his way there, turning down the wrong street, and he had to stop and turn around and backtrack. That was when he caught a glimpse of a dark sedan he was certain he'd seen earlier near the motel. For a few unsettling moments he was convinced the car was following him then he shook his head and laughed at his paranoia, it was just coincidence Victoria is a small city.

When he knocked at Andi's front door no one answered so he walked around to the back and let himself in. Andi was next door at Zen's and the house was dark. He found Tyler in his bedroom in the basement and he tapped on the door.

"Can I come in?" he said through the door.

Tyler unlocked the door and without saying a word went back to his computer. He entered the room and looked around it was completely dark except for the light coming from the computer screen. He sat on the edge of his bed and watched him working at his computer. Tyler did not seem surprised to see him and he did not ask him why he was there or how he got in the house, his lack of curiosity about such things was not typical.

"What are you working on, Ty?" he asked.

"Glial cell replication syntax."

His wide-range of interests did not surprise him but he found it odd how he could be interested in such a diversity of subjects yet talk so little about it.

"Your mom asked me to talk to you. Zen is upset with you. Do you know why?"

"Zen is upset."

"Do you know why she is upset?" he said.

"POrna."

"Yes. She is angry that you infected her," he said.

"Yes."

"She is upset because it made her sick," he said.
He watched the boy work through the details of their conversation in his mind.

"Are you sorry you did it?" he asked.

"No."

"Tyler, it is not okay to infect someone. Do you know why?" he said.
He could see the boy thinking it over. He obviously did not understand why Zen would be upset about being infected so he tried to relate it to a past experience.

"Like asking why someone is fat."

He could not help laughing at the boy's weird understanding of things.

"Well, not exactly, Ty though I suppose it is a bit like that only more serious," he said, "Zen is a girl and things like that upset her." When he said that he realized too late it was not what he'd meant to say.

"Zen is a girl," Tyler agreed.

He smiled and shook his head when he realized he'd reached the limit of his social awareness. He could not waste any more time he needed to find out what he knew about the corpse in the old factory. Considering his tortured conversational style he decided it was best to jump straight in and get to the point.

"What do you know about the dead person at the factory?" he said. "Do you know who it is and what happened?"

"Hobo."

"Do you mean the dead person was a street person?"

Tyler nodded.

"Do you know how he died?" he asked.

"Bacillus Anthracis."

Tyler answered without hesitation as if he was reading it from the computer screen and he peeked to see if he was but Bacillus Anthracis was not on the screen. He sat down again with a renewed sense of unease.

"Anthrax?" he said. "Are you certain Tyler? How do you know it was anthrax?
Where did it come from?"

"The farm."

He pointed his finger over his shoulder in the direction of the farm across the road.

"Why anthrax? What were you doing with it?" he said.

"Possible vector."

"What?" he said.

"I separated its virulence Plasmids, pXO1 and pXO2, but it was unstable and it resisted insertion of the mRNA sequence."

He was stunned by this information. How could he know this stuff let alone work with it in these primitive conditions? The answer, he realized, was simple he didn't do it someone must be working behind the scenes helping him.

"Tyler, did someone help you get the anthrax?" he said.

"David Klein."

"Who is David Klein?" he asked as he tried to recall all the scientists named Klein.

"Farmer."

He pointed over his shoulder in the direction of the farm across the road.
While they were talking his eyes had adjusted to the low light in the room and details started to emerge. It was a big room which would likely be a rec room had it not been stuffed with all kinds of science and technology related items.
There were two long work benches built from scavenged lumber. He could see mismatched paint on their surfaces from prior use. The benches looked sturdy and were situated on opposite sides of the room. Both were completely covered with electronics and other parts. Tyler was sitting at his computer, which occupied one end of the bench placed along the outside wall. He noticed a sedimentation chart taped to the wall above his head.
There was something that looked like it had once been a kitchen blender sitting on the floor. He got up and walked over to look under the workbench and examine it. It was modified to work as a centrifuge.

"Did you make this Ty?" he said.

"Yes."

"How fast does it spin?" he said.

"15000 rpm. Its broken."

He saw a homemade gel box built with an electrical transformer from a Lionel train set and there was a bottle of polyacrylamide gel beside it.

"Ty, where did you get this gel?" he said.

"Free sample."

He read the shipping label attached to the container. It was addressed to T. L. Worthy, President, Zen Gene Labs Ltd. at this address. It came from a scientific equipment distributor in Toronto that he recognized. He continued to examine the various science-related devices and laughed when he saw a large clear glass pickle jar filled with white marbles with the business end of a black plastic dildo protruding from the top. It took him a moment to get control of himself before asking what the jar was used for.

"Cellular breakdown."

He smiled at the boy's dead pan expression when he answered and continued to look around marveling at what he was seeing, amazed by the creative ingenuity of the kid. The devices he built, though not elegant, would certainly do the job they were meant to do. He wondered how he had managed to work safely in the house with Andi around. How did he keep her from getting into things? Conceivably, if she decided to come in and clean his room she could be exposed to something toxic.

"Did you work on anthrax here?" he said.

"I don't work here."

"What about all this equipment?" he said.

"Old stuff."

"Does Andi ever come into your room to clean?" he said.

"Not since the rat." He pointed to a stain above the doorway to his room and Mann walked over to examine it. The wall above the door was stained with something brown and he saw tufts of fur stuck to the brown stuff. "Rat stuff got on her hair."

He smiled at the look on the boy's face, he was getting a clearer picture of him and was relieved to see at least a few signs of typical teenage behaviour.

"Did you set that up to happen?" he said.

The boy's face showed no expression but turned slightly red.

"She touches stuff."

He looked directly at Mann for the first time since he entered the room and there was a *do you know what I mean* look on his face.

"Yes Tyler I know what you mean," he said.
"Tell me more about the POrna virus. What are its limiting factors? How virulent is it? Is it as communicable as polio or do you know?" he said.

"Programed entropy, mutates to harmless after three iterations."

"Did you design this entropy or does it occur naturally?" he said.

"Design."

"Have you created an anti-virus to control POrna in case the virus spontaneously mutates into a more virulent form, for instance what if it jumps and infects a non-human species like the avian influenza model?"

"No need, it relies 100% on human DNA to replicate."

Chapter 13

Trouble

8:40 PM

Western's sour-gut told him things did not go as planned at the factory. He should have heard from Hunter by now and he was getting worried. He hadn't heard from Dr. Mann but that wasn't a surprise he had been a long shot at best and was probably halfway back to Thunder Bay by now. It didn't matter, when he figured out he was not involved, he lost usefulness. He had no faith in the guy anyway and the fact he did not call was hard to place in the hierarchy of problems facing him.

Earlier in the day the base commander, under pressure from Sergeant Peters' wife, released the infected soldiers from quarantine and by now had presumably gone home. It was bad luck that Mrs. Peters' father happened to be the Brigadier General in charge of all of Western Canada's Armed Forces. He was trying to watch television in the bedroom he used as a den but he could not keep his mind on it. He was worried that Hunter messed this up somehow.

"Damn. Why hasn't she called?"

The words had just left his mouth when the phone rang and he jumped up to get it. It was not Hunter. It was Tom Waters, the assistant base commander. A call from him was not good news.

"Hi Tom," he said.

"John," Waters said without engaging in the usual pleasantries. "Do you have a Lieutenant named Patricia Hunter working for you?"

Western swallowed. "Yes sir."

"A vehicle checked out in her name exploded and burned in Colwood a couple hours ago. What do you know about it?" Waters said.
Western swore under his breath. What the hell went wrong? He needed to get this guy off the phone quickly.

"Yes Tom she is one of ours and she is on an assignment in Victoria. I can give you the details if you give me a direct order but I feel I should warn you her assignment is classified and you might not want to know these particular details," he said.

His lightly veiled warning produced the desired effect. The Major paused for a moment and then said, "Get this thing under control John before it eats someone's career."

The Major hung up without saying goodbye. He knew exactly how to play men like Waters. No mid-level bureaucrat would ever order him to reveal classified details that he might later need to deny knowledge of. Anytime covert ops were involved the politically sensitive higher-ups knew it was a better career move not to be aware of the details. Now that Waters had been dealt with it was time to figure out what went wrong with his operation.

Chapter 14

Sandwiches

11:19 PM

Andi came home from talking with Zen and went downstairs to look for them. He noticed she did not enter Tyler's bedroom, she stood outside looking in, and that made him smile.

"Zen is really upset," she said.

He saw the sadness in her eyes when she spoke, it was obvious that what Tyler did to Zen weighed heavily on her. She smiled wanly as he stepped out and took her into his arms and held her close and in that moment it felt like they'd never been apart. He thought he'd lost her forever and now with the situation spinning wildly out of control he worried he might lose her again, this time for good.

He was troubled, afraid that Sergeant Nichol would die of his wounds. He looked bad and was unresponsive when they rolled him into the Emergency room. It was unclear how the legal system would view Tyler's role in his death. Both deaths were related to what he was doing in the old factory and, with the additional complication of infecting Zen with POrna virus, things were stacking up against the boy and he knew it would destroy Andi if Tyler went to prison.
He did not know what he was going to say to Zen as he walked across the lawn to her house. When he knocked

on the door his basic goal was to convince her not to report Tyler to the authorities.

Zen looked pale when she opened the door but she stood aside to let him in and he took that as a positive sign. He could see she'd been crying. Without saying a word she led him into the kitchen where he sat across from her at the kitchen table. The house was almost exactly the same design as the one next door that Andi rented only this kitchen was yellow and hers was blue. He watched Zen's fingers as she sat slumped in her chair peeling an orange.

He had always been fascinated by women's hands, in some respects they were the most interesting feminine feature. Something about the animation and strength of slender female fingers made him think about the creation of art. He zoned out for a few moments until the tart scent of peeled orange roused him and he realized just how fatigued he was. Between letting him in and peeling the fruit Zen did not say much but she checked her cell phone at least ten times.

"Have you talked to your mom?" he asked.

"Yes. She's in Saskatchewan delivering tractor parts, there's something wrong with her truck again. She's been having trouble with it lately."

"Did you tell her what happened?" he said.

She lifted her eyes from the orange and looked at him like he was an imbecile.
"Are you crazy? I don't want her to have a heart attack," she said.

When she spoke she flipped the hair from her face and that girlish gesture reminded him how young she was, and looking at her face, even with the stress and being upset and tired, he could see that she was still a kid. "She will need to know sooner or later," he said.

"I pick later," she said and turned and tossed the orange peel into the kitchen sink. She was obviously still angry at Tyler and her movements showed it but there were things he needed to talk to her about which could not wait.

His immediate problem was that she did not know him and had no reason to trust him. She had been afraid of him when he opened the door at Andi's house and he hoped that first impression could be overcome. It was clear Andi had never talked about him and then out of nowhere this strange man shows up and everything goes to hell.

"I've been thinking about what Tyler told you about infecting you with his virus," he started. "I think he is wrong about what will happen. I don't know if you are aware that I am a geneticist and I know there are many things including viruses which do not get passed from mother to child. In all probability he is wrong about your future offspring having the virus."

When Andi told him the reason Tyler had infected Zen was so her baby would be a POrna carrier he'd said a silent, *oh fuck no!* and as he watched darkness gather in her features her expression hardened and she looked him in the eye.

"Like he's been wrong about everything else?"

The tone of her voice left no room for argument on that point. He winced at the sharpness of her comment and its obvious truth and, in a reassuring way, he was impressed and buoyed by her strength of spirit. This is a strong young woman, he thought, she will always be a survivor, no matter what happens.

She was right to say that Tyler had been correct about most things and her fears, given what was at stake, were well founded. There were many reasons for her to be upset about what he did to her not the least of which was it made assumptions about what she would be doing with her life. Before he came over to talk to her Andi told him that Zen had freaked out on Tyler when he told her she should be happy to have a baby with the POrna virus.

'A baby will spread POrna all over the world.'

When she cried he tried to undo the damage by explaining to her how an infected baby would be a good thing for people like her father. Mann looked at her face and could not imagine what she must be feeling or what kind of horror movie scenario was running through her mind thinking about someday giving birth to an infected baby. She must surely wonder, he thought, what else would be wrong with it.

"The problem is that Tyler does not understand that what he did was wrong. To him it was a perfectly reasonable action to take and it never occurred to him you would not want to do it," he said.

After he said that he shook his head at the awkwardness of this approach. He watched the negative effect his ill-chosen words had on her and decided to try a different tack.

"Ty believes you are his girlfriend, you know that, don't you?" he said.

She got up from the table and walked to the sink and spit an orange pip into it. She turned on the water and flipped the switch for the garbage disposal and used a finger to slide the pip and pieces of peel down the drain. The noise of the grinder saved her from having to respond to his question right away. The truth was she did not know how she felt or what she thought about any of this, not that there was anything she could do about it. The whole freaky idea of him giving her his stupid virus was creepy.

Did she even want to know someone who would do a thing like this? The problem was she had no choice about any of it. She was infected and there was no way to undo that.

"I kind of understand what you're saying. He thinks I'm his girlfriend and that made it okay to infect me because he doesn't get the whole concept of right and wrong, like laws and rules. I get that part, but it still hurts that he would do that to me. I was sick in bed for over a week. I thought we were friends and then he treats me like some kind of lab rat to do his weird experiments on," she said.

"Andi told me that when you were sick in bed he refused to go to school and he came over every day to be with you," he said.

"So what, he hates school," she said.

He heard the bitterness in her voice and he knew he was losing his opportunity to reach her. He decided to get away from reason and facts and make one last attempt.

"Can I just say this, Zen? I know it's not my place but I think you need to hear it," he said.

He got up and walked over to her. He stood in front of her and looked her in the eyes.

"In my heart I believe that he loves you, but he doesn't have words to express what he feels. He cannot show you the normal signs of love a young woman would expect to see, but his actions reveal his heart. I do not profess to know how his mind works, but I have eyes and I've seen how he looks at you. No matter what you decide to do, please remember that what Tyler did was not from malice or indifference, it was from love. Remember also he created this virus because of something you said to him. He obviously sees a future in which you and he are together and this should tell you something of his feelings for you," he said.

Her lower lip trembled and she turned her face away not wanting him to see her tears.
"I guess I know," she said.

He put his hand on her shoulder and gave it a gentle squeeze and then turned and walked to the door and let himself out. When he got back to Andi's house he let himself in and found her flaked out on the couch.

"I think she will be okay, and I don't think she will report him to the police or anything. So far she has not told her mom, but she has a lot of stuff to think about," he said.

She sat up and he flopped down beside her and smiled.

"What did you say to her?" she asked.

"I told her he did not do it to hurt her and he's probably wrong about the baby thing," he said.

"Is he wrong?" she said.

He thought about it, shook his head, and grunted a negative.

"But he could be?" she said.
There was a tinge of desperation in her voice.

"I wouldn't bet on it. To quote Zen, he has been right about everything else. If those two had a child together, which is not likely given how she feels about what he did to her, their offspring would almost certainly be a carrier. It would be somewhat less likely if she has a child with someone else but the bigger problem they face is not a child with the virus. When word about POrna gets out to the wider world they will be in grave danger," he said.

"In danger from who?" she said. The features of her face portrayed equal parts confusion and fear.

"Almost anyone who has an interest in killing or controlling people, which includes arms makers, religious groups, governments, and probably a whole lot of people we can't even imagine," he said.

He felt her tremble as the meaning of his words sank in and he put his arm around her shoulder to comfort her and she drew closer to him.

"How can we protect them from that?" she said.

He understood the fear and turmoil she was feeling and he squeezed her in support. Her fears for Tyler and Zen matched his own. It was strange how only a few hours ago he did not know he had a son and now he found himself caring deeply about what might happen to him.

"I'm working on a plan. It is possible we won't have to worry about any of this, but I do not want to discuss it while Tyler is in the house," he said.

She turned and looked at him questioningly. She was wondering why he did not want him there but she agreed. "Okay."

He wanted to keep her mind off the bad news, at least until he sorted out his thinking about the plan, so he changed the subject.

"I told Zen he loves her," he said.

He watched her face to see how she would react and he thought he saw something cross her eyes. It was only a flicker and it was gone as fast as it came but it was there and it meant something.

"No shit, Sherlock," she said, smiling a little too brightly, and he noticed that too.
"He has been crazy about her since they were little kids, and she has always adored him," she said.

This last statement was said with less enthusiasm and he remembered how complex Andi was emotionally. When they were together in Toronto he often found himself trying to guess why she reacted in a some way and it was this past experience which allowed him to more accurately read her now.
He detected the hurt she was feeling in the tiny down-turned margins of her smile and when she spoke he realized her words were an attempt to conceal what she was feeling. It was also clear to him she didn't want to appear foolish by revealing the petty jealousy she felt about Zen's close relationship with Tyler, but she was having trouble covering it up.

She watched his face and knew he was reading her, because he always could, and she decided it was time to steer the conversation towards another subject.

"Do you think it would help if I sent him over to her with some food," she said. "I don't think she has eaten all day."

"I think that would be a great idea," he said, hoping to defuse the tension his comment created by trying to be funny, "and if he comes back unscathed we will know my Svengali charms have worked their magic upon her."

She could not help it, though she did not feel like it, she laughed. It was his crazy sense of humour that drew her to him in the first place.

"I will prepare the bandages in case your magic has weakened, Oh Great One," she said.

She wore a smirk on her face when she said it and he knew he was successful.
She made up a tray and called Tyler up from the basement.

"Zen is upset with you. I made sandwiches for you to take to her," she said.

He did not say anything because he was staring at the tray of sandwiches.

"When you give them to her, if she lets you stay, don't eat them all," she said.

She read Tyler's mind and he chuckled when he heard her say it to him. He left with the food and she reminded him again as he walked out the door not to talk about viruses or babies. The door slammed and she watched out the window to see if she would let him in and when he did not come back she grabbed two beers from the fridge and rejoined him on the couch. He was sitting in the semi-darkness of the living room staring out the window deep in thought.
She handed him a beer and took a long pull on hers. It had been a dreadful day and she was weary but she knew

they needed to talk about everything that happened and what they were going to do about it.

"Are you up for a conversation?" he said.

"Are you kidding? Where do you want to begin? Explosions, viruses, terrorists, weird genetics, or infected babies?" she said with an ironic half smile on her weary face, "there is no shortage of interesting and entertaining topics to choose from."

He laughed amazed she had a sense of humour after a day like this. He knew she could not have much energy left after working a full shift and with all the other things that happened she must be exhausted. He would try to go easy on her but they needed to cover a lot of ground. There were important decisions to be made and they had to be made tonight.

"I've been trying to sort out what needs to be done," he said.

"I need to find a good lawyer," she said as she slumped lower on the couch, "if Nichol dies do you think they'll charge Ty with manslaughter?" she asked.
"I don't know how the law looks at things like this but there is something else, something potentially worse which you do not know about," he said.

Her face went white as he watched her brace for the next salvo of bad news in a day of seemingly non-stop hits. Her eyes were wide with expectation and her bright irises dilated with fear. She wondered what could be worse than what has already happened?

"When we were driving to the Emergency room, Hunter told me they found a corpse in the abandoned factory where Tyler has his lab," he said. He heard her sharp intake of breath as her eyes closed, squeezing tight in an effort to end this nightmare.

"When I was talking to him downstairs he confirmed it but more importantly he told me how the person died," he said.

"Who is it? Did he do it?" she whispered urgently, eyes still closed, hoping to gather the pain she knew was coming into a single survivable blow to get it over with, not daring for a moment to allow it to be true yet knowing full well it could be.

"No not directly. He said it was a street person who somehow got into the factory and broke into the lab he was using at the time and began opening stuff," he said.

She cut him off, "This is all wrong, Lee. I need to call a lawyer and then the police. If he didn't kill him then whatever happened to him was an accident.

They'll understand won't they?" she pleaded.

"He did not directly kill the street person but, unfortunately, there is more to it," he said, "if Nichol dies his death was accidental and I'm sure it can be handled by a competent lawyer. The death of the person in the factory was also an accident but it is what he died of that is our problem," he said.

She stared at him, her face a mask of confusion, her eyes asking the question her mouth could not form.

"Tyler told me he died from exposure to anthrax," he said.

The deep lines of fatigue and confusion on her face told him she was starting to sink from all the stress and bad news.

"Isn't that—?" her voice trailed off leaving the question unfinished.

"Tyler looked for and found anthrax spores at the farm across the road. He told me he was planning to use it as a delivery agent for POrna because it was highly virulent but he gave up on it after the homeless person died from exposure. He could no longer safely enter that lab so he sealed the door with duct tape.
The problem is the authorities will not understand what he was trying to do when they discover the cause of death was anthrax. It is a big red flag for them because terrorist groups have used it as a weapon in the past. Do you remember stories about people receiving letters in the mail with anthrax inside back in the eighties?" he said.

She nodded. She vaguely remembered news stories about it.

"Luckily he gave up trying to use it when he witnessed first-hand how dangerous the spores are. The immediate problem we face is potentially much worse than his POrna virus. When that body is discovered the authorities will notify the federal anti-terrorist unit in Ottawa. Anthrax is high up on their watch list.

They will not be convinced he was trying to do something positive for humanity and they will almost certainly demand he be charged as a terrorist."
He watched the growing look of horror on her face as the truth of what he was saying and what it might mean for their son sank in. She was still absorbing it when he said, "Here is my plan. POrna is potentially a much bigger issue but for all practical purposes the authorities do not

know anything about it. The anthrax problem on the other hand cannot wait. It must be dealt with immediately. My plan is simple I will go into the lab tonight and clean it up and remove any traces of anthrax spores," he said.

Her hand covered her mouth and her eyes were sunken and dark with worry.

"Can you do that? I mean, what if it kills you too?" she said.

"I have the training to handle hazardous agents and thanks to Hunter I have a high quality bio-suit to wear," he said. He paused and sipped his beer giving her time to absorb what he was saying as he decided how to approach the next item they needed to discuss. They sat in silence together as the seriousness of the situation sank in.

"There is one more thing we need to talk about," he said.

"Oh my God there's more? What is it?" she said.

"Will you let Tyler go with me?" he said.

Andi's hand flew to her throat in a gesture which was instinctively defensive. He had asked her to put her child in danger and to her shocked horror she was actually considering it. Too much had happened too quickly and she no longer felt in control of anything. Their lives had caught fire and there was no time to think about anything except putting out the flames threatening to devour their son. Lee came back into her life and it was wonderful and it felt right but now he was asking her to do this and she was terrified. It felt like she was gambling with Tyler's life and if she lost it meant she would lose both of them.

"I will go with you," she said.

The desperation in her voice tore at his heart. What an awful situation I've put her in, he thought.

"It has to be Tyler. He knows where to find the virus and anthrax spores and what needs to be done to clean the lab. There is no other way to do this, if I could do it alone I would in a heartbeat, but it would take too long to find all the contamination and I could easily miss something which could identify him. Has Tyler ever been fingerprinted?" he said.

When he asked her this question the last thin strands of control slipped from her grasp and she let out a sob. Everything they talked about up to that point was in the abstract but fingerprinting and everything that it implied made the danger to her son concrete and immediate. She envisioned him being forcefully handled and fingerprinted and she lost what little control she had left.

***

Zen turned off the kitchen light and walked through the darkened house to her bedroom. She turned on the ceiling light but did not go in, something made her pause, and she stood in the doorway gazing in. The room looked different somehow; it seemed unfamiliar, like it belonged to someone else, someone younger. It did not give her the feeling of safety it usually did and it felt like the things inside belonged to a former life, one she no longer lives.

It was not just what Tyler did to her that made her feel this way the feeling had been coming for a long time. The things in her room were from her childhood. Her stuff was thrown everywhere and she did not know why but the sight of her possessions scattered about suddenly made her feel ashamed. She began to pick up the clothes she'd thrown on the floor, embarrassed for her lack of caring, as one by one she put them into the laundry basket.

She was confused and uneasy about everything that happened today and as she straightened the shade on her Princess Jasmine bedside lamp she frowned at the thick layer of dust. She was thinking about Tyler, he was so confusing, she wondered if Dr. Mann was right. She supposed that in his own weird way he did love her.

She thought she saw something in his face today when he gazed at her while they stood in the sunbeam together. She lifted the lid on her jewelry box and looked at the baubles and girl stuff inside, and she picked up a pink plastic hair comb. She could recall the day she bought it at Zellers and how cool she thought it was though now she could not recall the name of the cartoon character embossed on it. She dropped the comb into the garbage can beside her desk.

Nothing feels right anymore, she thought, as she dug in the box and found the item she was looking for. A rusty metal bottle cap, the old-fashioned kind with the pointy edges, with the faded word "Coke" on top. It was the kind you needed a bottle opener to remove. She turned it over and read the words printed inside.

I LOVE YOU

When she showed it to her mom her mom said it was probably from a contest or something. She never told her mom that Tyler gave it to her. It was summer and Andi was at work and she was babysitting him. They rode their bikes to the airport and were lying together on the grass watching planes take off. She was dozing, half asleep in the warm sun, when he took her hand and placed the bottle cap on her palm and closed her fingers over it one finger at a time. He was eleven and she was thirteen and a half.

She was jarred from the memory by the sound of the kitchen door opening and before she could call out Tyler was standing in her bedroom doorway.

"Are you upset?"

She looked at him and tears formed in her eyes. Yes, she was upset but she knew he would not understand so what good would it do to tell him?

"No," she said.

"Want sandwiches?"

"No," she said.

He turned to leave.

"Wait Ty, I want to talk to you," she said.

He stopped and turned around and sat on her bed holding the tray of sandwiches on his knees. With one hand he started to fish around under the covers looking for her remote control.

"No Tyler, no TV I want to talk," she said.

She took the tray of food from him and set it down on her dresser. She turned around and stared at him and he looked uncomfortable like he knew he was in trouble.

"Okay."

He immediately began fidgeting. He noticed her iPod on the floor but he did not reach for it like he normally would.

"Why did you do that to me, why did you give me that virus? It made me sick. I trusted you," she said finishing with a chin-trembling sob.

"For the baby."

He was thinking that was enough to explain it to her but then he remembered what Andrea said about not talking about babies and risked a quick glance to see what the word baby did to her face.

"Do you even know what that means?" she said through her tears.

He glanced up at her eyes again and then away. She sat down beside him on her bed and roughly pushed his shoulder toppling him over. He was not expecting it and he fell completely over but quickly righted himself and braced himself for more. He watched her stomach muscles to see if her weight shifted so he would know if she tried to do it again.

"Tyler, you don't even know what that means. You think a baby is like your stinky iguana. You think you can get one and then do whatever you want to it like some lab rat. It does not work that way. Babies are forever. You were a baby, I was a baby, and you can't do weird stuff to a baby," she said.
Her voice was high and exasperated and he knew she was upset but when she mentioned the iguana he began thinking about the sequence of DNA which coded for a tongue flick. He could see all of them in order in his mind but he read only the letters at the three end of sequence. This kept his mind busy as he tried to decipher why she was upset and the meaning of the words she was using. She turned and looked at his face to see if he was listening to what she was saying and he flinched under her gaze.

"Who would take care of it?" she said.

"What?"

"The baby."
She was trying to think of something meaningful to get through to him. She remembered he let his pet lizard loose in the field next door because he did not want to take care of it.

"Andrea."

He was certain that was a safe answer.

"You'd give our baby to your mom to take care of?"
She shouted the words in disbelief and he saw her muscles tighten and he braced again certain she was going to try to push him over but she did not. He was confused by her reaction. He thought it was a safe answer because that is what Andrea does.
"Wait a minute. What am I saying?" she said.
There was a comical look of bewilderment on her face but he missed it.
"How did this get so freaking twisted?" she said.
She laughed at her own crazy reaction to letting his mom take care of the baby she did not have. This whole thing is insane she thought as she looked at him. She turned to him and lifted his chin and studied his open innocent features and his intense grey eyes.

They were cast downward because he found it hard to meet her gaze and that is when she realized he had absolutely no clue what she was talking about. Of course it was natural he would expect Andrea to take care of the baby. In his experience she is the mother unit and that's what she does. She continued to look at him and lifted his chin higher so he would have to look at her face.

"Tyler do you love me?" she said.

Her voice was low and questioning but also conveyed a tone of challenge.

"Yes."
He spoke without hesitation and although she had asked the question she was not prepared for the impact his direct simple response had on her. It brought fresh tears to her eyes and now it was her turn to look away.

He shifted uncomfortably on the bed because tears meant he said the wrong answer and he tried to think of a different word to say.

"Do you know what love means?" she said.
She spoke the words softly the question directed more at herself than to him. Did he know what it meant?

"Yes."

This time he did not risk saying more words. Instead he took her hand and held it on his lap and opened her fingers one by one to reveal the bottle cap she held in her palm. Then he looked into her eyes and held them for a long moment.
"Yes."

He turned his eyes away from hers but not before she saw something in them which caused her to shiver. Her rational mind knew he did not understand what love means to a girl, to him it was the same word you said to your grandma, but her heart at least hoped it meant something more. She was exhausted and emotionally drained. She squeezed his hand.

"You can watch TV now if you want I'm going to get ready for bed."

He did not reach for the remote and when she started to get up he did not let go of her hand. He gently pulled her back down beside him.

"Are you mad?"

"Yes, but I'll get over it," she said and smiled.

"Me too."

She laughed and he laughed because she laughed and it made her feel a bit giddy.

"Sorry about the baby."

"It's okay Ty," she said.

"Gene."

"Gene?" she asked.

"The baby."

"You already have a name for our baby?" she said amazed at how detailed his thinking was and she laughed.

"Baby is Gene."

"Don't I get to pick the name?" she said playing along with him to see where he went with this.

"No."

"That's not fair," she said.

"You pick next one."

"Next what?" she said confused trying to follow this weird conversation.

"Baby."
"You think there's going to be two babies?" she said poking him in the ribs trying to tickle him but he did not flinch. She gave up and started to rise from the bed to get changed.

"Brenda."

She laughed. The whole thing was crazy.

"You said I could name the next one," she said.

"You waited too long."

She laughed and grabbed him and tried to put him in a headlock and they struggled a bit and then, for some reason, this time he let her.

Chapter 15

Bad News

Mann held her as she sobbed and felt the heat of intense emotion radiate from her. After her tears subsided he heard her say, "Nichol's suit is shredded I had to cut it to get it off. "The words she spoke were muffled as she whispered them into his shoulder. He knew she was in shock from all that had happened but he was relieved to hear her say them it meant she'd come to terms with the situation and made a decision.

"I think I can patch it," she said.

"Hunter's suit is small, not quite the right size for Tyler but it is undamaged," he said, "it will be tight but I'm sure he can squeeze into it."

He spoke softly into her hair and knew again what he knew the moment he saw her in Ralph's, he still loved her deeply, hopelessly, and always had.

"Promise me you will keep him safe, both of you safe," she said.

He nodded his head and tried to let go of her but she would not release him. She held him fiercely to delay, if only for a few seconds, the storm she knew was coming.

"I know this all seems wrong to you but it is the only way to deal with this mess. I don't think Western knows about the anthrax but as soon as things quiet down he will send another team into the old factory and it will be game over for us. For all our sakes we have to beat him and the police to it," he said.

"Why? What's in it for him?" she said.

"Something Hunter told me makes me think he wants the virus for himself. He seems to be working far outside his authority. He doesn't know how POrna works but he knows it does, he's seen the results. He also knows that whoever controls the virus could conceivably sell it and make hundreds of millions of dollars.
The country that controls the POrna virus could create an anti-virus and inoculate their soldiers against its effects. That country could then destroy the armies of any and all nations opposing them. Someone like Western would become obscenely wealthy selling POrna to the highest bidder. I know Hunter will eventually tell Western what she heard in the motel room, if she hasn't already, and her story will convince him even more to try and get his hands on it," he said.

"If you manage to destroy the evidence in the lab that will take care of the anthrax problem but what makes you think it will stop Western?" she said.

"I've been thinking about that. The way I see it, once the physical evidence is gone, no one can legally tie anything to Tyler. It might not stop the authorities from trying but it is tough to prove anything in court without physical evidence. As for Western he can't implicate Ty in the death of the street person because he would need to explain why the Canadian Military knew about the body and did not report it and why one of their vehicles exploded outside the crime scene and why his people ran away.

Without physical evidence nobody will believe a sixteen-year-old kid failing grade ten could do any of this. I wouldn't believe it if I had not talked with Tyler and seen the results of POrna myself. I'm hoping Ty is right about the virus being self-limiting and it will not continue to infect soldiers. If it's true the virus will eventually die out and take the problem of its existence with it," he said.

"Lee, I don't understand how any of this could happen. He has been with me his whole life, I knew he was interested in science and experiments, you only have to look at his bedroom to know that, but how does a kid go from playing around with science to creating something like POrna?" she said.

He sighed and kissed the top of her head; it felt so normal and right to be holding her again.

"Well, like I said before, you can forget your worries that Ty might be mentally challenged, clearly he is not. In some respects the focus of his thinking is narrow but in a fundamental way I believe he redefines the definition of genius. He is not aware of any of this and if he was I don't think it would interest him. I believe, though he's had no formal training, he represents a type of natural scientist," he said.

"I don't understand. Can someone who is a disaster at school be a scientific genius?" she said.

"What I am going to say may sound simplistic because, frankly, it is. His intelligence is manifested in ways which make him appear to be intellectually challenged.

Most people operate within well-defined social positions from which they evaluate others by categorizing their behaviour. Ty doesn't recognize or follow the accepted social conventions. I'm not sure if he is like someone with autism who can't detect social cues or if he is so advanced our social cues are detectable but meaningless to him. Either way I am counting on society's continuing ignorance of him because that is what will save him from prison.

There are maybe a dozen Ph.D. geneticists on this planet who could comprehend what he has achieved and I know for an absolute certainty, knowing what I do about POrna, that I could not convince a single one of them it exists and that is what I am counting on to get him out of this mess. Have you ever heard the term 'savant'?" he said.

Andi nodded her head. Most people have heard of those rare disabled people with a single incredible but often useless ability.

"I think Ty is a kind of savant but without the associated disability. It is true he has few social skills but there are thousands of engineers and scientists exactly like him except his deficits and talents are more extreme. From observing him I believe his mind naturally operates on multiple discreet levels; one level has an intuitive ability to identify connections between unconnected things but at an extreme level of connectedness. Another level has a ravenous appetite for raw scientific data and a computer-like ability to retrieve and make sense of it.

While I was talking to him in his room he was reading new research on glial cells on his computer while at the same time watching The Simpsons on part of the monitor with the sound off and using ear buds to listen to some God awful music. I questioned him about glial cells and I found he had a post doc level of understanding of the material.

When I asked him he clearly knew what The Simpsons episode was about though I suppose he could have watched that episode before. My point is he is ingesting and learning vast amounts of information all the time. I do not believe much, if any, of this learning is conscious on his part. I don't think he is saying to himself, 'today I will learn bio-synthesis.' It is more like the way a baby acquires language. He is not actively trying to learn anything he is simply absorbing information from exposure to it. These discreet brain functions along with his ability to focus on several things at once are, individually, extraordinary traits but to possess all of them is unprecedented.

He is able to combine these talents and make the kind of connections and intuitive leaps needed to come up with something like POrna. I know he is developmentally and emotionally immature; he obviously lags behind his peers socially but I believe he will eventually overcome this. Imagine him as an adult with his gifted agile mind and a mature intellect. Given access to the right resources think of what he might achieve. He could potentially eradicate disease as we know it or reprogram the human genome so we live for hundreds of years. There is no limit to what his brilliant mind could come up with," he said.

She was listening in silence her feelings ranging from fear to pride to hope and all the while holding on tight to him.

"Another piece of this puzzle is what spurred him to create POrna in the first place. As unlikely as this might seem it was something Zen said to him."

"What on earth did she say?" she asked.
The look of surprise on her face made it clear she didn't think anything Zen would say could be that important.

"She told Tyler her father died in a war," he said.

Andi's brow wrinkled with confusion.
"What? That's not right. Her father, if you can call him that, was a drug addict. He died living on the streets of East Vancouver. Ellie told me all about him." She leaned

back and looked at him and asked, "Why would she lie to him about that?"

He leaned back from her and looked at her with a raised eyebrow and an indulgent half smile.

"Her dad was a drug addict who died on the street. Why do you think she lied?" he said.

"Oh,"

"Anyway the truth doesn't matter. He picked up on the emotion or the pain she felt when she said it and it had an impact on him. At the age of ten, because of his strong connection to Zen, he decided to fix the main problem with the human race. It is ironic he developed POrna because of a lie she told but that does not make it any less amazing," he said.

He put down his beer and took her hand while he was talking and he was holding it tightly with both of his when she looked him in the eyes.

"I have some iron-on patches that should seal up the suit."

She got up from the couch. He watched her turn to go and get the patches but stop when she saw something move past the window. She turned back to him with a quizzical expression on her face. She was about to ask him if he'd seen it when there was a deafening explosion and the front door disintegrated.

Chapter 16

Cutting Orders

Patricia Hunter paced stiffly around inside Western's office. She was agitated, she did not want to sit, the skin under the tape wrapped around her ribs itched like crazy and she wanted to get the hell going. Her next assignment was in Paris and she would be happy to get out of Victoria. Things went very wrong at the old factory and she was worried a disproportionate amount of the blame would stick to her if she hung around.

Sergeant Nichol was in a stage three coma and not likely to recover. The blast cost her twenty-five percent of her hearing in her left ear and ten percent in her right. She did not mention this to Major Webb at the Canadian NATO Mission in Paris when she requested her transfer.

"What did they say?" she asked when he hung up the phone.

"He is non-responsive; they are still buying the motorcycle story at least for now. That was good thinking on your part. I hope they never go looking for…what was the name you gave them?" he said.

"Sandra Lockerbie," she said.

They looked at each other with sad resignation it was not easy losing a colleague even one you barely knew. They'd both lost friends over the years; soldiering is a dangerous business and losing people was never easy.

"I've cut your transport orders. You leave for Gatineau in two hours and at ten o'clock Quebec time you leave for Ipswich. It's all in the printout. You'll be sleeping in the airport, what else is new. You all right?" he said.

It was not actually a question it was simply something he felt he was supposed to ask as commanding officer. He knew she would never admit it if she was not okay, that is not how the military works.

"What's going to happen to Dr. Mann and the kid and his mom?"

"They'll be okay. All they need to do is shut up and play dumb," he said.

Western's phone rang again and he grabbed it. He listened for a full five minutes then said "Fuck" and hung up.

"That was my contact at the RCMP they found something incriminating on the kid's computer. He has maps showing population densities and dispersal rates for pandemics. It is the kind of information terrorist organizations might use when planning a strike. The RCMP believes there were terrorists behind our exploding van and they were planning to use anthrax for some kind of domestic attack here in Victoria."

"Anthrax?" she said.

"It was all on the kid's computer how to modify it to make it a weapon and how to disseminate it. There are plans and layout maps on his computer for spraying it on travelers in the departure areas of Victoria International Airport," he said.

She was shocked. What was that little shit planning to do?

"Do they know about his virus?" she said.

"No. They think he was working on anthrax," he said, "which is bad enough."

Hunter checked her watch and looked towards the door. "I have to get going, so how do we leave things?" she said.

"There is nothing to leave. You weren't there it never happened and Nichol is another dead soldier, end of story. You need to cultivate some amnesia to go along with your hearing loss," he said.

She looked at him and wondered how he knew about it but then realized it was his business to know. Her medical files would be a simple thing for a man like Western to access.

"I'm sorry sir what soldier was that?" she said.

She waited a beat for the tiny smile of acknowledgement then she saluted him and left his office.

When the door closed behind her he turned to his computer screen and called up an encrypted file. It contained the phone numbers of contacts he collected over the last twenty years for back-channel communications all over the world. He found the number he was looking for and it was ringing now somewhere in the Pentagon in Washington DC.

He was calling a man he met in South America a long time ago. Arne might know some way they could cash in on this virus and now more than ever he knew it could not wait. If the cops grabbed the kid first it was game over. Arne answered on the third ring. After the niceties were over he began.

"The best way to describe this thing is a genetic weapon," he said. He chose his words carefully.

"What does it do?" Arne said.
The man on the line was a few thousand kilometers away in Washington DC but Western could plainly hear the interest in his voice.

"That part is hard to explain but here is the most important aspect of this weapon. Once it is deployed against a hostile force it incapacitates them," he said.

"You mean it kills them?" he said.

"No, I mean it renders them incapable of engaging in armed combat," he said.
There was a long moment of silence on the line and he could almost hear his old friend thinking.

"We should meet," he said.

"Yes good idea come to Vancouver and I'll take you to watch the Canucks lose a hockey game," he said.

"This is a serious deal right?" he said.

"It could not be more so," he said. "But we need to move fast because the whole thing is beginning to unravel."

"I'll call you when I get to Vancouver," he said and hung up.

He went to the window of his office and gazed out at the distant mountains on the US coastline. He wondered what it would be like to be rich. He would buy a BMW convertible to celebrate. He was not worried about the Americans not paying for the virus if they didn't want it the Chinese certainly would. He was too old and jaded to worry about national loyalties.

One way or another he was going to cash in on this thing. All he had to do was figure out how to deliver the product without getting caught or dead.

Chapter 17

Sanctioned Terror

Midnight

    Mann saw Andi's hands fly up to protect her face from flying debris as three men charged through the splintered doorway yelling for them to get down on the floor. They had machine guns and wore body armor and breathing masks, he could see angry contorted faces behind fogged plastic. He was frozen in place by shock and disbelief as one of the men screaming at Andi held a machine gun up to her face.

"Get down on the floor and put your hands behind your head!" Another man held an automatic weapon up to Mann's face shouting at him to get down.
He and Andi were stunned to immobility by the suddenness of the attack and the third man through the door wasn't willing to wait for them to comply. He grabbed Andi by the hair from behind and slammed her to the floor. The assault smashed her head to the floor and he heard and saw her head bounce off the hardwood and her eyes roll sickeningly as she was knocked unconsciousness.
The same man bent down and jammed his knee into her spine as he zip strapped her hands behind her back.

Mann made a desperate attempt to go to her but the guy beside him anticipated this move and bashed the side of his head with the butt of his weapon sending him crashing to the floor beside her. Stunned and bleeding from the gash in his face someone he could not see stomped down on his neck with his boot pressing his face to the floor while another man strapped his hands behind his back. Andi regained consciousness and saw his bloody face and screamed and the big cop on top of her jammed his knee down hard into the centre of her back knocking the air from her lungs.

He could not see her but he could hear her gasping desperately struggling for breath as the cop continued to press down hard on her.
He shouted at the cop that Andi was losing her airway and somehow the message got through to him. He heard him ease up on her and roll her onto her side to facilitate breathing. His training had obviously kicked in, the cop did not want to be responsible for her death and he was relieved to hear her breathing improve.

He heard someone shout "all clear" from behind him and the violent tension in the air eased somewhat. His left eye was swollen shut and he could not see well from his right eye because it was smeared with blood, but he could make out the shapes of four people in green biohazard suits with respirators come in through the ruined door. They were carrying mobile test equipment and they immediately began to tear the house apart.

Through a swollen and bloody mouth he asked the man nearest to him what they were after and he was told to shut up and not move. When he protested he got a hard knee to his ribs in response. After a few minutes he and Andi were physically dragged from the house and thrown bodily into the back of an unmarked van. The lone guard inside the van held an automatic weapon on them and put his boot down hard on Andi's back when she woke and began shrieking.

The pain cut her off in mid-howl. The cop sat impassively watching them, as they lay tangled, sore, and bleeding on the bare metal floor. He could not see anything by this

time and felt like he was going to pass out from pain and blood loss. He heard more vehicles arrive and the sound of lots of doors slamming and people running around. After a few minutes the van door opened and a huge man in swat gear looked in. He stood in the open doorway and had to duck his head down to look inside. He too was wearing a mask and respirator.
"Where is Tyler Lee Worthy?" he said.

His voice rumbled out from behind his mask in a menacing baritone threat.

"Who are you and what do you want?" Mann said, not able to see he was speaking into the blurry darkness mustering what bravado he could.

"Where is Tyler Lee Worthy?" The big man asked again ignoring his questions.

He did not reply.

The big cop reached out and roughly grabbed his leg and pulled him to the rear of the van. He was wearing a double layer of blue gloves when he searched all his pockets for his wallet. When he found it he opened it and drew out his province of Ontario driver's license.

"This says you are Phillip Lee Mann. Is that correct?"

"This is an illegal search and seizure," he said his voice quaking with fear and adrenaline. The man drew a piece of folded paper from a Velcro-sealed pocket on his vest and tossed it at him hitting him on the side of his blood-covered face. He recoiled from the surprise hit.

"That's a search warrant asshole. I suggest you answer my questions or suffer the consequences," he said.

"I want to call my lawyer now," he said.

"Under section 31, paragraph ten of the amended anti-terrorism act of 2011, we have the right to detain you, without communication, for up to sixty days; if you cooperate with me it will make things easier for you in the long run. Be smart Mr. Mann and cooperate."
He could not see Andi's face but he hoped she realized what he realized. This was not Western doing this and they had not found Tyler. He was still at Zen's or maybe they were able to sneak away.

"Well? Are you going to cooperate?" he said.

"Why are you here, are you the police?" he asked.

The big cop did not like to answer questions from suspects but he also knew it was sometimes a way to get information they didn't know they were giving.

"We are looking for Tyler Lee Worthy. He is wanted for questioning. A computer was found at a crime scene which identifies him as the owner. There was information on the computer which directly relates to an ongoing terrorism investigation," he said.

"What information?" he asked.

"Terrorist planning data which is illegal to possess for any purpose under the anti-terrorism law of 2011, save yourself some grief and tell me where he is and I will testify that you cooperated."

Mann grunted a reply the cop did not like and he slammed the door.

Bloody Face

Zen felt the rumble and heard the blast and jumped up and ran to the window to peek through the gap in the curtains. She heard yelling and saw two dark figures carrying guns run through the shadows of Tyler's backyard. He was watching a science program on television and was so completely involved he did not notice the commotion next door.

They were lying on her bed eating the sandwiches Andi made for her when the noise startled her. She watched the people in the backyard for a moment confused by what she was seeing and then heard vehicle doors slamming at the front of the house. She ran to the living room window to see what was happening next door.

There were police cars and vans and two large trucks parked on the street and in the front yard and people wearing gas masks running into Andi's house. She went from window to window to watch what was happening but was stopped cold by what she saw through the small window in the front door. She gasped with horror and disbelief as police forcefully carried Andi and Dr. Mann with toes dragging out the front door to a black police van.

She choked back a sob when two cops picked Andi up and threw her limp body into the back. She did not want Tyler to hear her cry out because if he saw what they were doing to his mom he might try to stop them. She forced herself away from the window for fear that one of them might look over and see her and come to talk to her. She locked the front door. She was worried the police might want to question her about the people in the house next door because that is what they did on television at a crime scene.

She was breathing hard, her mind racing, as she realized the most important thing was not to let them take Tyler. They were taking Andi and Dr. Mann away and she had to assume they would also be after him. There was no way she could sneak him out of the house with that many police in the yard. She felt trapped and was close to panic but calmed herself by controlling her breathing and clearing her thoughts. If she could keep him away from the windows he would probably be safe inside the house.

She did not know much about the law but she knew the police needed to have a warrant from a Judge to come into the house and in this respect she might have a small advantage. She hoped it would not come to this, but if they came to her door and demanded to come in, she would tell them who her grandfather is and that might keep them out or at least buy her some time. If her mom found out about it she would be dead meat because her mom and grandfather hate each other. She went back to her bedroom after first locking the back door.

"What's going on Zen?" Tyler asked. He'd finished off the sandwiches and was sprawled on her bed watching something else on television.

"Nothing. What's on now?" she said. He ignored her question and started to get up off the bed to see for himself.

"Wait. Okay I'll tell you but you have to promise me you won't look out the window. Promise me you will keep watching TV and I will tell you. Okay, promise?" she said.

"Okay. I promise," he said.

"The police are at your house and they took your mom and Dr. Mann away," she said.

"Why did they do that?" he said.

She looked over at him with wide eyes and hissed, "Are you fucking kidding me?"

Her eyes opened wide in silent exclamation and he laughed but he went back to watching television because he promised. She turned away from him and went to the window and scanned the backyard then pulled the curtains tightly closed. Nothing else was happening that she could see. She sat down beside him on the bed, tucked her long legs up and rested her chin on her knees while hugging her legs.

She was afraid. Nothing in her life had prepared her for this and she was relying on instinct alone to get them through, she knew Tyler was unable to help her. She tried to concentrate on the television program he was watching but it was a blur in her racing mind. She could not stop thinking about Andi's drooping head. It looked unnatural, like her neck was broken. Her hair was dragging in the dirt as they took her to the police van. She heard herself speaking in a dreamy disconnected way.

"The police dragged them out of the house and put them in a van. They were dragging them. Dr. Mann's face was bleeding."

Tyler did not say anything because he finished off the last of the sandwiches and fallen asleep. It was after midnight and she was exhausted. She had a stress headache and knew she needed to sleep. She got up and checked all the doors and windows again to make sure they were locked then went into the bathroom and without turning on the light and changed into her John Lennon nightgown.

She peed, brushed her teeth, and washed the tear tracks from her pale face.

When she came out she resisted the urge to look out the window and went to her bedroom. She untied and pulled off his sneakers and undid the top button of his jeans. She lay down beside him and pulled the covers up over both of them and felt around under the sheets and found the remote control in his hand. She took it and turned it off then found his hand again and held it.

She lay awake unable to sleep staring at the ceiling for a long time tightly holding onto his hand waiting for a knock at the door. The world outside grew quiet as she waited and soon all she heard was Tyler's slow rhythmic breathing. It made her think of the sound of surf rolling on a distant shore and eventually she drifted off to sleep.

September 25

7:00 AM

Morning sunlight filtered through the curtains into the bedroom and the warmth on her face woke her. Tyler was asleep beside her and sometime during the night she let go of his hand and put her arm around his waist. It felt nice to have him beside her and she felt dreamy and safe until she remembered the blood on Dr. Mann's face. She tried to get the cozy warm feeling back but it was gone and now she could not stop seeing the shock and fear on Dr. Mann's face as he was dragged from the house.

She shuddered at the violent impersonal nature of this act of defilement. It played upon her mind until she could no longer resist the urge to get up and look out the window. She lifted her arm off him and slid out from under the covers laying them back down again gently, she did not want to wake him. Watching him as he lay sleeping her heart ached at the sweet innocence of his boy face.

An innocent face that was contradicted by a growing awareness that the little boy she grew up with was not the strange indecipherable person he'd become. It was confusing because her heart wanted to believe he was still that sweet boy. Her mom drove the message into her since childhood that men, her father in particular, must not be trusted. They do things to make you fall in love with them and when you do they turn into ugly monsters and ruin your life. She did not believe Tyler was a monster she believed Dr. Mann when he told her he loves her and that's why he did what he did.

She kinda knew all along he liked her maybe even loved her but so much had happened. She worried about the fact he was only sixteen and clueless about everything; he did not understand the consequences of the things he did or what could happen to both of them because of it. She glanced at the time as she padded over to the window to look outside.
Her eyes widened and her breath sucked in with disbelief at what she saw. The stuff from his bedroom was scattered all over the lawn. His clothes, his bed, all his science junk, everything from his room was thrown about. She saw pieces of lab equipment which looked like they'd been smashed. His bedding was spread all over the place, along with books and shoes and the shower curtain from the little bathroom in the basement. His mattress was cut open, the wood frame of the box spring was showing, and stuffing and fabric was flying around and the entire yard was cordoned with yellow police tape. She did not want him to wake up and see this. She did not want to see it herself and blinked back tears unable to look away. She jumped with a startled cry when Tyler put his hand on her side. He was right behind her.

"Why?" he asked.

She did not have an answer. They stood at the window for a long time and then he turned away.

"I'm going home," he said.

"Tyler no, you can't they'll get you too. We need to go away somewhere we need to hide until we figure out what is happening."

"Why?" he said.

She could not answer him. She did not know for certain the police were looking for him but it was mostly his stuff spread all over the yard. She decided if the police went to all the trouble to destroy his stuff they would likely have someone watching the house which meant he could not go home. The police must be looking for something they believe he has or why would they rip open his mattress?

"I'm going to ride around and see if the police are hanging around watching your house. I want you to promise you'll stay inside and watch TV until I get back. Don't even look out the window. Okay?" she said.

"Okay," he said.

She used the washroom and got changed and put on her helmet, when she went out to get her bike he was lying in bed watching NOVA. She pedaled away from the house and made three wide sweeps of the area and stopped at the 7-Eleven for cherry Freezies before heading home. She was riding and balancing the Freezies with one hand when she turned the corner and saw a dark blue sedan parked down the street from her house. There was a man sitting in it and she pretended to ignore him as she rode past but snuck a quick peak at him. He definitely looked like a cop to her.

She rode her bike into the backyard and saw someone bent over rummaging through the stuff in the backyard. She prayed Tyler would not pick that moment to look out the window. As she got closer she saw the person rummaging was Tyler.

"What are you doing?" she whispered.

"I'm getting my stuff," he said.

"Oh my God Tyler come inside!" she said.

Chapter 18

I Have a Plan

Zen had to admit it. He looked ridiculous with a fake mustache. She liked the Chinese dragon tattoo which curled around his neck and onto his cheek. When she started applying it on his lower back it tickled like crazy and she had to stop and remind him every two seconds to hold still. His shirt was off because the tattoo was drying and she was admiring her handiwork as he channel surfed.

She also put lime green and baby blue spikes in his almost white hair which looked good, she thought, but she was not happy at all with that wispy glued on mustache. For one thing it was not cooperating, it drooped to one side.
For her disguise she opted for a Goth look with raven black hair and way too much black eye makeup and white face powder. In her estimation they looked nothing at all like their former selves and she was confident they could leave the house and no one, including the police, would recognize them.

That was when he told her that face recognition software was impossible to beat and nothing short of plastic surgery could fool a computer. At first she was pissed that he had not mentioned this important detail until after she was finished but upon reflection she suspected he went along with the disguise idea because it kept her busy. She smiled when she realized he had allowed her to put shoe lifts inside his sneakers to make him taller and the lifts made him misjudge his step and stumble a lot. The tattoo and hair colour would eventually wash off but she giggled when she wondered how long it would take him to learn to walk again.

While she was working on their disguises he was thinking about how to get his computer back. He assumed it was the police who took it from his room but when he said he wanted to phone them and ask for it back Zen told him he was not allowed to phone anyone and made him promise not to. The computer is what he was looking for in the backyard when she came home. He needed to get it back, but aside from calling the police, all he could think of doing was calling Colonel Western and he knew Zen would not like that idea.

Calling Western was the only solution to this problem he could think of now that Dr. Mann was gone.

He needed his computer to work on stuff and with it gone there was no other choice he would have to ask him. He was the most logical person to ask to get it back; without it he could not finish his work. He looked down at the items arranged on the bedroom floor. The bits and pieces from his room he retrieved from his backyard were scattered everywhere. He thought if he could view them maybe it would help him to determine how to complete his project. None of the individual pieces were particularly useful but together, he thought, they might hold an answer.

He was having trouble visualizing the formula and sequences he originally used. The problem was he could not recall the details without referring to the data on his computer. He was hoping the Colonel might be able to get it for him. If all he could get back was the hard drive from the lab computer he could recover enough data for the primary sequencing and modify POrna to do what he now wanted it to do.

The unknown factor in this plan was Colonel Western. Would he go for it and could he get access to his computer? He was not sure if a Colonel could boss the police around. He had no concept of how the civil or military hierarchy of command was structured.

Zen came into the room and flopped down on the bed and stared at him. She wore a pink bathrobe and a towel around wet hair; her face was no longer white with makeup her skin looked scrubbed and healthy.

"What is all this junk anyway?" she said surveying the mess on her bedroom floor and making a face.

"My stuff," he said.

"I know that. Is any of it salvageable?" she said.

"No," he said

"So why is it all over my floor?" she said.

He looked at her and considered the question. He could not adequately explain what he was doing because he did not know himself. It was simply necessary for him to do it because it was the way his mind processed information. There was something about the relationship between the various bits and pieces, though they were now destroyed, that made his thinking flow in a productive way. It always worked that way. He would look at something and without knowing how or why he would imagine a change or improvement to the design or a new combination which worked in a novel way.

He would find himself with the solution to a problem without conscious thought or even knowing how he arrived at the answer. If he tried to explain it to her she would not understand and he did not want her to think he was weirder than she already did.

"I need to look at these things to remember stuff," he said.

She rolled her eyes at his answer but thankfully she seemed to accept it.
She found the remote control and turned on the television and started scanning channels and when she came to The Learning Channel she stopped and turned up the volume. She knew it was his favorite channel. This was a change in her, she never would have let him watch a program without arguing over it. They used to wrestle over the remote, and because she was bigger, she made him watch all her girl shows. She wondered about this change and what it meant.

"What is your big plan, Tyler? What are we supposed to do now?" she said.

He got up off the floor and sat beside her on her bed.

"What's on?" he said.

"Never mind what's on. What the heck are we going to do now?" she said.

She was exasperated. It felt to her like they'd been cooped up in the house for a long time and she was getting antsy to do something, anything. They had no idea what happened to Andi and Dr. Mann. She was afraid to call the police and ask about them in case they traced the call. He kept telling her he had an idea but would not share it with her and she was beginning to think he did not have a plan at all.

"Ty my mom's going to show up any day now and she will want to know what's going on. When she left on her trip I didn't have a boy living with me. What do we tell her about that?" she said, "and what do we tell her about the SWAT team raiding your house?" She used her mother as a prod because she knew he was a little afraid of her.

"Colonel Western," he said.

"What about him?" she said.

"I will call him," he said.
"Are you kidding? He's the guy who started all this in the first place," she yelled in disbelief.

"I need my computer," he said.

"What if he locks you up and throws away the key?" she said.

"He won't," he said.

"How can you be sure?" she said.

"He wants to know about POrna," he said.

"What do you think will happen to you after he gets what he wants? They won't need you anymore. They will put you in prison for being a dumbass!" she said.

She was upset and worried that he would end up in prison or dead or something and all because he did not understand the seriousness of the situation.

"You made this virus thing and let it loose on their soldiers. Do you think they are happy about that? Do you think Colonel whatever is gonna say, '*Hey, Tyler. Here's your computer back by the way great job on the Porno virus*'," she said.

"They will not do anything to me. POrna does not work without you and me," he said.

"How do you know? They got their own scientists and computer people. What makes you so sure?" she said.

"Trust me I have a plan," he said and grinned.

"Yeah that's what I'm afraid of you have a plan," she said.
He gave her his best don't worry I've got this covered look and threw in a double thumbs-up for good measure. She was doubtful about his plan but she had to look away from him because she did not want him to see her smiling at his crazy optimism and have him think she agreed with him.

It was sweet that he tried to make her believe he had everything under control but she knew he was clueless about the real world. Although she did not like his idea at least he was suggesting some course of action. Her big plan was for them to put on disguises and go downtown and take a Pacific Coach Lines bus to Vancouver and stay with her aunt Amy, her father's twin sister, someone she has not seen since she was six years old. It was doubtful Amy would remember her let alone let them stay at her house. The good news was the policeman watching his house was gone but she still made him promise he would not go outside.

***

As soon as Zen rode away he ventured out to retrieve a bit more of his stuff. When she went out the most important thing she brought back from her trips was food. He was hungry and having Andrea gone was inconvenient because she knew what he liked to eat and how to make it and Zen was not good at cooking. He had never learned anything about food other than how to open a bag of cookies but she was trying hard and they were both learning and trying to help each other. When they were kids they always used to sleep together but it was a few years ago and now he was not used to sleeping with anyone. It was hard to get used to it.

On the second night he suggested she should sleep in Mom's room. When he said it her face got red and she was upset for a long time. Andrea tried to teach him about other people's feelings but he did not understand much of what she said. He did figure out if someone's face was red they were upset but it only told him after they were already upset and he kept on saying the wrong thing to people's feelings.

On the second morning they woke up together she insisted he have a shower and wash his hair, which he hated, but he did it to make her happy. She also wanted him to change all his clothes, including socks and undies, which was not difficult because his clothes were all outside on the lawn but she got upset with him when he went outside after his shower and got dressed in the backyard.

She told him he was lucky there were no neighbour on their street that could see because they would have called the police. When he pointed at the farmhouse across the road she said they were too far away to see anything. He asked her what it was they should not see but he dropped the topic when her face got red.

She was also upset to discover he did not wear pajamas to bed and slept in his undies but she got over it when he agreed to brush all his teeth and let her watch him to be sure he did it. Since he was a little kid he wondered why there were so many rules to remember and why it was always women who enforced them.

Andrea, Zen, and the teachers at school never failed to remind him when he got one of the "unwritten" rules wrong or missed it completely. His grade three teacher, Mrs. Horn, laughed at him when he asked her why no one ever wrote the unwritten rules down so he could read them.

What to do?

Zen was thinking over his plan, not that she liked it, but she could not think of anything else to do. She considered phoning her grandfather and asking him if he could find out what happened to Andi and Dr. Mann but she already knew the police took them and they were probably looking for Tyler. She was afraid her grandfather would ask her if she knew where he was and she did not think she would be able to lie to him. He was a Judge after all, and judges have a lot of experience catching liars, at least that is what her mom told her.

She held the belief, without her mom actually admitting it, that her grandfather had caught her mom lying to him when she was growing up and that was part of the reason they did not love each other anymore. She wished she could think of a way to ask him for advice without giving him any of the details of their situation but she knew it was impossible. He would ask her questions and eventually he would get it out of her.

"Okay, so we contact this Colonel guy what then?" she said.

"He gets my computer," he said.

"What if he can't?" she said.

He shrugged because he did not have a plan for that possibility.

"What did you mean Porno won't work without me? What do you need me for?" she said.

"To be with me."

"To do what?"

"I need you."

"For what?"

"I need you- because."

He tried to put extra emphasis on the word "because," dragging the sound out a bit longer than the other words. He darted a quick look at her eyes to see if she got it. He struggled to put meaning into words. He knew what he was trying to say to her but he could see she didn't understand. He was young when he first learned that it was better not to talk because words made people upset. He understood that spoken words contained hidden information that he was unaware of. He did not understand these extra meanings and it was risky using words without knowing, so he didn't. She was looking at the television when he glanced to see her reaction and that is when he was distracted by the loose strands of hair against the curve of her neck.

The electronic glow from the television was harsh and thin and that weak light became entangled in the damp strands. She had washed out the Goth hair colour and her natural golden brown hair turned the TV light into a coppery fluid. As it dried and shifted temperature he could feel something like sun-warmed iced tingles.

She was thinking about what he said when she noticed the intense way he was looking at her. He was sitting close beside her and the intensity of his gaze made her face flush with warmth and she became aware that she was naked beneath her robe. Her attention had shifted to the rough texture of the material and the way it made the new flock of goose bumps on her arms and chest feel.

He was so confusing; she did not know what he meant and she knew from experience that it was pointless to try and guess. She was losing patience with everything about this situation, she turned to him and reached out and took his chin and lifted it so he would have to look at her eyes.

"Why Tyler? Why because?"

Her voice was lumpy with emotion. At first she was surprised by it but after a moments reflection she wasn't surprised at all. She told herself she needed to be honest about her feelings. She knew very well where this emotion came from. It was there because, deep down inside, she knew exactly what she wanted it to mean.

He considered her question for a long time. His eyes turned away from her and looked at the floor, then at the wall, at the poster of a tree with a poem on it, then at the stuff on the floor again and finally at her face. He inhaled a gambler's breath and rolled the dice.

"You are my girlfriend." He risked another quick look at her eyes to gauge her reaction and he saw tears in her eyes and realized he used wrong words again.

He gambled and lost but he wanted to understand why he lost. He needed to figure out why she was crying.

"I'm sorry," he said.

"Sorry for what?" she said. She was sniffing and grabbed a tissue and wiped her nose.

"You are upset."

"I'm not upset Ty I'm confused. I'm not sure I understand what you mean," she said.

She used a corner of the towel wrapped around her hair to wipe her eyes. She could see by his expression his mind was working and she knew he was trying to think of something he could say to fix the problem. She felt an urge to help him but waited.

"I like sleeping with you," he said.

He was trying to hit the right combination of words to undo whatever it was that made her cry. This made her laugh and cry at the same time and at that point he decided to fold and not say anything more, the words he used just made things worse. She was looking at him with tears in her eyes and he was looking at her eyes and wondering if she could see okay with water in her eyes. He reached out a finger and lifted a tear from her cheek and examined it.
The gesture was so intimate, tender, and unexpected that she took his hand in both of hers, uncurled his fingers one at a time and kissed his open palm, and held it to her cheek.

He liked the warm feeling of her tear-wet face and, even though it was skin, it was her skin. He put his other hand up and gently held her face and looked into her eyes. He held her eyes for a long time, longer than ever before, and she melted a little as she was pulled into those intense grey eyes. It felt like for the first time she understood him at a deeper level. The look she saw in his eyes made her realize that something was changing between them, something was different. She felt a shivery surge of elation mixed with fear when her heart dared to name what that something was.

He thought she was about to speak and he touched his finger to her lips to stop her. He was aware that something important was happening and knew instinctively that words would chase it away.

He spoke more clearly with the touch of his hands than his words ever could and it set her adrift. She drank in the sweet emotion she felt from his touch and slowly moved her face towards his. She saw his eyes widen and was heartened when he fought the urge to pull away from her. Her lips touched his softly and in that sweet instant of contact she had new tears but this time of joy.
When that sweet kiss ended she looked into his eyes and time slowed and her heart grew with the certainty of their connection.

Something new was happening; it was new to her mind but old and familiar to her heart. There was a change happening within her, a shift of perspective that was subtle but fundamental to her existence, in a profound sense she knew her existence now depended on his. It did not matter to her he did not know, or might not ever know, the right words to say or the things he was supposed to do as her boyfriend.
"I wasn't crying because I was upset, Tyler. I was crying because I am happy you want me to be your girlfriend," she said.
She kissed the words she spoke into his neck.

"You are my girlfriend," he said.

"I am your girlfriend," she said.

She whispered the words back and realized he had known and been certain of this all along. The towel wrapping her hair came loose and he put his face into the wet strands and breathed in the heady scent of shampoo and clean girl.

"I love you, Zen."

Chapter 19

Teenage Lawyer

September 25
8:00 PM
RCMP Building, Victoria, BC.

"Dr. Mann, the police have not charged you with anything. They are holding you as a material witness but because you live in Ontario they have convinced Judge Ryan you are a flight risk."

"Flight risk? I'm not guilty of anything why would I run away?" he asked.

"They do not have to specify why they simply need to convince a Judge of the possibility," she said.

His lawyer, Kelly Woods, gave him a smile which said she agreed that it sucked.

"Great," he said, slumping back in the chair.

They were in a locked interview room in RCMP Headquarters on Nanaimo Street in Victoria, where he'd been cooling his heels for the last two days. The police offered to provide him with a lawyer but he opted to call his lawyer in Toronto. She called back an hour later and recommended Kelly the only problem was she was unavailable and he would have to wait.

"What about Andi?" he said.

"She is still in the ICU at Victoria General Hospital. The police are claiming she sustained her head injury resisting arrest," she said.

He jumped up from his seat and yelled, "That's bullshit! She didn't resist anything. A cop grabbed her by her hair and slammed her head to the floor, I thought he killed her," he said.

"Sit down, Dr. Mann, and please do not say any more. Do you understand?" she said.

He sat down and controlled his anger. She was right of course. The police could be listening to their conversation and probably recording it too.

"Are you ready now?" she asked and waited for him to make eye contact before accepting his answer.

"Yes," he said.

"Okay, remember to follow my lead. No matter what they say to you, when I talk, you stop. Do not get emotional, do not argue, this is what they want. They will try to get you upset and say something incriminating, do not let them do it. Are we clear on this?" she said. He nodded.

When she stood up she gave him a big bright confident smile followed by a wink. Amazingly, the wink made him feel better. She was a smart capable lawyer but when he first met her, less than two hours ago, he was struck by the thought she was too young to be a lawyer. She looked to him like a high school girl; he lost that opinion when she immediately began teaching him how to answer the questions he was going to be asked and she showed no mercy in critiquing his answers. One question she asked that he answered caused her to look at him and in a matter of fact dead serious voice said, "That answer in court could mean jail time for you."

In two short hours she managed to sharpen his focus and whip him into some kind of reasonable shape. He had complete confidence in her ability but he was not sure about his own. She tapped on the door and a few minutes later three men came into the room.

Chapter 20

What Boys Do

Zen wrapped her arms around his neck and clung to him. Immersed in newly discovered intimacy she pecked tiny kisses on his neck until he pushed her away. It was not rejection he wanted to kiss her mouth again and when they came up for air, she grinned.

"I love you too," she said out of breath.

She stopped and thought about those words and though she had said them easily enough she was surprised at the power they held for her.
Without letting go of her he found the remote control and turned off the television and she became aware of a new intensity in the air. The room was quiet; she had not noticed the constant background noise of the television until he turned it off. The room was dark but for the glow of early autumn twilight that filtered through closed curtains.

The only sounds were those of her beating heart and the rustle of sheets as she crawled further onto the bed. She lay her head on the pillow and looked up at him and he hesitated, but only for a moment, then lay beside her turning to face her. He reached out his hand to touch her arm and she was struck by the thought that he was checking to see if she was real.

She turned onto her side and faced him watching his eyes follow her hand as she reached out to touch him. He was wearing his faded Star Wars T-shirt. The material was worn dangerously thin from washings and she was keenly aware of warm flesh beneath her fingers. She watched his face as she gently explored the contours of his chest. Her touch was one of familiarity which began innocently but turned to intimacy as her face and chest flushed with heat. Touching him awoke within her a familiar need which grew sharper as she explored, as her fingers sought the warmth of his flesh. This need, this desire, was one she'd not felt for him before or perhaps never admitted to feeling, and the urgent intensity of her need for him surprised her. Her eyes were the messengers of her heart but she knew he could not read her gaze and she willed her roving fingers to convey her intimate mind to him. She slipped her hand under his T-shirt and made Yoda dance in an impossible way.

"Resist the force you cannot," she said and giggled.

He was watching her in the near darkness his beautiful open face betraying nothing of what he was feeling. It was her need which led her to interpret his lack of squirming as license to continue. She could see he was attending to her in a singular fashion, in a way she had never seen him do before. She watched for his reaction when she moved her fingers under his shirt lightly scratching his skin with her fingernails.

"Mmmm, do you like that, Ty?"

She murmured dreamily adrift on her tactile journey of discovery. He did not answer her directly but his answer was clear enough, he let her continue to do it. She tugged the front of his T-shirt up to expose his tummy and to her amazement he sat up and peeled it off tossing it on the floor.

Her breath caught at the sight of him. His shirt had been off earlier when she was applying the tattoo but now, in this context, everything was different.

They were on her bed and he was naked from the waist up leaning on one arm looking at her and she drew in a ragged breath. He looked different from when she was applying the tattoo and her eyes consumed him tasting the solid contours of strong arms and thick chest, inhaling the clean soapy scent of boy. She stroked his stomach, it was hard and flat, and she wondered what miracle of genetics gave him a body like this without exercise.

Her touch was light, too light, it tickled. He laughed and squirmed like a little boy and she could not resist the temptation. She leaned forward and burbled her lips in a noisy baby kiss above his belly button and when she looked up he had an odd expression on his face and she wondered if that was because his mom had done that to him as a baby? The thought that Andi had kissed him that way made her feel inexplicably jealous.

Chapter 21

Four on the Floor

September 27
2:00PM
Vancouver, BC

Colonel John Western drove off the Queen of Nanaimo ferry into a blinding west coast rainstorm. He had opted to use his own car for this trip to Vancouver because he was not on official business and now he was glad he did. If he got creamed over here driving a military vehicle he would have to explain why he was there. Welcome to Vancouver, he thought, as he adjusted his driving style and speed to match the more aggressive driving on the lower mainland.

His wipers on the highest setting barely kept up with the rain coming at him horizontally in vast sheets. He was driving faster than good sense would suggest but in an odd way it was exhilarating and of course preferable to being run down by a gravel truck. He winced as another fully loaded dump truck with pup trailer roared past him on the inside lane.

He was heading downtown to meet Arne Schlect. They served together, though for different countries, in some interesting places around the world. Their friendship solidified when they were both stationed in Peru. They were in a strip club on Maguire Road in Lima when, after too many tumblers of whiskey, they came up with an idea for getting rich in the export business.

He could not remember which one of them came up with the original idea, but when they sobered up and it still seemed like a good idea, they did it. They shipped a lot of high-grade cocaine and made a pile of cash and they never got caught because they knew exactly when it was time to get out of the business.

The reason they knew when to quit was Schlect was the Major in charge of the US Military Police in Peru. When the memo came from headquarters that someone was smuggling drugs on military aircraft it landed on his desk first.

He knew his friend Arne was bent enough to like a deal like this Worthy kid, and he knew Arne had blown through all the drug money he made years ago and was in need. He also knew Arne wouldn't burn him and the guarantee was the knowledge that the US military doesn't have a statute of limitations on criminal activity committed while in uniform. His old friend knew if he tried to burn him it would result in mutually assured destruction.

It was the Cold War all over again only better, he thought laughing at his joke. He told Arne just enough about the deal to get him interested. He did not know anything about the virus or how it worked, but that was not his problem. He would have the kid and that was all he needed. There was some personal risk involved in this deal but if they worked it right they would both end up extremely wealthy.

The parking lot at the Royal Hamilton was full and he had to circle the block three times to find a surface spot. On the third go round he caught a glimpse of a grey sedan that he was certain he'd seen earlier on Georgia Street. When he found a spot and got out of his car the sedan passed by him and turned at the next intersection. A man in his thirties was driving and he looked military. He did not recognize the driver but seeing the same car twice activated his internal threat detector.

This thing with the kid was potentially huge and could involve lots of money. If Arnie yapped to someone about it, and they understood its significance, it could pose serious health problems for both of them. He walked into the lobby of the hotel and loitered until he could be sure he was alone in the elevator on his way up to Arnie's room on the nineteenth floor.

Inside the elevator he turned his back to the surveillance camera and pretended to check his teeth in the mirror as he slipped the weapon out of its holster. He always carried a nine-millimeter Beretta often joking that it was like his dick: he never left home without it. He quietly jacked a round into the breach, flipped the safety on, and then slipped it into his coat pocket. He was glad he had the foresight to screw the stubby suppressor onto it before he left home.

He put it in his pocket because he might not have an opportunity to reach his holster if something went wrong in the meeting. He did all this naturally and with few noticeable movements. Anyone reviewing the security video later would think he was simply checking his appearance before meeting someone.

He stood outside the room for a few moments listening before he knocked. He knew something was up because when he knocked Arnie opened the door about two seconds later with a big bullshit grin on his red face.

This was a dead giveaway, he knew Arne would never smile when a scowl would do as well. He stepped into the room and saw two men he did not recognize. They were seated. The reason they were sitting down, he figured, was to put him at ease. It had the opposite effect he recognized they were in position to ensure at least one of them would always have a clear shot.

It was exactly how he would have set things up. He stood between the large fake wood cabinet which held the television and the entry door with the wall against his back. That way he could watch all three men.

"What's the deal, Arne?" he said.

The man sitting in the chair on his left answered.

"We want to talk to you about the virus," he said. The man's demeanor was one of reasonableness but given the shooting gallery setup he was not in the mood to be reasonable.

"Who are you?" he said.

The man answered him and the dismissal in his voice was clear.

"I am your best chance for surviving this," he said.

The same man answered both times, and judging by his smug over-confident tone, he was no pro. Western continued to look at him but he knew he was not the leader so it had to be the other guy. It did not matter who was in charge because he had already decided it was time to leave but he needed to check one thing before he left. He smiled at the man who spoke and relaxed his posture. When he saw the man relax it confirmed to him he was no pro. When he reached into his pocket and took out the Beretta no one missed the soft click of the safety coming off.

"I'm leaving now," he said.
He pointed the gun at Arne's big belly and said, "You are going through the door first."

He was disappointed to see the colour drain from his old friend's face because it told him all he needed to know about the situation and more than he wanted to know about Arne. He was in on this thing otherwise he would not be afraid to go through the door first. It meant there was someone outside, probably the guy that followed him to the hotel, and he did not plan to be front and centre in a fire-fight. He looked around the room without taking his eyes off the seated men for more than a second at a time.

On the nineteenth floor of a modern hotel there was no reasonable alternative for getting out of a room other than the door you came in. He tried to remember what kind of load the Beretta was packing. He normally packed light loads for subsonic or hollow points for close work but it had been a long time since he was in the field and could not recall what he'd loaded.

The interior walls of hotel rooms were notoriously thin and he did not want to kill a guest with a through shot. He was ready now, he just needed the poke and it came when the man who had not yet spoken shifted in his seat and it looked like he was about to get up. Western was jumpy and he mistook the movement thinking the man was reaching for a weapon. He fired one shot which hit him in the forehead then immediately turned and shot "best chance" guy as he was reaching for his gun, then he shot Arne in the chest.

Jonas heard the whole thing and, as Western spun around to cover the hotel room door, he quietly stepped out from the bathroom and shot Western in the back of the head. He was dead on his way to the floor.

Chapter 22

Zen's House

September 25
11:22 PM

    The house was dark but he had a feeling Zen and Tyler were inside. When he knocked again there was no response. He knew they must be frightened by what happened and were likely just being cautious. He gave up and walked around to Andi's backyard; if they were inside watching they would see it was him.

Not that seeing him would necessarily fill them with confidence, he thought. He wondered if they would ever trust him after what happened. He stood in the yard surveying the carnage then bent over and began to pick up the bits and pieces of Andi and Tyler's life. Bending over made him dizzy, his vision had been affected by the beating he received from the police, but it made him feel better to be doing something. He did not want to leave their belongings outside to be ruined though after two days outside it was obvious a lot of it was now trash. He turned over some books trying to decide which, if any, were salvageable after being out in the weather. He picked up a book of children's stories with a bear on the cover and gazed at it lost in thought wondering about the childhood of the son he never knew he had.

When Tyler touched his shoulder he yelped. Startled by the sudden touch he jerked away defensively. He had not heard him walk up behind him and he was shaken from the scare. His nerves were shot after all that happened and he bent over and vomited on the lawn.

"Tyler you scared the shit out of me," he said trying to catch his breath.

"Where is Andrea?" Tyler said.

It was then he noticed the boy was naked and shivering in the chill night air.
"Andi is at the hospital," he said

"To visit Daniel?" he asked.

For a moment he was confused and did not know what he was talking about but then remembered Daniel was the injured soldier's name. It seemed like it all happened a long time ago; since the blow to his head he'd been having trouble concentrating and keeping details straight. When he went to see Andi he inquired about the soldier and learned that the Sergeant had died of his injuries.

He didn't think this was the right time to tell Tyler that. What he needed was to come up with some way to explain to him what happened to his mother.
How should he explain to Tyler that his mother is not visiting the Sergeant but is herself injured and in critical condition, in a coma in the ICU? He could viscerally recall the sickening thump of the impact as her head hit the floor and it made his stomach ache. The instant her head hit the floor he was certain the impact had killed her.

He sat with her in the ICU until they made him leave but the whole time he was there he talked to her. He read somewhere that people who are unconscious can hear and will often respond to the sound of a familiar voice. The fact she has suffered a serious brain injury was bad but an injury was better than the alternative. She was alive and he would work with her and help her to recover.

It was entirely the fault of the police SWAT team that she was injured and they compounded the damage done by not believing it when she suffered blackouts and fainting spells while they interrogated her. When she finally collapsed and lost consciousness and they could not wake her they realized she was not faking and reluctantly called paramedics who rushed her to the Emergency at Victoria General.

The attending physician examined her and called Dr. Sing the neurologist and when he saw her he immediately admitted her to the neurology ICU. When he spoke with Dr. Sing he would not give an opinion on what further damage it caused her by not immediately receiving medical attention but the angry look on the Doctor's face told him what he already knew.

"Your mom is hurt Tyler. She is at the hospital because she got…. hurt," he said.

"What got hurt?" he asked.

"Her head, her head hit the floor," he said.

"Why?" he said.

He considered his words before he answered and decided there was no point in lying to him.
"The police hurt her," he said.
He could not keep the bitterness from his voice or the tears from forming in his eyes. "The same people who did this to your home," he said, gesturing to the yard, "hurt your mom."

"Why did they do it?" he asked.

He shook his head. He could not answer that question. He didn't know why the police acted in the violent and destructive way they had. He supposed some of them believed anything that might involve terrorism gave them license to act like terrorists themselves. There was nothing useful he could say to him about why his mom was hurt because it amounted to nothing more than brutality and indifference. He noticed Zen standing in the shadows and looked over at her and smiled.

"Thank you for taking care of Tyler," he said and then remembered the ruined book in his hand. He threw it on the ground and walked over to where she was standing.

"Andi has been hurt. She has a concussion, a head injury," he said to her. "I came from the hospital and she's unconscious. The Doctor said her brain has swollen from the impact when her head hit the floor. I don't know what will happen. The doctors don't know if she will recover," he said.

"You need to come inside," she said. She turned and led him into her house only turning on one dim lamp in the living room and locking the door behind them. She had all the windows covered and it was dark and cave-like inside the house. She led him to the couch to sit down. She asked Tyler to get dressed and when he left the room she sat on an old armchair which matched the couch next to the unlit fireplace. She commented he looked awful; his face was black and swollen with one eye shut completely. There was a fresh scab covering an ugly gash on his cheek.

"I'll make some tea," she said. He listened to her banging around in the kitchen and he was comforted by the normalness of the sounds. He sat quietly with his hands folded in his lap and it occurred to him he was likely experiencing some kind of shock in response to all that had happened. She came in and put a cup in front of him along with a pot of steaming tea.

"What do you take?" she said.

He thought about it and couldn't remember how he liked his tea and the fact he couldn't remember confused him. Where did that bit of information go he wondered as he searched his mind, but it was not there to be found.

"Clear," he said.

She poured a cup for him and one for herself. He held it to his lips and sipped.

"Can I ask you a favour?" he said.

"What is it?"

"Can I lie down on your couch for a few minutes?"

***

He woke the next morning with a start and for a few terrifying moments he did not know where he was. Only after the vision in his good eye cleared did he notice Tyler sitting across from him. He sat up and immediately regretted it because his head and face began to throb. He was holding his head in his hands when Tyler stood up and came over to him and held something out to him. His eye was not focused enough for fine details but he did not need to see it he recognized it from the frame. It was the photo of him and Andi at Niagara Falls. Zen came in the room and handed him a mug of black coffee and he took a sip.

"We need to talk," she said.

He nodded and took another sip of his coffee and then he put it and the photo down on the coffee table.

"Do you have anything for pain?" he asked.
She got up and left the room and he could hear a cupboard opening. The whole time Tyler never said a word. He simply sat down again and continued to watch him. When she came back with two pills she dropped them onto his open palm. He washed them down with coffee. He eased back on the couch and rubbed his temples.

"Okay where should we start?" he said.

"Are you a good guy or a bad guy?" she said.

He could not help laughing which was a mistake because it made his face hurt. Her question was asked without a trace of accusation or prejudice. She was so innocent in her directness his heart went out to her. It was obvious to him she was protecting Tyler and she wanted to know if he was a threat or if she could trust him. She sat beside Tyler on the arm of his chair and they both looked at him waiting.

It was odd having these kids openly challenge him. Although he did not detect anything in Tyler's gaze he saw wariness in hers. It occurred to him only the young could ask a question like that and actually expect an honest answer. The truth was, at the moment, he did not know if he was good or bad. He knew his intentions started out good but, so far, everything he touched had turned out bad.

It was not a question of blame or guilt exactly there were forces working against all of them which were beyond his control. What he was mostly feeling was responsible for not being smarter about things. He left his tidy academic life and been thrust into the middle of all this and he had to admit his performance so far was less than stellar.

He knew there were a lot of things he should have done differently. At the very least he should have anticipated the police response to what they might find on Tyler's computer. If he'd been thinking proactively he would have insisted they get out of town and hunker down until things cooled off but he was way behind the curve.

If he was less of a lab weenie and more of a man he would have anticipated all of this and Andi would not have been hurt. The police never gave them an opportunity to say anything before they were attacked, beaten, and arrested. Until it happened to them he had not known that the police acted that way and he realized what a sheltered existence he'd led up to now.

They kept him locked in isolation and spent hours grilling him and wearing him down. They threatened all kinds of possible charges against him and he would normally have cooperated but he was angry at what they did to Andi. He did not speak to them other than to tell them all to go to hell. He was glad he kept his mouth shut because when his lawyer Kelly showed up it only took her a few minutes to completely blow all their charges out of the water.

He remembered how calmly she listened to their evidence and when their lead inspector, Maerks, finished out-lining the charges against him she smiled indulgently at him and let them wait a full minute before responding.
He watched the discomfort this caused them as the locus of power silently shifted away from them based solely on her icy demeanor of confidence and dismissive efficiency. They were obviously wary of her from past encounters and that made him feel much better. When she began to speak he listened raptly as she refuted all their

charges as unprofessional indefensible fantasy. She let them roast in their own juices for another full minute and then posited her own much more plausible explanation as to why there was virus information on Tyler's computer.

"Tyler Worthy is sixteen years old," she said.

She let this statement steep for a moment and he watched two of the cops shift uncomfortably in their chairs.

"He was collecting freely available data from those august terrorist organizations, the World Health Organization, Health Canada, and the NIH in the US," she paused again and drew a deep breath which spoke of their extreme ignorance. "because he was building a computer game," she said.

She said this while staring at them wide eyed and slowly shaking her head. She wore on her face a look so damning and dismissive he imagined she must have practiced it in front of a mirror to perfect the perfect blend of disgust and sympathy for their simple mindedness.

The disgust was for the pathetic police assertions unsupported by any physical evidence and the sympathy was for the Crown Council who might be assigned to try these idiotic charges in court.

He was impressed at how quickly and completely she removed all the breathable air from their side of the interview table. Not one of the men sitting across from her would look at her let alone attempt to counter her assertions.

It was clear that in their haste to nab a possible career boosting "bio-terrorist" they overlooked a more likely scenario for why this information was on a teenager's computer. He could see by their blank faces they simply never thought of it. This was one of those situations where something obvious was missed and the truth, when it was revealed, was painfully embarrassing. Her scenario along with the complete lack of corroborating evidence for their charges sank them. He could see it mirrored in the unhappy expressions frozen on their faces.

"Gentlemen please inform your legal counsel I will be contacting them shortly to set a date to discuss damages and reparations for the grievous injuries and wanton destruction of private property. Clearly Dr. Mann and Ms. Worthy have suffered greatly both physically and mentally as a result of your agency's egregious misjudgment and the ensuing precipitous actions your agents undertook against them.
As it happens I will be lunching tomorrow with Superior Court Justice Roberts. You may recall he is the Justice you convinced to issue the search warrant for this debacle. I do hope, for all your sakes, that you did not mislead him in your application. I am certain he will be very unhappy to learn of the life threatening injuries Ms. Worthy has sustained as a result of the actions of your officers. Will that be all, gentlemen?" she said.

She sat composed and impatient with a slight but unmistakable look of dismissal upon her face as she looked across the table. No one on the other side spoke. They sat restlessly for a few moments then folded their papers and closed their file folders and each one rose from the conference table and filed out of the tiny room.

He sat holding his breath and vibrating with jangled nerves on the chair beside her as she began to put away her papers. He drew a whole breath and turned his head to her to ask what to do now but she stopped him with a tiny shake of her head and a wink.

Her meaning was clear: Do not speak. Relax and wait. She was right. It was less than five minutes before the door opened and a smiling information officer, one who was not part of the interrogation team, stepped into the room and announced he was free to go.

When the officer attempted to engage Kelly in dialogue starting with an apology to both of them for the misunderstanding she held up her hand like a stop sign and without looking at him said, "Save it."

They walked out onto Nanaimo Street a few minutes later into a light evening drizzle and it felt wonderful to be rained on. They did not talk much when they got in her car and she dropped him off at Victoria General Hospital with a promise he would call her when he found Tyler.

Darth Vader

He looked at Zen and Tyler sitting together and he sighed. They looked like many young couples, handsome beyond the mere fact of their youth, each one attractive alone but more so in the combining.

"The first thing you need to know is Andi is at Victoria General Hospital in the ICU. I went to see her last night after the police released me. She is very ill. They are keeping her in something the nurse called an 'induced coma'. This is something neurologists do to stop further damage to her brain from swelling. I believe she would benefit greatly if you and Tyler went to see her. She is unconscious but she would likely be aware of your presence," he said.
Zen was nodding slowly but Tyler never said anything. He continued.

"The other thing I need to tell you is…" he paused, his voice faltered thickened with emotion, "Tyler, I am your father."

He watched the boy's eyes but there was no change, no emotion, not a flicker of surprise. He simply stared at him with a blank expression it was Zen who reacted to the news.

"Are you kidding?" she said.

Her voice and face were full of wonder and shocked surprise.

"No, I'm not kidding. Andi told me just before all this happened," he said.

His eyes fell upon the silver framed photo on the coffee table and he picked it up and handed it to her.

"Is that you?" she said. "I wondered why Ty had this. He brought all his science junk over but this was the only thing he brought that wasn't about science," she said.

"Yes, that is Andi and me many years ago," he said.

"Where was this taken?" she asked

"Niagara Falls," he said.

She looked at his face and then back at the photo, "It's sort of hard to tell," she said. She was looking at his older battered face trying to match it to the photo. Then she looked at Tyler's face and back to the photo.
"I guess you do look a bit like Ty," she said.

Tyler was watching her examine the photo but otherwise he seemed disengaged from the back and forth of the conversation. He had not had time to think about it much since all this started and he examined the boy's face in profile. He saw something of his father's face in the angles. There was something about the mouth and the way his eyes were set in the skull.

"I only found out myself a few days ago," he said again.

"You mean Andi never told you?" she said.
Her eyes went wide with surprise clearly shocked by this detail.

"No," he said

"Why not?" she said.

"I don't have the answer to that," he said.

"Was this in Montreal?" she said.

"No. We were in Toronto attending university and she simply took off one day without saying anything to me about being pregnant," he said.

He was aware they were talking as though Tyler was not sitting right there in the room with them. Zen seemed to sense he was uncomfortable talking about this with Tyler not taking part in the conversation and she directed her next question to him.

He was impressed with her caring and intuitive nature it was unusual at such a young age. It was an odd thing to be thinking about but he was glad Tyler had her as a friend or maybe they were more than friends. She did not seem particularly abashed that he was outside naked when they found him. It told him something important about her values and priorities and obviously Tyler was a priority for her. As his father, though that concept still felt odd, it was heartening to know this about her.

"What do you think, Ty? Dr. Mann is your father. It's just like Star Wars," she said. She spoke brightly trying to relate this news to something he could relate to but then she thought about what she said and added, "Well, maybe not exactly." Her face turned red when she realized she compared him to Darth Vader.

There was a pause in the conversation and Tyler looked at her and said, "Does that mean you are my sister?"

They looked at each other and started laughing and Tyler joined in though he did not know why they were laughing.

"So what do you think, Ty?" she said.

She was excited by this surprising news. In all the years they knew each other the subject of who his father was never came up. The one time she heard her mom and Andrea talking about it, they were drinking wine and aside from tears and generally disparaging comments which seemed to apply equally to all men, she heard nothing specific about his father.

She knew Tyler was born in Montreal but that was all. She did not know Andi changed her name from Worthington and she was only peripherally aware that she did not communicate with members of her family back east.

"Think about what?" said Tyler.

"That Dr. Mann is your dad?" she said.

He did not answer because he was scanning her face to see if she was talking loud because she was upset with him. He could not determine for certain because her cheeks were red but she was smiling with all her teeth and those two things sorta cancelled each other out.

"Didn't Andrea ever say anything to you about him?" she said.

"Who?" he said.

"Dr. Mann," she said, her voice was rising. She was practically yelling at him barely able to contain her frustration. She could not understand why he was not excited by this news. It would be a big deal for most people to meet their father for the first time.

"Don't you have any questions for him?" she said. She was prompting him now because she was feeling bad about Tyler's seeming lack of interest.

"Yes," he said.

"Well?" she said glaring at him. "What is it?"
"Do you have an SEM?" he said.

Tyler quickly looked at her face to see if that made her more upset but her mouth was hanging open. He could not read this but he decided it did not mean she was upset and he relaxed.

Mann smiled at them, they were like a lot of couples he met over the years where one partner, usually the female, has stronger verbal skills and becomes impatient and answers for the other.

"Yes we have a scanning electron microscope at the school why Tyler? Do you want to use it?" he said.

"Yes," he said

"Do you need it to work on your project?" he said.

"Yes," he said.

"Have you and Andrea ever been to Thunder Bay?" he said.

He and Andi did a lot of catching up when he came for dinner but he did not know all of their history after they left Montreal. It was possible they were in Thunder Bay and he would not have known. Tyler did not answer but Zen piped up.

"What's in Thunder Bay Dr. Mann?" she said.

"That's where I live," he said.

He could see by the look on her face she had not considered the possibility he did not live in Victoria. He watched the swift progression as thought and emotion subtly reshaped her features as she connected the dots deciphering what that might mean. He knew Tyler was important to her and he watched her calculate; Tyler is only sixteen and if Dr. Mann is his father and Andrea is too sick to look after him it means he will move to Thunder Bay.

"No," she said the barely audible word leaked from her throat as this fearful calculation struck home.

He smiled at her reassuringly then winced because his face hurt.

"You don't need to worry Zen, Ty will not be going anywhere without you," he said.

The look of relief which spread across her face was quickly followed by embarrassment at being so easily read. It would have been comical if it was not so completely affecting. He realized then, no matter what happened to him or Andi, Tyler would be okay because she would see to it.

"We should go to the hospital now and see how Andi is doing," he said.

"No," Tyler said.

He looked at him and then at Zen and she shrugged her shoulders.

"Why not, Ty?" she asked.

He did not answer her he got up from the chair and went into the bedroom and closed the door.

Chapter 23

Dead Western

Vancouver, British Columbia

Jonas McLean had known all along that Western was a hard ass but he had no idea the guy would go nuts and start killing people. Two dead Americans, one of them an NSA agent. This was going to be hard to explain to his contact, especially when he was the reason they were there. He knew they would be looking for him to explain what happened and now the only way to put things right was to grab that kid.

When he and Fran decided to go freelance he knew there would be dangers he just didn't expect them to come from his own freaking side. Before he left the scene he wiped the gun he shot Western with and put it in the hand of the rookie CSIS agent and took his gun. He was closest to the bathroom door and, he reasoned, that should roughly coincide with the trajectory of the rounds that killed Western as long as the cops did not check too carefully. He took one last look around trying to remember what else he touched in the room. He gave the bathroom door handle a wipe and put up his hood and left the room.

He took the fire escape down three floors before summoning the elevator. He pulled the fire alarm as he exited the elevator on the main floor and left the building through a side exit to the parking lot. He made his way out to the street as the first police car screamed up to the curb. The cops who got out were met with a crowd of people rushing out of the building. He joined the fleeing mass and walked towards the bus depot. He checked his watch, if he hurried he could catch the four p.m. bus to Victoria.

Andi's Place

Mann ducked under the yellow police tape walking into the house through the unlocked back door. He planned to start cleaning up while he waited for Zen. She was going to shower and change and try again to convince Tyler to come with them to the hospital.

He was appalled by the mess he found inside; the house stank of rotting food. He found garbage bags and started by removing spoiled food from the refrigerator. He could not understand why the police unplugged it in the first place. What was the point of that? The destruction they left in their wake was extensive and looked like the worst kind of vandalism. It added to the anger he already felt about Andi.

When it was empty he pulled the racks out and wiped the inside down with warm water and bleach; the fridge was the source of the smell. When he finished he closed the door and plugged it in. He walked around closing drawers and picking things up that had been knocked over. The police had installed a sheet of plywood over the smashed front door but they did not clean up the pieces of splintered wood all over the place.

He could see the spot where Andi's head hit the floor as well as patches of his own dried blood. He went back to the kitchen looking for a broom wondering how much time he had before Zen would be ready to go.

She said she would try to find out why Tyler did not want to go and visit his mom but she would need some time to talk to him about it. He suspected the reason was simple: he was probably afraid to go and see her. It was difficult to know for certain what he thought or felt about what happened to her but he reasoned it must have some affect. It dawned on him as he dumped a gallon of sour milk down the drain that, if Andi did not recover, it would be up to him to take care of Tyler.

The significance of this crashed on him as he realized he was now the parent of a sixteen-year-old boy with all the challenges and responsibilities that went with it. This line of thought raised other questions for him, some of them legal, that might need to be addressed before he could officially take on the job of becoming a father. Did he have a legal parental right to him or would someone in Andi's family fight for custody?

He supposed a genetic test would clear up any doubts about paternity, and if someone challenged his right to the boy, then it would be a matter of applying to the court for a decision on custody. The glib promise he made to Zen when she was worried about losing Tyler was looking harder to keep. It was while he was thinking about which school in Thunder Bay would be best for Tyler to attend it hit him. Everything he was thinking about was based on Andi not recovering. He had let his mind race ahead and became caught up in the myriad details of becoming a parent.

He stopped and let those thoughts go because losing Andi was too painful to contemplate. He found her after all this time and now he was in danger of losing her again this time forever. The reality of this possibility was depressing and he tried to shift his mood by thinking of something happier. It took a while for him to find something positive to think about.

At least we do not have to worry about the police for a while, he thought. That reminded him he was supposed to call his lawyer when he located Tyler because she needed to talk with him before the police did 'in case they were dumb enough to continue to pursue the issue,' she said.

He flattened the empty milk carton, tossed it into the garbage bag, rinsed the stale milk off his hands and rinsed them in the sink. He dried his hands on a tea towel and took a step towards Andi's phone but it rang before he reached it. He thought it was probably Zen and he picked up.

"Dr. Mann?" a woman's voice said.

"Yes," he said.

"This is the person you drove to emergency. I can't talk long, I wanted to tell you that Western is dead. He died yesterday in a hotel room in Vancouver. It might be unrelated but I don't think so, I believe the kid is in danger," she said.

"Danger from whom?" he said.

"I don't know Doc. I'm in Europe and I'm AWOL. All I know is he's dead and I plan to disappear for a while maybe forever. I can't tell you who killed Western or if his death is connected to the kid but I thought you ought to know. If you decide to get him and his mom out of there you need to take the girl too because whoever is looking for him will use her to get to him. One more thing Doc, the kid and me, we are even now I have to go," she said.

He was staring at the dead phone in his hand when the back door flew open and he jumped with a start. It was Zen and her eyes were wild.

"Tyler's gone. I was in the bathroom getting ready and when I came out he was gone. His bike is gone too, "she said.

"Where would he go?" he said.

She shrugged her shoulders. She could think of lots of places he might go but none that made any sense. She talked with him about seeing his mom but he said no. He made it clear he did not want to go to the hospital. When she went into the bedroom to talk to him he was on the computer looking at a map of Ontario.
"Do you think he would try to go to Thunder Bay?" she said.

Other than asking him about the electron microscope she could not remember anything else he said that would indicate where he might go.
He was not listening to what she was saying to him because he was processing what Hunter told him seconds earlier. While Zen was talking he was working through all the ramifications of Western's death and Hunter's phone call. If she was on the run she wouldn't have risked a phone call unless she was certain they were in real danger.

Western must have told people about Tyler and what he has created. If those people believed Western that would be reason enough to want to get their hands on Tyler. There were lots of people who have a huge monetary incentive for controlling POrna which means controlling or eliminating anyone who knows about it.

The people who make money from human conflict are not going to celebrate Tyler's work. They will kill him without hesitation and it would not make any difference to them if POrna virus was real or not. They would eliminate all of them simply on the slim chance that POrna was real.

"I had a call from Patricia Hunter. She's one of the soldiers Tyler helped and she told me Colonel Western is dead. He died yesterday and she wanted to warn me someone might be looking for Tyler," he said.

Zen's eyes widened in shock as she put a hand over her mouth. What little colour she had drained from her face, she looked terrified.

"When you and Andrea were gone he talked about contacting Colonel Western. Oh my God. We have to find him. What if he tries to contact him and they're waiting for him?" she said.

"Did he say how he planned to contact Western?" he said.

"No, he only said he was going to try," she said. She was slowly shaking her head and there were tears welling in her eyes.

"We need to find him. Give me your cell number," he said. She recited it and he punched it into his phone and hit send. A few seconds later her phone chirped.

"Okay, now you have my number too. Do you think he would go to the hospital to see Andi? Maybe he had a change of heart?" he said.

She shook her head.
"I don't know. I don't think so but he can be weird sometimes. Maybe he did go to see her," she said.

"I'll go to the hospital and see if he's there. Maybe he changed his mind about seeing her. How do you feel about riding around the neighbourhood? You could check his usual places and see if you can spot him? If you see him make sure you grab him and stay together until I can get to you," he said.

She sniffed and nodded her head.

"When we find him we need to get out of Victoria for a while until I can figure this thing out. Please be careful and if you see anyone suspicious hanging around call me immediately. Does Ty have a cell phone?" he said.

"Yes but he never turns it on except to take pictures. He doesn't talk much," she said. She gave him Ty's cell number anyway and he gave her a quick reassuring hug. She was crying as she flew out the door. He could see she was in a panic as she grabbed her bike from the back porch. She did not see the street person rummaging through the recycle box at the front gate of the farm next door as she rode from the yard. Her mind was elsewhere trying to figure out where Tyler might go. It was the wrong time of day and he would not be doing his fence thing at Layton's. She set off in the direction of his lab at the old factory to see if he went there. It did not seem likely, given the fact his stuff was gone, but she was at a loss for where else to search.

She heard an engine start and gravel fly and she turned her head and saw Dr. Mann driving away in the rental van and that was when she noticed a man standing at the side of the road watching him drive away. She was stricken with fear when he turned his head and looked directly at her.

Andi

The Intensive Care Unit was dark and relatively quiet compared to the rest of the hospital. When he entered the room he noticed Andi was deathly pale and he held his breath a long time waiting to see her chest rise and fall. Her respirations were almost too shallow to see and he thought for a moment she was was gone.

He spoke briefly with Dr. Sing and Sing told him they were planning to bring her out of the coma within the next twelve hours if all went well. He was concerned about the swelling in her brain it had gone down considerably but he wanted to try for a little more reduction before they try to wake her.
Tyler was not there and in a way he was glad he did not see his mother like this. He spoke briefly with the ICU nurse when she came in to check on Andi but she had not seen Tyler. She told him unaccompanied children were not allowed onto the neurology ward anyway. He gave her his cell number and extracted a promise she would call him if he showed up. The nurse left the room and his phone beeped. It was Zen.

"A man was watching the house when we left and now I think he's following me," she said. Her words were whispered breathlessly and he could hear the fear in her voice.

"Where are you now?" he said.

"I'm near the old factory I'm scared, Dr. Mann. What should I do?" she said.

"Stay out of sight I'm on my way," he said.

He clicked off and took one last look at Andi before running out of the room. He was within a block of the old factory when he spotted a dark sedan parked on the street out front. He was heading for it when he was startled by the blip of a police siren and flashing colour bar behind him. He pulled over and stopped and as the cop was getting out of his car Zen raced up to the front of the van on her bike. Her eyes were wild with fright. He rolled down the window and mouthed the words *did you find him*? She shook her head and then stood back and waited as the cop approached the van.

"Good afternoon sir. Would you mind stepping out of your vehicle?" he said.
As he was getting out he watched the parked car pull away from the curb and make a U-turn and drive away.

"May I see your operators permit?" he said.

He fished out his Ontario driver's license and handed it to him.

"Lee Mann is that correct?" he said.

"Yes," he said.

"Would you mind opening the back door of the truck, sir?" he said.

"Sure," he said.

They walked to the rear of the van and the cop watched as he undid the clasp which held the door closed. When he lifted the door the interior was in shadow and the officer used his flashlight and shone it into every corner but it was completely empty. That's odd, Mann thought, what happened to the bio-suits? The officer told him he could close the door and handed him back his license.

"Thank you sir. Drive safely," he said.

The cop walked back to his car and got in and drove away. Zen was trembling with fear; he told her to get into the van while he stashed her bicycle in the back. The two of them sat in the van waiting to be sure the cop was gone and wondering what they should do next.

"I didn't go inside the factory because I was afraid whoever was following me might see how I did it and follow me. Ty's bike isn't where he usually puts it but that doesn't mean he isn't inside," she said.

He was trying to figure out what happened to the bio-suits and facemasks. He knew it wasn't Andi who took them because they had only just decided what to do when the police bashed the door down and raided the house.

"We'll go in and look for him but we'll need flashlights. There is no way I'm going in there and poking around in the dark," he said.

She explained to him how they usually got inside the building but then he was faced with a dilemma. He did not want to leave her alone outside but they could not both enter the building at the same time. He thought about taking her home but given the news about Western's death he was not sure she would be any safer there. He could not let her go in first because who knows what might be waiting for them inside. The logical thing was for him to go first and make sure it was safe and then she could come in and that way she would be alone and exposed for the least amount of time.

None of these options gave him comfort and he was still deciding what to do as he parked the van. She handed him a flashlight; she loaded the batteries on the drive back from the 7-Eleven. She knew the clerk working and asked him if he'd seen Tyler but he had not. It was time to decide which one of them should go inside.

They walked to the loading dock keeping an eye out for the police and the dark sedan that had been parked outside earlier. They ducked down and crab walked under the dock and Zen showed him the way in. She was about to go in first but he stopped her, it was her action that made him decide what to do.

"I think it's safer if I go in first. We don't know what we will find in there. When I see that everything is okay I'll call to you and you come in. If I don't call you or you hear anything…." he hesitated looking for the right word, "disturbing from inside the building do not call out to me. Run away as fast as you can and when you are safe call the police. Okay?" he said.

When she did not answer he took her by the shoulders and looked into her eyes. Her young face was clouded with fear and he worried this was too much for her. "Okay?" he said.

She lowered her eyes and nodded her head.

"Good. And don't worry, everything will be fine. I'm being extra cautious, you know, like a dad," he said and smiled. She smiled back and nodded her head then demonstrated to him how to climb in. It was a tight fit and awkward with his injuries but he managed to wiggle along the vent. When he pushed himself over the edge and hit the bottom he scrambled out and turned on the light. He peered around the dark room listening and determined it was safe for Zen to come in there was no one waiting in the shadows. He stuck his head back inside the vent and called to her to tell her it was okay to come down.

There was no answer.

He thought he heard scuffling sounds coming through the vent from outside. There was no answer when he called her a second time and that's when he realized his mistake. He chose the wrong option. He did not have to try it to know he could not climb back up the vent. In a panic he ran to the stairway in the far corner of the basement. He ran faster than he could pick out obstacles using only one eye and the narrow beam of bouncing light and he tripped on a pile of debris and landed hard on the concrete floor. He picked himself up and ran up the stairs and cast the light around looking for a fire exit.

He was disoriented but he spotted an exit with a push bar door and ran to it as precious seconds seeped away. He knew anything could be happening to her. He jammed the bar and flew through the fire door and was stopped dead by what he saw. Zen was lying on the ground outside the door not moving. Her eyes were closed and her face was smudged with dirt. She was out cold.

"Don't move," a voice said. It came from behind him and to his right. He started to turn and something smashed the side of his head.

"I said don't move."

The voice was male but with a feminine quality to it and the trace of an accent. He could not help thinking he heard it before. The man was standing only a few inches behind him but he knew he could not surprise him by throwing himself in his direction. He did not know exactly where he was standing because he was on the same side as his swollen eye.

"I can hear you thinking Doctor Mann. Don't do it. I have a gun and if you want the girl to keep breathing do exactly what I tell you," he said.

He stood holding the side of his head. The blow reopened the gash made by the police and he was feeling lightheaded and in danger of passing out.

"Where is Tyler Worthy?" he said.

"I don't know," he said.

"Okay. Where do you think he is?" he said.

"I thought he might be here," he said.

Zen moaned and began to stir and he made a move towards her to help and something smashed his kneecap and he fell to the ground in agony. He saw bright shooting sparks of coloured pain behind his closed lids. His assailant had used some kind of club on him. He passed out from the intense pain only to awaken moments later sprawled on the ground facing Zen.

"Do exactly what I tell you or I will hurt her," he said.

The voice was cold and bore no trace of emotion. When her eyes fluttered and she rolled over onto her back their assailant came into view and though his vision was unclear he knew he'd seen him before. He was vaguely European looking with dark hair and he was short. He wore jeans, a plain shirt, and a light jacket. He looked like nobody and most people would find him difficult to pick out of a police line-up. The first and only time he saw him was with Western when he accused him of being the creator of the virus. He stared wondering if he was looking at Western's killer.

The man stood over the girl with one foot on each side of her rib cage. He watched helplessly as he jabbed the toe of his boot down hard on her breast and roughly shook her from side to side. Zen's eyes popped open and when she saw him she screamed but her scream was brutally cut off with a yelp of pain. He anticipated her reaction and lifted her shirt and Tasered her below her left breast.

Her face went slack as her body jerked as she went into convulsions. He feared for her life wondering if a jolt like that could stop her heart. The man laughed at her as she thrashed in the dirt and then looked at him and said, "Where is Tyler Worthy?"
He rested the heel of his boot on her chest and stomped down hard. He could hear the air forcefully expelled from her lungs. The man put his heel on her chest again. He waited and then stomped down hard on her chest again this time coldly looking him in the eye as he did it. His message was clear: tell me where he is or I will kill her. His flat emotionless eyes were locked on his as he began to repeat the words- "Where is Ty-" before he could finish the sentence Mann heard the sound of solid contact with flesh and bone. Their assailant's eyes went wide as he pitched forward landing on top of Zen.

His vision blurry he saw a figure come into view and stand with his back to him. He was wearing green coveralls and black rubber boots. He watched him bend down and grab their attacker by his jacket and roughly pull him off Zen. He dragged the inert form a few feet away from her and dropped him. That is when he saw the length of steel pipe in his hand.

"Is Zen dead?" Tyler asked.

He was wearing Patricia Hunter's biohazard suit standing over the unconscious attacker with the pipe in his hand. He was afraid the boy was prepared to kill him if the answer was yes. "No Ty she is unconscious she is hurt but she will be all right," he said.

Tyler stood for a long time over the prone man but came to a decision about something and threw the pipe down. Mann let out the breath he was holding as Tyler knelt beside Zen and gently lifted her and held her.

"Do you think you can carry her, Ty?"

He was gathering his wits trying to work through the pain as he watched Tyler gently pick her up and cradled her in his arms waiting for him as he struggled to get to his feet. He picked up the pipe and used it as a crutch to hobble over to the unconscious man lying in an expanding pool of blood. He felt his neck for a pulse but could not find one and worried that Tyler had killed him until he detected a thin racy pulse at his wrist. He was relieved the boy had not killed their assailant though he had no doubts the man intended to kill him and Zen after he got his hands on Tyler.

He searched his pockets and took everything he found: keys, wallet, gun, and Taser. He looked at the name on his driver's license; Frank Sedulca. He rolled Sedulca on to his side to ensure he did not lose his airway after they left and he threw the keys and wallet into the long weeds and pocketed the weapons.
It was beginning to look like he was going to need them. He used the pipe to hobble along behind Tyler as he carried Zen to the truck. He drove awkwardly using his left leg and hand while Tyler held Zen on his lap in a surreal replay of a few days earlier when he held Patricia Hunter in the same way.

When they arrived at her house Tyler carried her into the bedroom and allowed hi father to check her condition under his watchful gaze. She was breathing normally and there was nothing much he could do for her but wait for the effects of the Taser to wear off. He anticipated she would be in severe pain when she woke and he searched the bathroom for pain killers, took a few for himself, and handed the rest to Tyler with instructions to give her two pills when she woke and come and get him.

He left them and went to the kitchen where he found a full tray of ice cubes in the freezer. He wrapped a handful in a dish towel and alternately applied it to the side of his face and his knee to try and lower the swelling. He took two of the pills to ease the pain and decided to lie down on the couch for a few minutes until Zen woke. He needed to get them all out of there and find a safe place to hide but he did not want to be driving with an unconscious girl and Tyler in case they got pulled over.

That was his last thought before passing out from exhaustion.
It could have been a minute, an hour, or a week he did not know how long he was out, it was only when he heard someone speaking in a loud voice close by that he drifted up from the abyss.
His non-swollen eye slowly came into focus at the same time he realized someone was vigorously shaking his shoulder.

"You better wake up fella I've already called the cops."

A woman was standing over him and she held a black baseball bat poised and ready to nail him. She was big and she looked like she knew how to use it. He was disoriented coming out of a deep sleep and he wondered if this was a dream. Before he could figure out what was going on he heard Zen's voice.

"Relax mom, that's Tyler's dad."

The woman looked at her daughter then back at him.

"So what happened to you?" she said and grinned.

"It's a long story," he said.

Chapter 24

Lady Spy

Ottawa, Ontario

They sat in an office on the fifth floor of a modern five-story low rise office building located in a primarily residential suburb of Ottawa. The building bore no external signage to indicate what kind of business was conducted within though it was common knowledge in the neighborhood that it was part of the Canadian Security and Intelligence Service.

Les Henry, the director of CSIS, sat silently while his private secretary Dineen poured their coffees. They waited until the door closed behind her before resuming their discussion. The other man was Charles Wyatt, the Western Regional Chief of Domestic Operations. He was a little more than halfway through his report when he continued.

"Item number seven is emergent. Last Wednesday we received Intel from NSA, as part of the Open Borders Initiative, that an active duty Canadian Forces Colonel named Western contacted one of their agents inside the Pentagon.
It appears this Colonel had a back-channel proposition for their agent who it turned out was an old drinking buddy. The call from this Colonel, who is the senior Intel officer at the Naden Naval Base, was routinely intercepted by NSA. It was placed to a non-secure phone inside the main Pentagon building from a phone located in Victoria, BC.

The agent he contacted is a mid-level analyst with a level six pre-retirement security clearance. The call transcript is in your briefing notes. It appears Western was calling him to set up a meeting to discuss a new biological weapon based on a common virus."

Wyatt paused before he said the next part knowing the reaction he would receive.

"This weapon was allegedly created by- a teenage boy in Victoria."

Henry looked up from his notes and snorted.

"Is this a joke Charlie?"

"No sir, it is most definitely not a joke," he said.

Henry set his coffee down.

"Continue."

"Have you seen the news reports of the multiple shooting in Vancouver yesterday?" he asked.

"I've been at the cottage for two weeks painting and Val forbids me to read the papers or watch the news at camp. She says it is for my mental health. She dropped me off here an hour ago so no I have not heard or read anything about a shooting in Vancouver."

"Four people were killed in a hotel room in downtown Vancouver and unfortunately one of them was in our employ."

"Who?" Henry said.
"James Hamilton. He was the only asset available on the lower mainland at the time."

"I don't know the name is he new?"

"He is one of Mrs. K.'s recruits and that may have contributed to this situation. He was inexperienced. It should not have been a problem as this was supposed to be a simple meet and greet."

"Go on," Henry said, he did not look happy.

"The meeting was set up to discuss this bio weapon the details of which are sketchy. Western's initial call to his buddy was peppered with enough keywords to jangle the NSA pre-sets for domestic traffic. His call set off an automatic stage two terrorist alert. When NSA interviewed the Pentagon analyst they discovered he and Western were friends from way back. The NSA got the analyst to roll over on Western and set up a meet. John Masse called me personally to propose this as a joint venture which I thought was nice of him considering the meeting was to take place in Vancouver."

Both men smiled at that. They knew the Americans sometimes forgot to extend that courtesy when they were running operations in Canada.

"They sent the Pentagon buddy to the meet along with an unnamed US asset from Oregon who, it turns out, was a biologist and not a field agent and we sent our freshly recruited Mr. Hamilton, who it would appear possessed zero trade-craft.

The meeting was set up with Western and when he showed up something went wrong. Hamilton, the US scientist, and Western's Pentagon buddy were all killed. Western did the shooting. The unknown here is who killed Western."

"What happened?" Henry's face had turned hard his jaw set with tension.

"As near as we can figure Western, an experienced field operative, went rogue and started shooting people. The Vancouver police are keeping the details out of the media for the moment but someone is bound to leak something and when the media puts it together, from the odd mix of victims, they will eventually come barking at our door."

"What is our exposure?" Henry said.

"That is difficult to estimate at this moment. Western's gun killed all the men in the room and he is an active duty soldier so the military will wear that. Some of the evidence seems to indicate our guy Hamilton shot Western, which we will call self-defense, but there is a problem.

My contact at the VPD tells me forensics thinks Hamilton was already down when Western was killed. He said the site lines do not line-up and there was no powder residue on his shooting hand. The other odd thing was the weapon used to kill Western did not belong to Hamilton. The weapon he signed out was a Sig 9 but there was a S&W .45 in his hand when the VPD showed up. I suppose, because he was an ex-cop, it's possible the .45 was a 'throw down' but I don't think so and neither does VPD.

It is more likely there was a fifth person in the room. Someone pulled the fire alarm a few minutes after the shootings but that could have been a panicked member of the public. I'm waiting to hear more from my guy in Vancouver."

"Or it could be the shooter covering his tracks," said Henry.

"The best thing for us to do at this point is information manage the event. Clearly the reason for the meeting will not come up."

"What are the Yanks saying?" Henry asked.

"Not much, they are waiting for us to tell them what went wrong at an event advertised as a simple meeting. It is a classic full-on cluster fuck and like most of those there is nothing in the way of logic or learning to be gained from it."

"Are the RCMP interested?"

"No, sir."

"Who do we have on it?"

"I'm sending Mrs. K. She is on her way here now."

"Does she still do field work?"

"Only when the occasion warrants and this one certainly does."

"What is her brief?"

"Contain and control. Find this weapon, if it exists, and ascertain the facts about the teenager, if he exists, and do what is necessary to contain the situation. We need to maintain deniability and keep the Vancouver situation separate and unconnected to this bio weapon thing. Mrs. K. will put a team together to debrief Western's staff in Esquimalt."

"Who is in charge of the base in Esquimalt?" Henry said.

"Steven Evans."

"Good luck with that. Evans is a shit show. How worried are the Yanks about the viral weapon angle?"

"They take everything seriously these days. The interesting thing is I spoke to Jed Pepperdine for follow up and he hinted at something that made me think they have someone on the ground in Vancouver working on this, but for obvious reasons he did not come out and say that. He was short on details but I gather they've had an asset on the ground for some time and this asset reported there may be some truth to the weapon thing, including the part about the kid.
Pepperdine didn't give me any details because I don't think he has much in the way of details. The only reason he told me as much as he did is because his deep asset is several days overdue reporting in and they have not been able to contact him. Pepperdine was grateful when I told him I would have Mrs. K. keep an eye out for him."

The intercom buzzed on his desk and Dineen announced Mrs. K..
Both men rose as the door opened and Barbara Knight came into the office. She was a short powerful woman with intense hazel eyes which bore humour and intelligence and something else that could best be described as resolve. She started her security career during the Cold War and spent years undercover in Eastern Europe. Her brusque manner and expensive taste in clothes reflected this experience. She shook hands with both men and Henry pulled up a chair for her.

"Good to see you, Barbara. Coffee?"
She nodded and a few minutes later Dineen came in with a fresh pot.

"Charlie tells me you are leaving for Victoria. What will you need when you get there?"

She looked at Henry and smiled.

"I don't know yet, this thing about a teenager creating a bio-weapon is odd. I don't know what to make of it, I'm just hoping it's not my grandson, Earl," she said and they laughed.

"Charlie, why don't you continue," Henry said.

"Well, to sum up, I think the bio weapon angle is weak. A teenager building an advanced weapon is not credible. I have a sixteen-year-old and he hasn't learned how to make a sandwich. I believe what we have here is an unfortunate misfire. This Colonel was probably off his nut from the get-go and something or someone at the meeting spooked him and he started shooting.

We all know unexpected things happen in this business, and I think this is one of those times. We need to snip the cord on this mess and move as far away from it as possible. Hamilton was a D1 with solid cover in a another industry and his death won't lead directly back to us. As for this kid we need to check it out but I have a bad feeling about it generally. Anything that involves a minor has a nasty way of sticking to whoever touches it, including this agency if we get on the wrong side of this. Barbara, you need to use a ten foot pole on this. If there is a kid and he has created a weapon I want you to grab him on a security warrant.

After we debrief him we can make the call about what to do with him. The other thing we need to do is figure out who killed Western. If there was someone else in the room we need to find out who. From what Pepperdine was hinting maybe the shooter is his missing asset but at this point we don't know anything for sure," he said.

Mrs. K. finished her coffee, stood up, and smiled.
"My flight leaves in an hour but before I run there is
something which strikes me as odd about this whole
business. What was the dead Colonel's connection to this
kid in the first place? Did he try to sell the weapon to
him?

"That we don't know, we are hoping you can find out,"
said Henry.
Mrs. K smiled at both of them.

"My daughter Gwen is married to the base commander at
Comox AFB and she told me that all flights and
personnel transfers from Vancouver Island bases have
been grounded since early September and Naden Naval
Base is in virtual lock down. If you start adding all this
together the possibility of a bio weapon may be more real
than you think. My gut tells me there is something to this
kid thing."

"Okay, I agree with Barbara. We need to discover the
truth about the kid. Charlie, you find out what is going on
with the military and let's hope whatever this is it does
not come back to bite us," Henry said.

Chapter 25

Cold Camp

Parksville, British Columbia

Mann awoke, roused from an uneasy sleep when the rig came to an abrupt stop. It bounced hard on stiff springs and the sudden squeal of compressed air as Ellie set the parking brakes startled him into an upright position. A moment later the engine shut down and the cab vibrated with one final bone-rattling shudder as the big diesel rumbled to a stop.

The silence that followed was as intense as the engine noise had been. It felt like something evil had stopped squeezing his head and he waited for his ears to adjust to the lack of pressure. He looked out the windshield and was surprised to see they were stopped in a Parks Canada campground. There were rows of empty drive-through sites each one with an identical fire pit and picnic table.

Not many campers this time of year, he thought.
Ellie opened her door and climbed down from the cab. He had a few moments of stretching the muscles of his neck and back, stiff from sleeping on the jump-seat, before unkinking his legs and following her out. It was just beginning to get dark.

"Where are we?"

"Welcome to Parksville, Doc," she said.

He turned when he heard Tyler climb down from the sleeper and wait at the bottom to help Zen down. They stood in a loose half circle around a cold fire pit and he noticed he could see his breath in the crisp evening air.

"We need to set up the tent and get some food started because I need to sleep," said Ellie.

At that point she'd been awake and driving for twenty hours and he thought she looked ready to fall down. While they were unloading the truck he watched Zen wander aimlessly around the campsite. Her movements were jerky and uncoordinated and he worried she would trip and fall. Her face was pale and her eyes, which normally sparkled with life, were flat and unfocused.

"Are you okay Zen?"

When she looked in his direction he noticed she responded slowly and her eyes did not seem to focus on him.

"I'm okay," she said.

Her voice was barely audible and her words were slurred. From reading about it he knew that the cumulative effect of multiple Taser hits could reduce mental and physical responses and he was concerned about her. After several hours of sleep she had not fully recovered as expected; the Taser's after-effects were still obvious. She suffered trauma to her chest from the pounding she got from Sedulca and he wondered if that assault had compounded the Taser's effect. When he suggested they take her to the hospital she flatly refused. He thought Ellie was going to insist but something in Zen's voice made her back down. He was concerned she might trip and fall in the gathering darkness and further injure herself.

"Zen I want you to sit down at the picnic table while we set up the camp," he said.
The most telling and therefore worrisome sign was that she did as he requested without argument. Ellie noticed it

too and they exchanged a worried glance as she meekly sat down. He kept an eye on her while he tried unsuccessfully to set up the tent one handed. Tyler had wandered off with a flashlight in search of firewood while Ellie finished unloading the truck and started preparing their meal.

When he returned his two arms were loaded with branches and twigs and a few chunks of split cedar he found left behind at other camp sites. He dumped the whole thing in the fire pit and went back for the pieces he could not carry in the first load. When he returned he tried to help set up the tent but the two of them could not figure it out and they stood by as Ellie put it together. The cooler was on the ground beside the fire pit. She stopped what she was doing to take a long appraising look at Mann and shook her head. She reached in and grabbed him a cold beer and opened it for him.

"You look like shit, Doc," she said.

He realized he was probably not any healthier than Zen, they were both pretty well thrashed from their encounter with Sedulca. When they stopped in Nanaimo for lunch and to buy snack food, water, and a six pack of Kokanee, he went into the washroom and tried to clean himself up. His face looked scary with a swath of itchy scabs and colourful bruises. The injuries, plus the fact he had not shaved for three days, made him look like a street person living rough. He joked that maybe he should try pan handling for a few bucks outside the liquor store but nobody laughed. His face did not bother him much, the pain was mostly gone, but his knee was still painful and swollen; it refused to bend far or easily.

He tried to be useful by lighting the campfire but he gave up because he lacked the necessary dexterity to bend down. He was experiencing a lot of pain from his knee even though he washed four painkillers down with the beer Ellie gave him. Tyler was sitting with Zen and they watched him for a while until Zen asked Ty to help and he took over and soon had a good fire going.

He gave up trying to help and sat down with Zen at the picnic table and they watched Ellie and Tyler do the work. It was completely dark and getting cold by the time they finished eating and cleared the table. Ellie prepared a great meal of salad, beans, and cold fried chicken, but he noticed Zen did not eat much and only picked at the food on her plate. The meal revived him and he was starting to feel human again and with that came a more positive outlook. When he looked around their little camp he felt they could safely stay for a day or two until they figured out what to do next.

He was anxious about Andi's condition. She had not responded well to the treatment and he was frustrated at having no information but he dared not risk a phone call to check on her. A single call could lead some unknown threat right to them and put all their lives in danger. He did not risk calling from Nanaimo lest it give away the direction they were traveling. The important thing he discovered, in his short but intense exposure to the people involved in this, was they were deadly serious. He would just have to suck it up and wait to find out how she was doing.

They sat in silence exhausted by the day's events. He could hear the soothing sound of the surf pounding on a nearby shore and the rhythmic sound lulled him. The surf, his full stomach, and the beer and pain killers were making him drowsy. It was only ten pm. but he could barely keep his eyes open and he yawned. The yawn was contagious and Ellie yawned too and said, "You boys should be warm enough with those sleeping bags and we've got a good bed of coals going in the fire pit. I'm going to turn in before I fall down. Good night."

He was ready to turn in as well but he noticed Zen stir uncomfortably and he glanced at her. He watched the firelight and shadows on her face and it seemed like she was getting ready to say something. She seemed to be trying to find the courage to tell her mom something. When he talked with her in her kitchen she mentioned her mom held strong views about her boyfriends and males in general.

"Mom, that isn't going to work," she said. Her voice was soft but resolute.

"What?" Ellie said. "What isn't going to work?"

"Tyler and I-," she began but stopped.

"What?" Ellie said. She was tired and not getting it.

"We… me and Tyler, we are… together now," she said. Her eyes were cast down and she looked like she was getting ready for a huge reaction from her mom.

He saw some of the colour leave Ellie's face when she realized what her daughter was telling her. She was obviously stunned by this news but thankfully retained the presence of mind not to overreact. He could see her weighing her response and for a long moment she looked like she would say something but decided against it.

Instead she got up from the picnic table where they were sitting, walked to the truck, climbed in, and closed the door. Zen looked at him and her eyes were wide. It looked to him like she had surprised herself when she told her mom she would be sleeping with Tyler.

He had only recently met Ellie and he did not know her well but waking up with her standing over him with a baseball bat he could easily imagine she might not be the easiest mom to spring this kind of news on. Zen got up from the table and he watched her unsteady footing as she weaved towards the tent. Tyler followed her a moment later and then he heard the zipper close behind them and he found himself in the uncomfortable position of not having any place to sleep.

Chapter 26

Bloody Hitch Hiker

Barbara Knight stood on the blackened pavement where two days earlier a military van exploded and burned. Turning slowly she took in her surroundings the most striking detail of which was the number of abandoned buildings there were. The buildings were mostly old and all were in various stages of decomposition. Her eye stopped when she came to Genetexa Agricultural Pharmaceuticals. The sight of the faded logo on the side of the building brought back a flood of unhappy memories.

Although it was years ago she could vividly recall seeing that logo all over the news media when the Government of Canada banned the use of artificial growth hormones. A research team at the University of British Columbia established beyond question a causal link between meats produced using synthetic hormones and Alzheimer's disease. Big Pharma fought back but it was too late the UBC studies the ban was based on was replicated many times by independent labs all over the world. The link to Alzheimer's syndrome was accepted as scientific fact.

This finding began a cascade of events around the globe and when the World Health Organization called for a worldwide ban on the hormones it marked the end of the practice of injecting livestock with growth hormones. The reason she remembered these events so clearly was a personal one. Her father died from Alzheimer's one week before the announcement. She was sad about losing him to that horrible disease, near the end he did not recognize her or anyone and he had to be restrained most of the day. He was angry and agitated and confused by everything around him. His death, when it came, was a relief and for a long time she felt guilty about feeling that way.

She walked towards the factory through the waist-high weeds and as she came closer wondered if there were laboratories inside the building. When the connection between Alzheimer's and the use of growth hormones hit the main stream media, factories like this one closed down in a matter of days. The parent corporations declared bankruptcy and the properties were boarded up and abandoned. Ownership of the land and buildings was tied up in class action lawsuits for years.

As she approached the side of the building she looked back and saw Owen leaning against the rental van smoking a cigarette. She wished he wouldn't smoke it got on his clothes and stunk up the van. At least he was outside, she thought. When she turned back something on the ground caught her eye. It looked like a bit of coloured fabric among the weeds.
As she came closer she could see a man sprawled on the ground. She unclipped her gun and removed it and jacked a round into the chamber. She flipped off the safety and held it down by her side as she approached, walking around to stand in front of him to see his face. He looked dead but moaned loudly when she kicked his leg.

"Are you okay?" she said.

The man slowly opened his eyes but they remained unfocused. He might have been drunk but the intense coppery smell of blood told her otherwise.

"Are you okay?" she repeated.

The man was insensible. She took out her phone and called Owen to come over. When he got there they picked him up and carried him to the van. She suspected that he he was the missing American agent she'd been asked to watch out for. He was well groomed and nicely dressed which meant he was not a street person and the fact he was lying within a hundred meters of where they found the kid's computer made it seem very likely. Regardless of his identity he was in bad shape and would certainly die of exposure if they left him.

***

In the Emergency room she watched the doctor examine him. With the loss of blood and the weak condition they found him in she assumed he would be admitted but judging by the doc's body language the man they brought in was not in bad shape. The trauma nurse she spoke with told her he took a good whack to the head. It took twenty-one stitches to close the gash and a liter of whole blood. The guy must have a thick skull, she thought. Anyone else would likely be brain damaged but an hour after they brought him in he was sitting up on a hospital gurney.

She came back from ICU where the Worthy boy's mother was being treated. The ICU nurse told her the mother's condition was unchanged and the longer they kept her unconscious the better the prognosis was for her recovery. An interesting detail about the mother was that it was the RCMP anti-terrorist squad that caused her injuries.

When she reported this to Charlie Wyatt he was glad to hear it; it gave him a card to play if they had to negotiate with the Mounties over any of the details of this mess. When Owen returned from the Tim Horton's in the lobby she told him it was time to go.

"Our ever expanding band of terrorists are traveling north in a Mack truck. Tech support has been following them using the truck's satellite tracking system. The truck belongs to Ellie Watson, she is the mother of the boy's girlfriend, Hazen Michaels. They are currently stopped, presumably for the night, at a campsite a few kilometers outside of Parksville. I am told we can drive there in about two hours. Good thing we opted for the ten passenger van."

She tossed him the keys to the van, she knew if she drove Owen would follow his normal pattern and be asleep within ten minutes of starting the engine. When he turned to head for the elevator she said.

"Wait, Owen, we have a passenger."

When he turned he was amazed to see the man they brought exit the washroom pale and shaky but upright and apparently mobile.

"This is Frank. He's coming with us to Parksville," she said.

Sedulca looked at Owen and curtly nodded as he sized him up. He was looking forward to meeting the guy who hit him and it crossed his mind it could have been Owen until he learned they'd just arrived from Ottawa. He was confused about what happened yesterday. In the washroom he looked at himself in the mirror while he waited for Jonas to answer his phone. It was lucky whoever took his keys and wallet missed the cell phone clipped to his belt.

The Doctor told him to take it easy for the next few days but he did not have that luxury. Things were moving too fast to sit around waiting for his headache to go away. He looked bad but aside from the throbbing head he felt okay. When Jonas picked up he said.

"I had your friend Mann and the kid's girlfriend but someone hit me; I think it must have been the kid. If it was, I hope whoever ends up with him doesn't mind damaged goods 'cause I'm gonna break the little pricks arm when I find him," he said.

He told Jonas about the CSIS agent who found him and brought him to the hospital. "She thinks I am a missing NSA asset. I think she means you?" he said, "how long has it been since you checked in with them?"
Jonas didn't answer so Sedulca told him that he heard the CSIS agents talking when they thought he was unconscious.

"They've located the kid but she didn't say where. They're heading up island, somewhere close to Parksville to pick him up and the CSIS woman offered to take me along with them which is handy. I need you to get the spare keys and pick up the car and drive to Parksville," he said.

He explained to him where he left the car. He was about to hang up when Jonas dropped his bombshell.

"Western is dead."

He filled him in on how Western went nuts and started killing people. There was a long pause.

"Did you take your meds today, Jonas?" he said.

"Yes, I did! This was Western's fault. He went nuts and started shooting people. I had to kill him, I was lucky to get out of there with my life," he said.
Sedulca could not tell over the phone if Jonas was off his meds and hallucinating, he'd had that kind of psychotic break before. If Western is dead that explains why the

woman from CSIS is looking for the kid, he thought. It also meant they were running out of time.

The deal they cut with their American contact was becoming more complicated by the minute. He could not be certain of what Jonas did in Vancouver. He was supposed to observe at the meeting not participate and certainly not intervene. He wasn't sure what Jonas had promised the American to get him to agree to let him attend the meeting but he was sure it did not include dead citizens. He was hoping it was not a delusional Jonas, off his meds, who killed them.

His head was pounding hard as he considered the implications of Western's death. When the CSIS agent asked him if he was up to the trip he nodded. He might look like shit with a bandage wrapped around his skull but now it was urgent that he catch up to that kid. Having him as a pawn to negotiate with might be the only thing that saves their asses.

They stopped at the Salvation Army Thrift Store on Cedar Hill Road and Mrs. K. went inside and bought him a shirt and jacket to wear for the trip. There wasn't too much blood on his jeans so they would pass. It was taking a long time to get going and he was having trouble staying awake. The agent she introduced as Owen kept getting them lost before they left the city so the woman drove. She stopped at the bottom of the hill in Millbay for coffee and muffins but he pretended to be asleep on the rear bench seat and Owen was snoring with his mouth open beside her in the front.

An hour later she pulled into a Shell station for gas outside Nanaimo and went in to pay and came back with coffee for all of them.

"How are we going to handle this?" Owen asked.

"When we spot them you and Frank will stay in the van and I will do the dotty old lady thing and see what they're up to. I have you on speed dial if I call you and say nothing it means it's time to show up for the party. We can take them to the safe house at Black Creek for a preliminary debriefing and see what happens. Did you load the safe house address into the GPS?"
Owen nodded, "Do we need to wear the bio-hazard suits in case there is some kind of weapon?"

Looking in the mirror she saw Frank was awake and he was eating a muffin.

"No. It would not do to let them see me dressed for Armageddon. I'll play it cool, they won't suspect me it works every time," she said.

"Almost every time, remember that beast in Brantford?" Owen said.
"I'm trying not to. It's your turn to drive. Don't get lost. Wake me when we get near the map coordinates."

Chapter 27

CSIS

Mann sat alone by the fire and watched the flames die down. His thoughts were with Andi. He missed her. He was half asleep at the picnic table thinking about crawling into the truck to sleep on the jump-seat and not looking forward to it. He was struggling to unkink his swollen knee stand when he saw a woman walking up the lane towards him. It seemed such an unlikely thing to happen that for a moment he thought he was asleep and dreaming. She stopped in front of him and smiled.

"May I join you Dr. Mann?"

When she spoke his name it startled him and roused him from his stupor with a jolt.

"Who are you?" he said.

The way he said it was not exactly a challenge but it was not a warm welcome either. She was an older woman, older than him, probably closer to sixty than fifty, he thought. She was short with a stocky build like some Eastern European women of a certain age but he could see this woman was no babushka wearing peasant. She was dressed expensively, her hair was styled, and she was well spoken. The only thing missing was the fashionably long fingernails women of her apparent standing typically wore. Hers nails were trimmed and she had working hands obviously strong and presumably capable.
The odd experience of having a stranger walk up to him out of the darkness in an empty campground gave a

dream-like quality to the experience and all the more so when she spoke his name. She had a warm sympathetic smile on her face and he wondered again if he was asleep.

"My name is Barbara Knight. I work for CSIS," she said. She waited a beat and when he did not respond she added, "The Canadian Security Intelligence Service."

"You don't look like a spy," he said. As soon as he uttered the words he realized how dumb it must sound but it was true she did not look like a spy.

"Most of us don't," she said, "it kinda defeats the purpose."
She smiled warmly again and in spite of the weird circumstances she seemed genuinely nice. He could not help but return her smile.

"Why are you here?" he said.

"I'm here to talk about your situation. We are concerned that you may be in danger and I've come to offer our assistance. We are also trying to understand what's going on," she said.

He could not help it. The way she spoke and the warm smile made him think of his mom.

"How did you find us?" he said.

"The truck you are traveling in has an asset-tracking system," she said, "most large commercial trucks do now."
He was not sure what that meant and at the moment it did not matter because the fact they had been found by CSIS changed everything. A thought occurred to him.

"Do you have identification?" he asked.

She pulled a small plastic ID wallet from her pocket and handed it to him. He opened it and read: Barbara Knight, analyst, CSIS. There was a recent colour photo of her face and underneath was embossed with what he assumed was the official seal of CSIS.

"We are all called analysts," she said, anticipating his next question.

"What do you know about our situation?" he said. He used her word to describe what was happening because fatigue was making him think slower than he normal and he was way out of his depth generally. The overall effect of the last few days was the uncomfortable suffocating sense he was drowning. He was normally a law abiding citizen but the last few days shook his faith in the authorities. He knew he needed to find out if she knew about POrna but he was having a tough time concentrating on how to go about it.

She paused for a moment to consider his question before answering him and though his mind was not sharp he got the impression she was being equally careful about how much she disclosed to him.

"We know you were working for Colonel Western. Are you aware he was killed yesterday in Vancouver?" she said.

He nodded affirmative.

She continued, "We do not know the reason he was killed. Do you know why he was killed and who killed him?"

He shook his head no.

"We believe his death is related to his investigation of Tyler Worthy," she said.

At this point he interrupted her.

"I would like to clarify that I wasn't working for Western. He coerced me into assisting his investigation by threatening my research funding. Because of my past experience with the military I had no intention of helping him with anything but that was before I found out Andi was Tyler's mom," he said.

She seemed to accept this, at least she made no comment, and he began to wonder how much, if anything, she knew about POrna. He did not want to give her any information that might be used against them later.

"We know about the exploding van and the military personnel, one of which subsequently died of his injuries, and the other missing. I don't suppose you know where she is? We would like to speak with her," she said.

She was watching his face and he realized she was probably a skilled interrogator and he would be no match for her if he tried to deceive her. He shook his head. It was true he did not know where Hunter was exactly but even if he knew he would not tell her.

"What we don't understand is why you and the others decided to run rather than reach out to the authorities for help?" she said. She looked at him closely watching his eyes for deception.

He looked at her and pointed at his face. "This is the assistance I got from the authorities and Andi is in a comma because of them and I'm not sure if she will survive," he said.

He turned his face away and looked down at the fire. He knew he was overtired but he could not edit the anger and disgust from his voice as he tried to make sense of the details of the last few days. He was trying to determine what, if anything, he should tell her, but at the very least he wanted her to know that, for him, going to the police was not an option. His thinking was not clear enough to be subtle or insightful so he decided to tell her about being attacked.

"There is a man who is looking for Tyler," he said. "He works for Colonel Western, or at least he did; I first saw him a few days ago in Western's office at Naden Naval Base. He was in uniform but I do not know what his rank is or what his role is in this or why he would be involved after Western's death but I can tell you he is definitely involved.

He attacked Zen and nearly killed her. He repeatedly Tasered her heart and then physically assaulted her while she was unconscious on the ground. When I tried to help her he pistol whipped me and smashed my knee. I am convinced he would have killed both of us if he got his hands on Tyler," he said. "That's the reason we ran."

"How did you get away from him?" she said.

"The reason we survived was Tyler. He saw him wailing on Zen and came up behind him and nailed him with a pipe. He knocked him out cold. For all I know he's dead but I wasn't willing to risk our lives on it. We needed time to sort out what to do next and we could not afford for him or anyone else to take another run at us because next time we might not be so lucky," he said.

He watched her face as she listened to his story and he wondered if, as Zen put it, she was a good guy or a bad guy. Unfortunately in this situation there was no way to sort out who was good or bad and, like it or not, he would have to trust her. He noticed as he spoke to her that she was looking decidedly more troubled after he told his story compared to when she first sat down.

"Where did Tyler hit him?" she asked.

He thought it an odd question considering what she might have asked.
"I could not see clearly but I think he hit him on the head," he said.

"No, I mean where did it happen?"
"In the old industrial section of Victoria with lots of abandoned buildings I don't know the name of the street."

"Fuck! Where is Tyler now?" she said.

Her voice held a different quality one he could not immediately define maybe it was urgency, but it also sounded like anger.

"He and Zen are asleep in the tent," he said. He nodded to the tent set up on the far side of the truck on the grass. He sat in silence and watched her breath billow in the cold air. She was thinking something over and her face revealed that whatever she was thinking it was not making her happy.

"Dr. Mann, it appears I have made a grave error," she said.

He waited but she said nothing more. He watched her take out a cell phone press send without looking at it and then held it to her ear. His pulse jumped when she used her free hand to remove a small black automatic from inside her coat. The sight of the gun sent a wild surge of anxiety through him.

She scrunched her face and held the phone with her shoulder as she removed the gun's clip and checked it while waiting for her call to be answered. He did not know what was going on but the look on her face gave him the horrible feeling he had condemned them all to die.

He made the fatal error of believing her when she told him she worked for CSIS. He was well aware of the fact any kid with a computer can make a fake ID with a colour printer and a plastic laminator. The students at college did it all the time. His anxiety mounted. Judging by the look on her face, whoever she was calling was not answering and that fact seemed to be bad news. She ended the call and jacked a round into the chamber of her gun and thumbed off the safety. The smile on her face had vanished along with any resemblance to his mother. The woman holding a gun before him was all business. Before he could ask her what was happening she abruptly stood up from the table and turned her back to him to face the direction from which she came from. She spoke to him without turning her head.

"The man who assaulted you caught a ride with us from Victoria. When I came to speak to you I left him and my partner waiting in the van down the road and now my partner is not answering his cell," she said.

The air around them turned thick with tension. He felt a drop of cold sweat trickle down the centre of his back. It left an ice slick of dread in its wake.

"Do you have a weapon, Doctor?" she asked.

"Yes, in the truck," he said.

"Can you use it?" she asked.

"I don't know. I've never shot a gun before," he said.

He never fired any type of weapon or even held one before today.

"Get it," she said, trying to make her voice sound calm and reassuring but he heard the shaft of steel at its core.

He got up from the table and almost tripped and fell. His injured knee was stiff and would not flex as he hobbled around the front of the truck to the passenger side door. The light went on in the cab when he opened the door, and he felt exposed and at risk. He pulled himself up and stood on the welded toe-hole on the fuel tank. He reached in and hurriedly dug inside the travel bag he brought with him from Victoria. He found the gun and Taser he took from Sedulca. He grabbed them both and tucked the Taser into his pants pocket. From the sleeper came the gentle snoring of Ellie. He was glad she was not awake it would add more complication if she was awake and knew the man who attacked Zen was in the area.

He quietly closed the door and awkwardly climbed down with the gun in his hand. The woman held out her hand for the weapon and it momentarily flashed through his mind it might be a mistake to hand the gun over to her but he went with his initial instinct about her and gave her the weapon. He hoped he was not wrong about her. She took it and efficiently removed the clip to check the load. Satisfied with what she saw inside she slapped it back in and jacked a round into the chamber.

She handed it back to him handle first with the safety on. She demonstrated how to click off the safety and said, "Point and shoot like your digital camera. Don't keep your finger on the trigger." She smiled at him reassuringly. "I'm going to check the van and see what happened to Owen.

If you hear gunfire or anything at all no heroism Doc, you get everyone out of here and to the nearest police station. Look at me Doctor Mann," she said.

She waited until she made eye contact and then said, "Do not stop and think about it, go. Your life and the lives of the others may depend on it. Okay?" she said.

He nodded remembering he said similar words to Zen before she was brutally attacked outside the old factory.

"What is your cell number?" she asked.

He told her and said he would have to get the phone out of the truck to turn it on.

"Get it. I'll wait," she said.

He climbed back into the truck and fished around in his bag. He could not find it and had a panicky few minutes until he remembered it was in his other coat. Once again he quietly closed the door and went back to rejoin her. When he rounded the side of the truck she was gone. He could not see her anywhere and he froze where he was. As his eyes began to adjust to the darkness again he saw the shadow of someone lying on the ground behind the picnic table.

He edged backwards slowly and stood around the corner of the truck. He did not hear a gunshot or any kind of struggle but he was sure it was Barbara on the ground. She was not moving and that was not good. The camp fire had died down and there was little light with which to see if anyone was lurking in the shadows. He concentrated hard but he heard nothing except the distant surf and the rapid pounding of his heart. His heart jumped hard in his chest when Sedulca said, "Put the gun down and step over near the fire Doc."

He was startled by the seeming nearness of his voice. In the darkness it sounded like he'd whispered it in his ear. Though he was close he could not pinpoint his location. He made sure he did not look at the fire pit because he did not want to blow what little night vision he had. He lost a lot of it from exposure to the cab light when he opened the truck door. He was not sure if Sedulca knew where he was but he guessed he didn't or he would have simply shot him by now. His knee protested as he lowered himself down to a crouch beside the front wheel making himself into a smaller target. He moved slowly because he knew that the human eye is designed to detect movement in low light.

"Come over by the fire Doc," he said, "or I'll put a couple into that tent."

He heard the unmistakable sound of a round being chambered but the mechanical sound did not last long enough for him to figure out where he was standing. He decided to stay put. He was bluffing. He would not shoot blindly into the tent because he could not know who he might hit. One good thing about his threat was he realized Sedulca couldn't see any better than he could and did not know where he was hiding and he was not about to show himself.

It was a standoff.

Then his heart sank. He heard the sound of the tent zipper opening and he watched Tyler climb out. He came out and stood beside the dying embers looking sleepy as he picked up the remaining firewood he'd gathered earlier and added them to the coals. The fire brightened and when it did Sedulca stepped out of the darkness and moved towards him. He stopped ten feet away and pointed the gun at Tyler's head.

"Come on out Doc or I will shoot the kid," he said.

He had no choice now. He'd never fired a gun before and though he could now see him he knew the odds of hitting him at this distance were bad. The only reasonable thing to do at this point, he thought, was come out and hope Sedulca would let his guard down and give him an opportunity to hit him with the Taser. He wished he'd taken the time to look at the damn thing because he did not know how it worked.

He began to rise from where he was hiding when he saw Tyler bend over and grab one of the rocks which defined the fire pit. It was about six inches across and easily weighed a couple of pounds. He held it loosely down at his side.

"What the fuck kid? Drop the rock," he said. Tyler stood motionless watching him ignoring his instruction. "Are you nuts? I have a gun. Put down the fucking rock or I will shoot you," he said.

Tyler took a single step towards him.
"Shoot," he said.

Mann quickly hobbled away from the truck and spoke to him.
"Do as he says Ty put it down."

Tyler ignored his instruction. He was calmly watching the other man's face when he took another step towards him and stopped.

"Put it down kid. You are coming with me so get used to it," he said.

Tyler didn't move. He stood eerily still and composed. He was now less than six feet away and an easy shot. He was convinced from his last encounter Sedulca was a sociopath and he would not hesitate to kill the boy. The only thing stopping him was the fact he was the prize and killing him would defeat the purpose. He knew Tyler was taking a big risk by taunting him because people with mental illness act irrationally and often against their own interests when provoked.

Tyler lifted the rock and held it at chest level. He was not preparing to throw it he was simply taking the weight off his extended arm muscle and Mann hoped the gunman could tell the difference.

"Are you nuts kid? Put down the fucking rock I have a gun," he said.

He spoke the words like he was talking to a slow child. He held the weapon up high and waved it in the air mockingly. His face was a mask of disbelief at Tyler's weird behaviour. The boy was watching him with clear unblinking eyes, which Mann couldn't help thinking, resembled the eyes of a stalking predator.

There was nothing identifiable as fear or emotion on his face but there was something sharply fierce and coldly analytical within the boy's features.
He was hyper-alert now tripping from the adrenaline circulating in his bloodstream. As he watched Tyler stare at the gunman he saw something new and disturbing invade his son's flat emotionless eyes. What he saw caused a fresh shot of adrenaline one which was pulled from the deep reserve saved for the most ancient fears.

"Shoot," Tyler said.

The voice was soft and clear and he could detect neither emotion nor bravado; it was as flat and affectless as his sharp grey eyes. A sick grin of pleasure crept over Sedulca's features as he lifted his weapon and turned and pointed it at the tent.

"How 'bout I shoot your girlfriend instead?" he said.

The words were hissed and meant to threaten but he did not doubt they expressed his true intentions. There was no cost to him if he killed her. She would just be collateral damage. He thought the threat to kill Zen would make him drop the rock and he was stunned when Tyler said.

"Shoot."

Nothing in his body language showed fear or concern for her. He stood completely at ease with the heavy rock once again dangling in his right hand by his side. Mann held his breath watching as the deadly stalemate grew longer. He was surprised when he saw cracks begin to appear in Sedulca's pathology-driven confidence. Stress had transformed the leer of impending violence on his face into a taut mask of confusion.

The hand holding the gun began to vibrate in the air as beads of perspiration appeared on his brow. His eyes took on the damp hollowness of intense fear as he blinked rapidly. He swiped his coat sleeve across his mouth several times. He watched as the gun barrel drew ever larger circles in the air between Sedulca and the tent. The sinews in his forearm twitched and jumped and he lifted his free hand to help steady it. A spasm erupted on his face which altered his features alarmingly then cascaded agonizingly through muscle groups as it marched aggressively down the full length of his body.

The stringy muscles of his forearm continued to tighten as if stretched by torture re-shaping them into elongated ropey strands that looked like they might snap at any moment. As his skin bulged and warped and sweat poured from his face he hoped one of Sedulca's wild spasms would not cause him to accidentally pull the trigger.

"I'm not fucking around. I'll do it," he said.

It was a last attempt to regain control of the situation but his tremulous voice betrayed him. The smug self-assurance was gone and his hollow threat was belied by a voice stained with fear. His leg began to jackrabbit wildly and he staggered backwards as if struck or drunk. His dimming eyes searching dumbly for his lost self-assurance.

Mann was sickened when he saw the whites of his eyes turn the purple grey of a full tick as they receded as if sucked back into their sockets. His rapid blinking slowed and then stopped altogether as first his left and seconds later his right eye shut and refused to open. It was clear he was in severe pain from the muffled sobs which leaked from the tight margins of his closed jaw. As he tottered blindly Tyler stepped over to him and raised the rock.

He used it to smash his frozen gun hand. The freed weapon thudded to the dirt and Sedulca, now entirely insensible to the world, stumbled and tripped to his knees. Tyler stood near him watching him sway back and forth for a moment and then he put his hand on Sedulca's back to steady him. Mann was struck by the simple humanity of this act. He'd not seen him comfort or show tenderness to another human being aside from Zen. At first he missed the movement of his hand along Sedulca's spine, but when he saw it, he realized the boy was counting vertebrae. He was confused by this and he could not imagine what he was doing. When he finished counting he stopped and took his hand away. Sedulca swayed from side to side and then fell to the ground.

He was trying to understand what Tyler was doing when his eye caught up to his next movement and he was, if anything, more confused by what he saw. It looked like an eerie biblical tableau. Tyler was on his knees with his hands together as though in prayer above Sedulca. It could have been Jesus Christ praying for the soul of a supplicant bowed before him. Then he saw it. The fire pit rock. It was still in Tyler's hand.

Tyler's face revealed nothing as he grunted with effort and accelerated the rock downward. The force of the impact smashed Sedulca's spine, obliterating vertebrae, nerve fiber, and tissue. In the low light from the fire and his swollen eye he could not be absolutely certain he saw it happen but he definitely heard it. The sickening crack of shattering bone and rending meat was unmistakable from across the camp he could clearly hear the sinews snap and bones pop.

Breath expelled from Sedulca in a whoosh as he slumped face first into the dirt.

The boy squatted down beside him and closely observed as the stricken man lay twitching uncontrollably. His torso folded in two as muscles contracted drawing his limbs together in jerky spasms. He watched in amazement as a single large incisor emerged bloody and whole, squeezed from the tight grimace of his locked jaw. It was forcibly ejected by the mechanical leverage of his powerful mandible. The tooth dribbled from between his drooling lips and down his chin, leaving a bloody trail of spittle, then was buried in the dirt beneath him as straining muscle rendered his mass into a coil of twitching meat.

He watched Tyler's reaction as he observed this destructive progress on the prone man. He was watching intently, fascinated by the progression and he laughed heartily when the man's bladder and bowel let go. He wondered what thoughts or feelings were going through the boy's mind. There was nothing displayed outwardly which could be described as empathy or humanity. There was no clue as to what he was feeling except maybe curiosity.

He was kneeling beside the ruined man when he turned his face towards him with a grin and a thumbs-up. He looked like a trophy hunter over a fresh kill. He was grinning with a happiness which contrasted starkly with the fact he intentionally crippled a man.

He was unsure how to feel about this. He would have gladly shot Sedulca himself moments earlier if he had the chance, the man certainly deserved it for the cruel sadistic way he hurt Zen, but he found the look on Tyler's face unsettling. The lack of human empathy did not come as a complete surprise to him but the look of pride and mastery over his opponent was new and disturbing. What he saw was not simply the testosterone blush of teenage bravado.

It was the first glimpse of dawning power. With his limited social understanding, non-existent moral centre and, in possession of a mind such as his, that look was worrisome.

He was lost in his thoughts about the boy realizing as a teen he was on the cusp of choosing the direction he would take as an adult and the potential he has as an individual to do good or evil was staggering. He hoped he would have the opportunity to help guide his moral development, because, if he was left to develop without any guidance, he could be disastrous for humankind. These thoughts carried him away but it was not until he heard the CSIS agent stirring from where she fell that it dawned on him the significance of what he witnessed.

That was POrna!

What happened to Sedulca fit the verbal descriptions of the onset of POrna and he looked exactly like the videos of the stricken soldiers he viewed in the lab at Naden. He emerged from these thoughts and focused his eyes in the darkness and saw him beside Sedulca holding his nose as the man lay insensible in the expanding pool of wastes squeezed from of him.

"It works," he heard Tyler say to himself.

That was then it dawned on him that Tyler did not know that POrna actually worked. When he taunted Sedulca to shoot he was risking Zen and his life on a wild-asses guess. There was no way he could have reasonably known Sedulca was exposed to the carriers of the virus and had become infected. He did not know his connection to the military. He was bloody guessing.

The crazy disparity between what he was capable of with his brilliant intellect and his lack of understanding of what he risked moments ago was breathtaking.
What a crazy son of a bitch, he thought.
The woman from CSIS used the picnic table to regain her feet and was now staggering over. She stared down at the prone man.

"I don't understand this Dr. Mann," she said, "what am I seeing? Has he been shot?"

He considered what he should tell her because he knew everything he said from here on would have consequences. He knew the closer he kept his story to the truth the easier it would be to remember the details when they questioned him about it later.

"Sedulca pointed his gun at the tent and threatened to shoot Zen and Ty clobbered him with a rock," he said nodding at the rim of rocks around the fire pit.

It was close enough to the truth to pass at least for the short term. It was obvious the man on the ground was not going to contradict him any time soon. He also hoped Tyler would keep his mouth shut, this would be a bad time for the boy to start explaining what he did.

"Why is he curled up?" she said.

He shrugged and pretended he didn't know why. Clearly she figured out it was Sedulca who zapped her with a Taser because she never asked him what happened to her. It was her curiosity about what was happening to Sedulca that needed to be explained. He had been hoping, perhaps unreasonably, that if Tyler did not say anything to her about POrna their problem would die right here and now.

Tyler remained silent. He looked at Barbara Knight for a moment but said nothing. He replaced the rock back in the indent it came from around the fire pit. He gathered up and threw on the last bits of firewood and went back inside the tent zipping it closed behind him. The amazing thing about what occurred in the last few minutes was that neither Zen or her mother woke up. The loudest part of the whole exchange was the sickening sound of bones cracking under the force of the rock.

Mrs. Knight was leaning over Sedulca weaving back and forth trying to make sense of what she was witnessing. He did not know how much she knew about the virus but figuring this out was the last thing he wanted her to do. In an effort to get her off the track, he said "Do you want me to come with you to check your partner?"

Seeming to surface from where her mind had traveled she nodded yes. She might be an agent of the Government but he could see she was badly shaken from being Tasered and appeared to be somewhat short of breath. He was not sure she would be able to deal effectively with whatever was waiting for her back at her vehicle.

Before they left to check on Owen she handed him plastic zip strips and insisted Sedulca's hands and feet be bound. He did it though he knew full well if he survived Sedulca would likely never walk away from anything again.
When he held out his arm to steady her she took it and held onto him. They walked back to the place she left her partner and the van.

They found Owen in the back of the van alive and embarrassed but basically unhurt. He swore a blue streak when they freed his hands and he ripped the gag from his mouth. It took them a few minutes to get him completely loose and a few more for him to walk off the leg cramps he got from being bound. It was during this time he explained how Sedulca came to sit behind him and that's when he got zapped.
When they got back to the camp site Sedulca was gone. Mann ran to check on Tyler and Zen as Owen and Mrs. K. checked the rest of the camp. The kids were okay and there was no one lurking in the woods. She examined the ground where he had been when they left him and when she was finished she sat at the picnic table and let out a breath. After he checked on Ellie in the truck he joined her.

"Someone picked him up and carried him away. We didn't hear a car so they were probably here all along and they could still be somewhere in the area. It is essential we set up a perimeter," she said.

When she awoke, she retrieved her gun from the grass where it landed when she fell, and now she checked it over and clicked off the safety. He looked at her.

"I don't believe two people would voluntarily allow themselves to be Tasered simply to make me believe they are the good guys but Barbara, without putting too fine a point on it, I can't help wondering why the fuck Sedulca was with you in the first place?" he said. At this point he did not know what to believe because nothing made any sense.

"I made a mistake. I assumed Sedulca was a missing American agent the one we were supposed to keep an eye out for. We found him unconscious beside the old factory where a military van exploded, which is presumably, where you left him last night after Tyler nailed him the first time," she said.

They sat looking at each other in the soft light each wondering how to play this situation. How much info either could share before it might have unintended consequences.

"He had no wallet or ID. He must have figured out we were looking for Tyler.

He might have been awake and listening to us talk when we drove him to the Emergency room. Because he knew what we were looking for he simply played along and let me believe he was the missing American agent," she said. Owen was hobbling around walking off his leg cramps and he decided it was probably okay to give him the gun Sedulca dropped. It turned out to be Owen's gun. Although he was livid at being taken out so easily by Sedulca he managed to mutter a curt thank you to him for returning it. He checked it over and jacked a round into the chamber and clicked the safety off then walked away from the firelight into the darkness to guard them against the possibility of Sedulca's return.

"Oh shit," Mann said. It was his turn to confess to a blunder.

"I think I know who carried Sedulca away. Sedulca was involved with an old colleague of mine from my university days, Jonas McLean. They were both working for Western. When Western dragged me out here McLean was the one who briefed me. He mentioned he was romantically involved with a soldier but at the time I assumed he was talking about a woman. The name he mentioned was Fran something," he said. "Frank Sedulca."

"Okay, so it looks like we both made a mistake, but right now Dr. Mann we need to get organized and establish some basic cover until I can arrange for backup from the RCMP. I want you to sit in the truck and cover us from that direction," she pointed her thumb over her shoulder. "Owen and I will cover the other directions. It is going to get dark when the fire dies down but it will be to our advantage. Don't worry about the kids. They will be safe inside the tent because Owen is prepared to shoot anyone who comes anywhere near them. Please stay in the truck so he doesn't accidentally shoot you.

Keep your gun out and ready to use but remember to keep your finger off the trigger. My gut says they are gone but like you I'm not willing to bet our lives on it. In case there are more than two of them it's better to be prepared. Okay?" she said making sure she had his full attention. He nodded an okay.

Mrs. Knight was talking on her cell when he climbed up into the cab. It was odd how he didn't feel the least bit tired. He was trembling but he attributed it to the cold and being pumped full of adrenaline. He sat quietly with the gun in his lap, safety off, concentrating on the deepening darkness beyond the windshield as the last of the firewood burned down to ash. He managed to stay awake for almost ten minutes before he fell into a black hole.

He dreamt he was in a frozen wasteland with snow all around him and nothing but the howling wind for company. The sound of the wind became a woman's scream of agony and he woke startled by the piercing whine of a turbo-jet engine under full power. He thought his eyes had only closed for only a few seconds when he jolted upright. The gun fell from his lap and he was lucky he did not shoot himself. When his vision cleared he looked out and saw the campground bathed in harsh light. Shielding his eyes from the glare he could make out the shapes of Tyler and Mrs. Knight standing together in front of the truck heads tilted up looking into the beam.

The scene resembled a movie poster of an Alien Invasion. Then he saw the light source and the black outline of tires under a huge twin rotor helicopter emerge. It descended smoothly to the road in front of them as though lowered by a crane. He climbed down from the cab and Mrs. Knight shouted something in his ear. He could not hear what she said but he found out later that Zen was having convulsions and Tyler came out and found her and she called in a favour from the commander of the airbase at Comox.

The flight to Victoria General Hospital was rough, noisy, and fast. He would never know for certain if it was the four serious looking combat soldiers running into the Emergency room with Zen on a stretcher that made it happen but she did not have to wait long to be assessed by the duty neurologist. She was rolled into the Neuro-ICU less than an hour after lifting off from the campground in Parksville.

Chapter 28

Show Down

Mann sat beside Andi watching her breath; Dr. Sing had begun the process of bringing her out of the induced coma. They began raising her body temperate an hour ago, at around the time the military helicopter touched down on Vic General's helipad. He listened to her soft steady respirations and this normal sound of life, her life, calmed him. Her eyelids fluttered as he held her hand and spoke quietly to her.

"I'm here Andi, I'm waiting for you to come back. Everything is okay now I want you to be here with me. Do you hear me Andi?" he said.

The nurse instructed him to speak softly and use her name and short phrases emphasizing the expectation that she would awaken and rejoin him. Before she left the room she reminded him to be patient, it can be along process. He spoke steadily to her and after ten minutes she squeezed his hand. He hoped this signaled the beginning of awareness as she begins her journey from the depths of unconsciousness.

The ICU nurse instructed him in great detail how to support Andi as she regained consciousness and he found it helpful but she could not or would not give him any indication of what to expect when she awoke. The staff did not know if she had suffered brain damage or if she would be able to fully awaken.
He was using positive thoughts and words to *will* her back to him. It did not matter how changed she was he

wanted her back; no matter the damage she may have suffered he would care for her. He tried to make his words sound light and cheerful and not let the deadening fatigue he felt seep into his voice.

His head was bowed and his eyes were closed when her eyes fluttered and opened. When her vision cleared she turned towards him.

"Lee?" she whispered.

He looked up and saw her eyes and knew at once that she was okay. Those wonderful beloved eyes told him she was awake and present and most importantly, Andi was back.

"Hi," he said.

He was smiling then grinning, trying hard not to cry, relieved to see the spark of intelligence in those beautiful eyes focused so intently on his face. When she smiled that was all the assurance he needed. He did not notice the nurse enter the room, she was standing behind him watching. An alarm at the nurses' station alerted her to Andi's wakefulness and changing condition. She waited as long as she could trying not to break the spell of Andi's awakening but something she saw on the monitor caused her to abruptly ask him to wait outside. Upon waking, coma patients sometimes experience a drop in blood pressure which can be life threatening; Andi's pressure was headed for zero.

He stood up numbly watching as she called the code.

Another nurse guided him out of the room reassuring him it was a routine precaution as a crash team raced down the corridor and into Andi's room pushing an equipment laden cart ahead of them. The nurse in charge told him it would be awhile before he could go back in and be with

Andi and directed him to a waiting room on the second floor.

He decided he would go there and try to rest for a few minutes but only after he checked on Zen. He was fatigued and wandered the empty predawn hallways until he spotted a familiar landmark and found his way to her treatment room. A nurse intercepted him at the door refusing to let him in. She assured him Zen was okay and resting and told him there was a patient conference happening in the waiting area on the second floor.

When he arrived he saw Dr. Sing, the neurologist, heading into the room and he followed him. He told Sing that Andi had regained consciousness and the ICU nurse made him leave. There was a problem with her blood pressure.

"They told me it was routine. You are probably going to be paged momentarily," he said, his statement conveying the worry he felt and the unspoken question- *will she be okay*?

The neurologist recognized him and thanked him for the update and told him not to worry it was routine but then he looked confused when Mann announced to Ellie and Tyler that Andi was awake.

"Dr. Mann, are you also connected to Hazen Michaels?" he asked.

"Yes, but it's complicated Doc. How is she doing?" he asked.

Ellie was watching Sing with tears forming in her eyes waiting to hear about her daughter's condition.

"First of all I can tell you Hazen is going to be fine. We administered medication to control her seizures and they've already stopped. She is sedated and resting now and will likely awaken in an hour or so," he said.

Ellie let out a sob of relief at this news and Mann put a comforting arm around her shoulder and felt her sag against him. When he looked at Sing again he noticed he had a mischievous smile on his face.

"The other good news," he began and paused waiting to be certain he had their attention.

"Hazen will not lose her baby."

"Baby?"

They spoke in unison and the neurologist could not help but laugh.

"I suspected as much," he said, smiling broadly. "According to the blood work your daughter Hazen is pregnant. Congratulations. Her pregnancy is very early and I do not know if she is aware she is pregnant so I would caution you to be…" he considered his words, "circumspect about speaking to her about this. She is a strong young woman but she has already suffered a severe shock to her system."

It was clear Ellie was stunned by this news. She turned to look at Tyler with an unreadable expression on her tear-streaked face. Tyler must have heard what Doctor Sing said but he gave no outward indication. He never took his eyes off the rerun of *The Price is Right* playing on television. His only comment came over his shoulder.

"Gene," he said.

Dr. Sing looked from Mann to Ellie and shrugged questioningly. Mann nodded his head as if to say, *yes he is the father*, to which Sing commented rather comically.

"Oh, my."

Sing looked back at Tyler and wondered, but did not ask, if the boy had a mental disorder. He did not dwell on it as his pager was vibrating in his pocket and he needed to discuss one more thing before he leaving. He got their attention again when he said.

"There is another issue we need to discus and in some ways it's as serious as Hazen's health issues. It is clear from your statement upon admission, and the burns and bruising on her body confirm it, that she has been assaulted. She has received injuries from a restricted weapon and by law I must file a police report," he said.

At that point Mrs. Knight who had been sitting quietly observing events stood up and spoke for the first time.

"Doctor Sing may I have a word."

Mann saw her reaching for her ID wallet as she took the bemused doctor by the elbow and steered him out into the hallway.
When he turned around he saw Ellie staring at Tyler. There were outward signs of strong emotion on her face but, as far as he could tell, they did not contain lethal intent. They sat down to wait each lost in their respective thoughts. An hour had passed before a nurse came in to tell them Zen was awake and they were encouraged to go and see her.

He stayed with Zen for a few minutes assuring himself that she was going to fully recover. The room was crowded and he squeezed her hand once more before he left; he wanted to get back upstairs to see how Andi was doing. Ellie and Tyler stayed with Zen and he smiled at the knowledge he was escaping a tense situation in a room full of unsaid things.

He was buying a cup of coffee from a vending machine and wondering what the energy would be like in the room with Tyler and Ellie and the knowledge of baby Gene. He was still smiling thinking about that when Mrs. Knight caught up to him.

"We need to talk and it can't wait," she said.

He frowned he did not feel like talking but she looked upset and he owed her for saving Zen so he followed her back to the waiting room. It was empty and he flopped down in a green vinyl chair and began to work the tension knots from his neck while she paced the floor.

"Owen is dead."

She had left him behind to coordinate the search for Sedulca and his partner while they were flying Zen to Victoria General. When the police arrived they discovered his body inside the rental van, he was shot to death. She flopped down opposite him on a two person love seat and, leaning back, closed her eyes.

"I've been on the phone to Ottawa, it looks like your buddy McLean and his partner tried to cut a side deal with the Yanks," she said, "they tried to cut Western out of the deal agreeing to deliver Tyler and the virus to them in two days," she said. Fatigued, she spent the last half hour on the phone with the director of CSIS, and appeared to be half awake as she spoke.

"The Director has received additional information from reliable sources which convinced him Tyler is the creator of a bio-weapon," she said.

She waited for a response; he was slumped in the chair across from her sipping ugly vending machine coffee making a face.

"I'm sorry about Owen", he began, "but there is no weapon," his tone emphatic,
"does the US Government condone the kidnapping of Canadian children?"

"Don't be absurd Doc, the NSA was laying a trap and CSIS was in on it from the start. Contrary to what you may think neither Government engages in illegal activities," she said.

He glanced at her over the rim of his coffee cup with an expression of disdain and snorted, "I'm too tired to debate that one Barbara, so your point is what?"

"One of the observed effects of Tyler's weapon is the victim curling into a fetal position unable to move," she said.

He looked at her through mostly closed eyes to see if she'd been watching his face when she said it. She was, damn!, he thought.

"Barbara, no legitimate researcher in the field of virology or genetics would believe for a moment that anyone, let alone a sixteen-year-old, could create such a weapon. Labs with real scientists and real budgets could not create something with the attributes you are ascribing to this thing. If it were possible to do that kind of work it would require, a team of scientists, a huge budget, and years of research," he said.

"Not many sixteen-year-olds have a geneticist for a father as a matter of fact I can only think of one," she said.

He did not recall telling her he was Tyler's father but then he had not tried to keep it a secret.

"I met him for the first time three days ago. Prior to that I didn't know I had a son," he said.

"Unfortunately Lee the only person who can corroborate your story is upstairs in a compromised state," she said. She spoke the words with no threat or accusation or even unkindness behind them she was simply stating the facts as she understood them.

"Believe me or not Barbara, that is your decision to make, but before you act on a hunch please keep in mind we are talking about the lives of a couple of kids. You are a parent, I'm sure you can imagine what would happen to them if they get caught up in this mess. Their lives will be over," he said, "and as for your assertion that I created your imaginary virus, all I will say about that is, I will be asking the warden for a day pass to collect my Nobel Peace Prize."
He didn't know why, possibly it was the fatigue, they both laughed at this way more than it warranted and then sat quietly for a few long contemplative minutes.

"Okay, Doc I agree we don't want the world to jump all over these kids so what do I report back to my boss about the virus?"
Mann shrugged and closed his eyes and yawned.

"If you didn't create the weapon," she continued, "and for the moment I will take your word for it, that means you are unaware of its major side-effect. A small but significant percentage of the infected military personnel had extreme reactions to being exposed to the virus. They became hyper-violent.
This information is, for obvious reasons, not widely known and I ask that you keep it to yourself. The deadly nature of this side-effect was discovered when they debriefed the soldier who recovered the stricken members

of his sniper team. It turned out he destroyed an entire village. He killed every man, woman, and child, as well as all of their animals. It is our belief the late Colonel Western was one of that small percentage of people who were affected in this way. We think that is why he shot and killed three people in a Vancouver hotel room. We are hoping the autopsy will tell us what caused him to do this," she said.

This was not what he was expecting to hear but it made some sense. At any time a viral agent could spontaneously mutate or maybe Tyler missed something along the way. He wondered if the boy knew about this side-effect and that was why he was determined to finish his project.

"The effect we are seeing, though our sample is small, does not seem to be a statistical anomaly. There must be a common denominator amongst those who become hyper-violent and we are looking for it. There is a team of researchers working on the problem as we speak."

He lolled his head back and stared at the ceiling. He was tired and there was so much to consider but this new development, if it is true, was not good.

"Do not take what I am about to say as acknowledgement or admission of anything. I am not promising anything but an anti-virus may be possible. I will do my best to help your people sort this problem out but right now I need to see Andi," he said.

***

He groaned with fatigue as he got up and threw what was left of his coffee into the trash. He was exhausted and opted for the elevator over the stairs to go up the two floors to Andi's room. He was at the end of his energy reserves and he would need real sleep soon; he was at the point of being dysfunctional. The nurse smiled at him and told him it was okay to go in but not to tire her. The light in Andi's treatment room was dim to help her adjust to wakefulness. There was no one else in the room and she was awake but groggy and disoriented.

"Hi, babe," he said.

He spoke softly and smiled at her warmly. He took her hand and she smiled at him and there were tears in her eyes.

"Everything is all right now," he said.

"Where's Tyler is he-?" Her voice was hoarse from disuse and she slurred the words a little when she spoke.

"He is downstairs waiting to see you. They have rules about allowing kids on this ward," he said. It was a lie but a handy one given the circumstances. He was not certain he could convince him to leave Zen to come and see her.

"Where is Tyler?" she said again.

"I will go downstairs and get him," he said.
He tried to let go of her hand but she would not let go.

"No, don't leave me," she said.

He sat down in the chair beside her bed and they talked. He asked her questions about their time at University of Toronto and his apartment gently probing to see if her memory was intact. Aside from some blurring of details there did not seem to be any deficit. Her memory and her mind were both intact and he allowed himself to feel relief; it was clear she was going to be all right.

With the knowledge that Andi was recovering everything else they faced would be much easier to handle. They would work through the problems together and with any luck, in spite of all the lost years, maybe they could be a family. He felt a deepening sense of optimism arise within his heart. After all that happened in their lives he was hopeful things were going to work out for them. He smiled when he wondered how Andi would react to the news she was to become a grandmother. Maybe I will wait a while before I tell her, he thought, given how she feels about Zen. She was asleep again and he decided this would be a good time to find Tyler and try to convince him to come up to see her.

■■■

V G H Staff Parking

Jonas McLean parked Sedulca's car in the staff parking lot and waited for what he needed. He saw the woman and timed it in his mind. He got to the door at exactly the right moment with his arms full and smiled gratefully at the young nurse who held the security door open for him. She assumed he was supposed to be there why else would he be at the staff entrance wearing a lab coat? This simple courtesy allowed him to bring the gun into the building without being detected. He tucked the CSIS agent's weapon into his pants, dumped the empty box, and stopped at the computer terminal at the first empty nursing station he came to.

He found the day's password written on a sticky note underneath the keyboard. He did a search for Worthy and found her in neurology, room 323 on the third floor. He

took the stairs and entered the section smiling distractedly at the duty nurse as he passed by. He was scanning an empty patient chart and she naturally assumed he was supposed to be there. He found room 323 and took a chance and ducked into the room.
Good, she was alone.

***

Tyler was sitting in the treatment room with Zen as the nurse was preparing her for discharge from the hospital. He refused to leave when she asked him to and by the time Mann came in she'd given up trying. He went to Zen and took her hand.

"How are you feeling?" he said.

She looked shaky but aside from that and the dark circles under her eyes she looked good considering all she had been through.

"I'm okay but my mom is really freaked out," she said.

It occurred to him Zen was the only one who was not aware that at least part of the reason her mom was upset was her pregnancy. He wondered if he should tell her, it was an awkward situation to contemplate and he decided against it. It would be up to her mom or Tyler to give her the news, he did not feel any great need to put himself in the middle of yet another tense situation. There was enough for him to sort out as it was and that is when the thought struck him, I'm going to be a grandfather, and his mind recoiled.
"Ellie has been through a lot and she's worried about you," he said and squeezed her hand then he turned to look at Tyler.

"Ty I want you to come with me. Your mom is awake and she is asking to see you."

He could not hear his mumbled reply but from the position of his head it was clearly negative. It was at that point he knew Zen would fully recover from her injuries, she immediately sat up in the hospital bed.

"I'm going to see Andi and so are you," she said

Twenty minutes later, with Tyler pushing Zen in a wheelchair, they entered Andi's room. The room was quiet and dimly lit. He was certain with them coming into the room she would wake but her eyes remained closed and it appeared she was sleeping. He and Zen talked quietly to her while Tyler sat down to wait. He did not speak to Andi but at Zen's urging he pulled his chair beside her bed and held his mother's hand.

When Ellie was finished the paper work for Zen's discharge she came in and the three of them took turns speaking soft encouraging words to Andi.
He was careful not to mention their adventure in Parksville and Ellie did not mention the pregnancy though he could see the knowledge of it lying below the surface by the way she looked at her daughter.

It took only a few minutes for Tyler to get antsy to leave. Too much quiet talk and no television in the room was a lot for him to endure. He let go of Andi's hand and got up from his chair and Mann thought he knew where he was headed but he was surprised when Tyler turned to him.

"I need to talk to the fat lady with the helicopter," he said.

He stood and took out his cell phone whispering to Zen and Ellie as he did they would be right back as they headed out of the room.

"Her name is Barbara. Why do you want to talk to her?" he asked. He was searching for her number as the door closed behind them.

"I have something," he said.
He found the number she gave him in Parksville and hit the send button.

"Barbara its Lee Mann. Tyler would like to have a word with you," he said.
He handed him the phone.

"Are you here? Meet me in the room with TV" he said and handed the phone back.

He put it to his ear but she was gone. Without saying anything to him Tyler turned and headed for the stairs but stopped when he saw Mann intended to follow him. His face showed confusion and it looked like he was trying to think of something to say. He turned to him and looked him in the eye and said.

"Andrea is dead."

***

Jonas watched the exchange from halfway down the corridor standing with his back to them pretending to read a patient chart. No one noticed him and when Mann ran back into Andi's room he casually strolled down the hallway following the kid into the stairwell. He needed to find a quiet place where he could grab him and at five a.m. a hospital stairwell looked like a good possibility. He entered the stairway and discovered he was too late, the kid must have run down the stairs, he was gone. He ran down the stairs and looked into each corridor. He saw the kid on the second floor and waited in the stairwell watching through the small door window. Tyler was met by an older woman and he took her hand and led her into the women's washroom. What was that about, he wondered?

***

Mrs. Knight was walking to the waiting room when she spotted Tyler and he led her into the nearest washroom.

"I have something," he said, "wait."

He left her standing there bewildered as he headed into a stall.

"What is it Tyler? What do you have?" she said.

"Wait," he said.

There was a long pause during which he said nothing. Then she heard the toilet flush and a moment later he emerged. He carried something to the sink and began to vigorously wash it. She could not resist looking over his shoulder and she saw him rinsing a smooth metal tube about three inches long and a quarter inch in diameter with a flush fitting screw top. He cleaned it thoroughly with the antibacterial hand soap he pumped from a wall dispenser. When he was satisfied it was clean he turned and handed it to her.

"POrna," he said.

The last twenty-four hours had been grueling and she was aware that fatigue had dulled her mind. She stared at the tube in her hand and felt the heat radiating from it and it slowly dawned on her where it had been stowed moments earlier. When she looked at him there was a question on her face.

"Maintain at body temperature," he said. He waited and watched her face to see if she understood what he was suggesting. When he saw that she got it his face reddened and he looked away.

"Don't let POrna get cold it will die."

She examined the metal vial and regarded him with a tight smile.

"Well if I must," she said, "Is this lid on tight?"

He nodded.

Although this was a hospital and not a nightclub she turned and looked hopefully at the walls for a condom dispenser but no luck. She sighed and entered the same stall he used and closed the door.

"By the way Tyler what is POrna?"

"Poliomyelitis-Okinawa ribonucleic acid. POrna is for short," he said. He waited to see if she would laugh like Zen did but she did not laugh or make a comment. He could hear the rustling of clothing beyond the stall door.

"A lab can grow it," he said, "I will post instructions on line when you get my computers," he said.

"We don't have them but I think I know who does and I should be able to get them returned to you. Is there virus information on them?" she said.

"No," he said, "I need them to do stuff."
He was talking when the washroom door opened and he turned to see a male Doctor enter. He wondered why he was coming into the women's washroom and then he saw the gun. The Doctor lifted it and pointed it at him and began to say something. Tyler did not hear what because he started to turn away as the gun fired. The bullet hit him high on the left shoulder shattering his collar bone. The impact spun him forcefully around in the direction he'd been turning the kinetic force of the bullet knocking him to the floor.

He rolled over and looked up and followed the black hole of the muzzle as it pointed at his face. The Doctor looked confused, like maybe he had not meant to shoot him. In fact Tyler thought the Doctor's face expressed surprise that he had. Then he saw the look harden as he aimed the gun again. When he saw his finger began to pull the trigger he used the blood on the floor to deke to the right by sliding his butt sideways. He ended up halfway under the sink he used to wash the vial and the second shot missed him digging a deep crater in the plaster wall by his head showering him in white dust. He tried to change direction and crawl to the nearest toilet stall but his arm was useless and escape was impossible. He could see there was nowhere to hide so he stopped trying. He leaned his head back against the wall and watched the Doctor.

When McLean saw him move he reacted to it and pulled the trigger and missed but now the kid had stopped moving. His third shot tore a chunk of meat from his thigh puncturing his femoral artery. They both watched as a geyser of dark blood spurted from the wound painting a red arc across the stall doors.

Jonas McLean watched the kid's face go white as blood pumped out of him and he wondered again why he shot him he had not intended to do it. He was supposed to grab the kid and take him to the boat and wait for Fran. Then he remembered that Fran was dead in the car outside even though he could still hear him inside his head.

He was confused.

He couldn't stop himself. He did not want to shoot him. The kid was not moving now he was sprawled on the linoleum with only his head tilted up against the wall.

He was panting like a dog and watching Jonas. They both knew there was nowhere to hide. Jonas moved closer to him and stopped not wanting to get blood on his shoes. He pointed the gun at his face and the kid looked at him but he did not show fear only curiosity. Jonas had the odd feeling that, knowing he was about to die, the kid found it interesting. Jonas squeezed the trigger.

Tyler did not react when the fourth shot rang out he simply observed the results. He watched as the projectile ripped into the right side of the Doctor's head. It entered just above his right ear. He thought it was authentic how the force of the bullet snapped the Doctor's head to the left like in the movies. The hollow point slug shattered on impact and expanded with the shards acting like little blenders. The lead chunks rendered a sizable portion of McLean's fore-brain into a lumpy pink puree before spraying most of it on the mirror. Jonas McLean did not see Mrs. Knight open the stall door beside him nor did he hear the click of the trigger.

As he slumped she tracked his progress from crazy to corpse with her weapon but he was already dead when the surprise on his face splashed the blood on the floor. All four shots were fired in less than twenty seconds. From the moment McLean entered the washroom until the second he died was forty-two seconds. He had, in fact, completely forgotten about the old woman by the time he entered the washroom and that was his fatal error.

When Mrs. Knight turned to look at Tyler he was white from blood loss. He was holding his hand over the gushing wound on his leg but his pallor and the amount of blood on the floor told her he was close to bleeding out. She slipped in the blood when she went to him and fell hard beside him. She slapped his weakened hand away from the wound and grabbed and squeezed his leg with both hands in a brutal raw-force effort to shut off the flow.

A woman opened the washroom door and Mrs. Knight turned and screamed at her to get help. When she turned back to look at Tyler's face she was astonished to see him laughing. Her pants were around her ankles when she fell and he thought that was funny. He was still laughing when his heart stopped.

Chapter 29

Making up The Truth

33 months later

Andi put her book down and glanced at Lee. He was at the kitchen table writing. She was curled up on the sofa with a blanket reading when she noticed him holding his face in his hands.

"How's it coming?" she said.

He looked up and gave her a wan smile. "Okay I guess."

She could see by his face he was having trouble. It could not be easy putting the events of the past few years into words. "Read me what you have so far," she said.

He smiled at her and cleared his throat and began.

"My name is Lee Mann and I am a scientist and teacher most recently at the University of British Columbia. You were to be addressed this evening by Lyle Greef, but he has asked me to speak in his place. He believes the message I bring is of vital importance for humanity and one which must be heard.
It is an honour to address the members of the World Health Organization.
As you are aware the nations of the world have all experienced a dramatic reduction in armed conflict and indeed deadly violence of all kinds. This, along with the wholesale dismantling of military forces worldwide, has

been a surprising but welcome change. I'm happy to report that the trend towards non-violence continues to spread across the planet.

We have seen progressive measures taken in countries such as the United States where the President has shown vision and courage by converting military forces into domestic agents of change. US soldiers are no longer engaged in killing or destroying they are rebuilding and repairing the aging infrastructure of their great nation. These and other changes in nations herald the beginning of a new era for humankind.

I am here this evening to explain how and why this fundamental shift in human behaviour has come about. There has been much speculation and many explanations posited by the various interest groups, be they religious, political, military, or academic, but I am here to tell you all of their theories are incorrect.
The planet-wide reduction in violence we are witnessing is the result of a virus-born agent which was created in a lab for the express purpose of inflicting peace upon humanity. This man-made agent, which some are calling 'the Zen Gene,' is the source of this change.

The Zen Gene was first detected in Canadian soldiers stationed in Afghanistan approximately three years ago. I was tasked by the Canadian Military to lead a group of scientists to study it and determine its origin and how to stop it. We were unable to discover who created it but we have learned much about how it works. When we charted its progress we determined that, at its present rate of growth, it would take sixteen years to infect 180,000 people.
This number is significant because it is the number of positive exposures required to ensure the vector virus will self-sustain. After several months of study we realized

this would not happen. The Zen Gene was clearly designed to be self-limiting. I informed the Canadian Government and military leaders that the virus appeared to have been purposely designed in such a way it would naturally stop and no longer be a threat within six to eight months of first occurrence and therefore creating an anti-virus or cure was unnecessary.

It was only later revealed to me the reason the Canadian Military wanted an inoculation against the Zen Gene. Along with their Western and NATO Allies, the military was planning to infect non-western armies with the virus while inoculating our troops against its effects. This, I was assured, would create a super army with which peace and stability could be maintained indefinitely the world over. It was at this point our group of scientists realized what would happen to humanity if this plan were to succeed.

We agreed to begin work on altering its genetic structure so the Zen Gene would no longer be self-limiting and I am happy to announce we were successful in creating an unlimited version of the gene while also eliminating a dangerous side-effect which caused hyper-violence in some people. Unfortunately the new unlimited version of the gene accidentally escaped from our lab eighteen months ago and you have seen its effects. Our version was a high-bred of the Zen Gene and unfortunately, at least for those who wanted to control it, we were unable to develop an anti-virus or inoculant before it escaped from our lab.

I feel certain that those people who once made their living selling or employing the tools of death and violence will judge us harshly for our failure to contain the Zen Gene and create an antidote. This is, of course, a most bitter irony given what they had planned for it.

The majority of humanity will see the new gene for what it is; the unconditional release of humankind from the tyranny of armed conflict. Those who profited by war have no case to be made. We have, after all, achieved the outcome they have always claimed they were after. Peace for all people on earth. We simply took the additional precaution of ensuring a peaceful future by not allowing the power of the new gene to be consolidated and delivered into the hands of the few rich and powerful people who claim, as they have always claimed, entitlement over others. It is my pleasure to report to you today the rate of exposure has surpassed the one million mark and growth projections indicate the human species will be completely free of violent conflict by the year 2032."

He looked at Andi to see what she thought and she had tears in her eyes.
"It's very good. I don't think you realize how powerful your message is," she said.

"Okay. You like what I have so far but do you think they will believe the part about a new Zen Gene? And you'll notice I didn't mention anything about the Androgen Effect," he said.

Andi looked thoughtful before she smiled and said, "The new Zen Jean is very cute like her grandpa, and the projections indicate the Androgen Effect will take at least one generation before it becomes a significant population balance issue. That's at least twenty years, and like you said, the number of live male births has been on the decline for decades."

"That decline was only seen in environmentally compromised industrialized countries like ours. The lack of male births will become obvious a lot sooner in less developed parts of the world," he said.

To his amazement Andi laughed and fought to control her laughter long enough to say,

"Honey you worry too much. Someday it may have an effect on the population but it will be nothing compared to what's going to happen when the world learns the Zen Gene does not affect females.

The End

After words

Orly Airport

The woman was tall and handsomely dressed in an elegant blue sari. In the grey pall cast by the windows her dress was a singular point of beauty and the electric-coloured material attracted the toddler. She could run amazingly well but when walking had the uncertain teetering gait of all two-year-olds. With a wide grin of exploration and high colour on her cheeks she haltingly steered her way towards the electric blue dress.

When the tug at her skirt came it did not startle the woman because it was such a familiar feeling. She was a mother. She turned to see who it was and smiled at the adorable girl with wonderful bright eyes looking up at her. The woman knew it was not generally done these days, picking up someone else's child, but convention could not override instinct. Like moms everywhere seeing a tiny baby plopping her butt down onto a dirty public floor caused this automatic response and she bent over and scooped her up.

"And who are you little one?" she asked. Her voice was warm and redolent with the lilt and music of the East. The baby giggled and gurgled in delightful response enchanting the woman all the more. When she looked around the waiting area to see if she could spot the child's parents she saw one solitary man sitting near a pink travel stroller absorbed by the laptop on his knees. He was the only person in view who might be her parent though he looked too young to be a father. She headed towards him carrying the child. Before she reached him a young woman came hurrying up to her smiling.

"Oh thank you, "she said.

She came from the direction of the washrooms and the woman smiled knowingly. She remembered her own husband doing a poor job of minding their children when they were toddlers.

"She is such a little wanderer," Zen said.

She glanced at the young man when she spoke and older woman smiled knowingly as she handed her the child.

"I hope she hasn't mussed your dress. It's beautiful," she said.

"No, she is a perfect little angel," the woman said with a smile clearly taken with the baby. The woman paused to listen as the first boarding call for her flight to India was announced.

"I'm going to my niece's wedding in Bangalore," she said and smiled. They chatted for a few moments and as the woman turned to leave to board her flight Zen asked her if it was to be a large wedding.

"Oh, yes," the woman said. "Over six hundred family and guests have been invited. My brother-in-law is very well situated in the movie industry."

She watched the woman walk away until the baby started to fuss to be put down again. She was at that age. She wanted to explore her world and nothing was going to stop her. She put her down, steadying her until she gained her balance while she struggled impatiently to be released. Zen watched her daughter trundle off to examine a bank of black vinyl seats in front of the floor to ceiling windows which looked out upon the runways. She kept her eye on the baby as she sat down.

"Where is Bangalore?" she said.

He made a few keystrokes on the laptop and turned it to show her a map of the Indian subcontinent.

"I think Jeani Beani just saved us a trip to India. Wasn't India on the primary list?" she said.

He nodded.

"I will send an IM to Dr. Mann."

She stood up and reached out her hand to help him stand. He was unsteady; he suffered a mild stroke when his heart was restarted and it affected his gait. They were supposed to fly to Zürich but their flight was delayed and now they
needed to find a room for the night.

"Why do you call your dad Dr. Mann?"

Tyler looked at her and smiled, "That's his name."

www.ingramcontent.com/pod-product-compliance
Lightning Source LLC
Chambersburg PA
CBHW062015170626
46813CB00001B/168

* 9 7 8 0 9 9 1 7 4 3 9 0 2 *